THE
HANNIBAL
PARADIGM

A Ross Siegal
Psychological Thriller

HERB PADZENSKY

The Hannibal Paradigm
Published by HERO Publishing LLC
Denver, Colorado

Library of Congress Control Number: 2022911283

PADZENSKY, HERB, Author
THE HANNIBAL PARADIGM
HERB PADZENSKY

ISBN: 978-0-9985034-5-5

FICTION / Thrillers / Psychological
FICTION / Thrillers / Terrorism

QUANTITY PURCHASES: Schools, companies, professional groups, clubs, and other organizations may qualify for special terms when ordering quantities of this title. For information, email heropadz83@gmail.com.

This book is printed in the United States of America.

HERO

PUBLISHING

PART ONE

Definition:
Par-a-digm (per-ə-dīm) n.
An example or pattern of something, a model.

The narrative of the great Carthaginian general Hannibal Barca's defeat is the paradigm for this novel's plot line.

ONE

SIMI BLOCK PACED LIKE A caged animal in her office at the University of California Berkeley. She was about to experience a great adventure. Two registered letters now stowed in her briefcase explained everything. The first arrived over a month ago, inviting her to present her innovative ideas to a group of elite psychologists at a meeting in Paris, France. Acceptance would be her chance to break the glass ceiling for women. Her topic would explain a new niche in the area of behavioral psychology she developed called "sociobiology."

Dr. Block presented the opportunity to her department chairwoman, who promptly gave her approval. From that moment, everything moved with lightning speed.

The second letter contained all the documents needed: an expense voucher to cover travel expenses, a first-class airline ticket to Paris, and a sizeable honorarium. It included all transportation information from her office to the San Francisco International Airport and all travel information while in France. This once-in-a-lifetime experience would start in about an hour.

Just two years prior, she received her PhD, summa cum laude honors. In the midst of her excitement, she also received word that Ross Siegal, her lover and soul mate, had been killed in a fiery incident while working on a secret project for the US government.

She vowed to carry on his groundbreaking work in behavior psychology. She adopted his assertion that there is no chaos in predicting behavior. It only meant all the information had not been input. The 80 percent bar for predicting behavior had been the accepted norm. Her creative addition of including the physiology of a single individual into the equation raised the prediction bar to better than 90 percent. It was the publication of her results that got her the prestigious invitation.

Simi was startled out of her thoughts by the intercom buzzer from the front door receptionist. "Doctor Block, your transportation has arrived and is waiting for you."

She did a final mental check. *All relevant research papers needed for my PowerPoint resentation are in my briefcase. I hope I have brought the best arguments to explain sociobiology. My clothes have been packed for several days and are waiting at my apartment.*

She nervously fumbled for her key to lock the office door before walking down the hall toward the front door where ... She gasped. Instead of a cab or rideshare car, a white stretch limousine waited. A uniformed man stood beside the opened passenger door.

"For me?"

A large man wearing a chauffeur's uniform greeted her. "Good afternoon, Doctor Block. I am here to transport you to the airport. Do you have more luggage beside your briefcase?"

"I have two large suitcases. We need to stop at my apartment and pick them up. It's only ten minutes away."

"No problem, Doctor Block. We have plenty of time." He added, "It is a warm day. If you are thirsty, there is a variety of drinks in the vanity in front of you. I know your address. It is already posted in my GPS."

The chauffeur parked in the apartment's yellow parking zone. He ushered her in to retrieve the luggage. He stowed it in the trunk and then opened the door for her. The windows were tinted, making the interior dark. Simi blinked, adjusting to the darkness. From the corner of her eye, she detected a smallish man wearing a pinstriped suit sitting near the far window. He wasn't there before. Her photographic mind never lied. She tensed impulsively. Before she could react, the chauffeur pushed her to the middle and placed himself beside her while closing the door behind him.

Simi screamed and struggled to get out.

The chauffeur said, "Please do not fight, Doctor Block. We do not wish to harm you. The darkened windows and insulated interior will hide everything from any passersby." He repeated as he tightened his arms around her, "Please relax."

The man in the pinstriped suit took a cloth from a small travel bag and forced it against her face.

The last thing Simi Block sensed was a sweet smell from the cloth. Her eyes closed, and her muscles refused to struggle anymore.

TWO

IT HAD BEEN EIGHTEEN MONTHS since Ross Siegal was forced from a mountain retreat in Colorado. A foreign power had dispatched armed troops there to kill him. Siegal, with the help of his friend Tom Danielson, narrowly escaped and was now living a hermit's existence on Little Deadman's Cay, a deserted nine-and-one-half-acre island in the Caribbean. And it was Danielson who reported that Siegal had been killed in that attack.

This day as with most days, Siegal had just thrown his unbaited fishing line into the bay and was preparing to take his regular afternoon siesta. He took off his shorts, leaving him nude, having long discarded underwear as an unnecessary article of clothing. The sound of an airplane startled him. This was not the day for his weekly supply plane.

"What the hell?"

A floatplane, not the regular supply plane, came into view. It landed in the nearby bay and taxied onto the beach near where Siegal was lying. He stiffened. "Should I approach the plane or go hide in the trees."

The passenger door opened, and a blond-haired man about six feet four emerged. A familiar voice called out. "Hey, good buddy."

Siegal scratched the balding spot on the top of his head. "Tom? What brings you here? You never come unannounced."

"I was just in the neighborhood and thought I'd make a call. But if you're too busy ..."

Siegal knew Danielson never did anything without a purpose and waited for the shoe to drop. He continued the banter. "I actually had a party with twenty beautiful native girls and a fully catered dinner. I'm sorry, there's barely enough food for us. But, I can cancel it all for someone to share a few beers and a couple of rounds of chess."

"Perfect. Exactly what I had in mind."

Siegal knew it wasn't. He could wait for the real reason until Danielson was ready.

Tom Danielson and Ross Siegal were polar opposites in both physical appearances and political biases. Their differences are what made them an unbeatable team that recently solved an international terrorist threat. Siegal was the genius who understood the behavioral makeup of the enemy, and Danielson knew how to make the wheels turn for success. He was the sole person who knew Siegal was not dead.

They walked to the only shack on the island. It housed a bedroom, a small kitchenette, and a third room doubling as a parlor and office with a solar-powered computer. Just outside the back door was a chemical latrine and a well for fresh water. The bay served Siegal as a shower/bath.

The two men set up the chessboard on a covered porch. Siegal brought out some fresh fruit as snacks.

"You seem to have most everything for creature comforts. Fruit trees, planted by former tenants of the island and many varieties of produce grow wild on the fertile land."

"The best of all worlds," concluded Siegal.

Danielson just nodded.

"Let's stop beating around the bush, Tom. You came here for a purpose. I know you too well."

"You caught me. You have about everything you could wish for. The weekly supply planes bring you meat, dairy products, toiletry items, and occasional tidbits. And I get you occasional consultancies to exercise your mind."

"What am I missing? When I want some physical release, I hop on the supply plane and visit Nassau for a couple of days. Out with it. What is bothering you?"

"When I met you, you were on the cutting edge in behavioral psychology. For a while, maybe even too long a while, your creative mind has become stagnant. I am losing the person I love."

"Forget it, man. I live a perfect life. No enemy threats, no stress of public life, no arguing with others why my theories are correct, no ..."

Danielson blurted in, "No creative thinking."

"What do you want from me?"

"Checkmate. Enough chess. Let's take a walk on the beach. It can clear our heads.

THREE

THE TWO MEN STROLLED THE beach and came upon the spot where the floatplane had come ashore.

"What are these two boxes?" asked Siegal. "They're certainly not mine. Are you planning to stay awhile?"

Danielson gave a casual whatever hand wave. "Oh, just a few things I had the pilot off-load while we were at the shanty." He pointed to the smaller box. "Carry this, unless you're getting too soft out here. I'll get the other. We can open them up on the porch."

Siegal hefted the box. "Damn. This box weighs a ton. Reminds me of the old filing boxes I used back in the day when I was your super profiler."

Sweating, they reached the porch and lowered them onto the deck.

Danielson said, "You get a couple of cold ones, and I'll break the seals on the boxes as soon as I catch my breath."

Siegal nodded and went into the kitchen, retrieving a six-pack of ODL, Old Dog's Leg, beer. He opened two, handing one to Danielson. Both men took deep swigs, drained the first round, and reached for a second.

"I told you before that I thought you were losing your edge. As your friend, I wanted to help. You know the threat to your life is over. You're free to go back to the mainland. Then, you argued against that, saying you didn't want to become a public person again, or at least words to that effect."

"I love my life," argued Siegal. "Why would I ever want to change it?"

"Because you are destroying one of the most creative minds I have ever known. As your best friend, I cannot let that happen if I can in any way change it."

"Okay. If I am this super researcher you claim I am, I have to hear your whole argument before making a conclusion. I suppose these boxes hold the magic solution."

"Remember when I worked for a group of world leaders? We called them the Summit of Six, the SOS? I told them I needed a super behavioral profiler, and they agreed. I spanned the globe and found you. The problem was and still is your stubbornness against working with anything that smacks of politics. If I had asked you straight out and said I needed you, your answer would have been no."

"I get all that. But, what about these boxes?"

"Patience. I had to find a way that manipulated you to join me and work as a team. You are the supermind, and I am the great manipulator. Remember, I manipulated you into getting on a plane to see me in Washington on the pretext you were going to defend your research at the university."

"And we ended up at a desolate chemical laboratory in China? I had no trust in you. We were like oil and water then."

"And still are. But we were then and still are a great team."

"That trip changed my whole mindset. And these boxes are my trip to China, so to speak. Like a rat in one of my mazes. And, these boxes contain my reward."

Danielson nodded and opened the box marked A. He took out a tri-fold pamphlet lying on top. The title read *Monkey Town Primate Center,*

Cape Town, South Africa. The picture on the cover displayed a spider monkey. The caption read:

I'm Garra, the Monkey Town mascot.

Take my tail, and let's go for a walk.

Want to climb a tree with me?

Before I came to Monkey Town, I was locked in a cage.

Now I roam freely.

I love putting my arms around your neck.

Come see me, and I'll give you a hug.

"What is this bullshit?" Siegal asked. "You think I should have a pet to follow me around and keep me company? I can call him Sunday just to be different. Do you think I've gone off my fucking rocker? What would I do with a pet monkey?"

"Hold on," said Danielson, putting his hands on Siegal's shoulders. "You are first and foremost a behavioral research scientist. It's consumed your whole professional life. I feel you need to be doing that again."

"You want me to go back to City University and look after rats again?"

"No, I don't think going back to what you were doing before is enough. You're far past rat experiments. A small laboratory no longer fits you."

"Then what the hell are you driving at?"

"You can stay here, and all of Little Deadman's Cay can be your lab. Look here." Danielson thumbed through the pamphlet. "The entire area of the primate center has covered walkways running like tunnels throughout. The observers are in the cages, and the monkeys are free to roam about."

"Are you suggesting I become a zookeeper?"

"Not just a zookeeper. You're going stir crazy and don't even know it."

"Tom, maybe you're the one who needs to be in a zoo."

"Don't you get it? You're bored because your mind hasn't been challenged. It's been on vacation way too long."

"But," sputtered Siegal, "I don't a have a clue about how to take care of a dog, much less monkeys. They have to eat, they leave messes, and who knows what other problems they offer. All I know about monkey experiments comes from studies by Harry Harlow, his maternal deprivation studies in the nineteen forties and fifties. And, of course, who doesn't know about Jane Goodall and her lowland gorilla observations."

"Perfect. The monkeys don't know anything about you, and you don't know a thing about them. You'll all be even."

Siegal shook his head. "This calls for another beer."

For the rest of the day and into the evening, the two men squabbled. Siegal kept bringing up reasons why Danielson's idea couldn't work. And Danielson kept breaking down each argument as the seasoned debater he was in his former life as the president's chief of staff.

The more they argued, the brighter Siegal's eyes became. He was no longer working on a low-energy battery. Instead, his voice raised a few notches with each series of exchanges.

Siegal rubbed his thinning hair spot. "Maybe it could be a good idea. But if it starts to go sour, I want out with no questions asked. Agreed?"

Danielson gave Siegal a fist bump. "Agreed."

Mission accomplished. The person talking with Tom Danielson was no longer Ross, the hermit turned beachcomber. He had regained his stature as Dr. Ross Siegal, behavioral psychologist and researcher. The transformation was like Dr. Jekyll and Mr. Hyde—only the transformation was for good and not evil. It was no longer why but how to make it happen.

"How many monkeys groups do you want?"

"I don't want any set groups at all. I think if I am to learn about monkey behavior from scratch, they will have to start their own culture. They must be of the same breed but not from the same family."

"Aren't you the clever researcher. Throw out a number you want for starters."

"Not sure. Maybe about six or eight mature animals. Half should be males, so there would be competition for leadership. And the others to b ..."

"Let me guess. Sexy females anxious to begin a family."

The men worked throughout the night making plans, taking time out only to release some of the beer in the trees behind the house. The sun was already climbing in the sky, and a sense of hunger suddenly hit them. Siegal turned on the gas stove. In minutes the shanty was filled with the aroma of greasy bacon and sunny-side up eggs with filets of fish.

After breakfast, they attempted to get back to business, but their brains had been drained.

Danielson glanced at his watch. "Sorry, good buddy, my time is used up for this trip. I have some appointments on the mainland."

"One more thing," said Siegal. "It's time for me to come back from the dead. My former friends need to know I'm alive. Do you think we could have a reunion here on this island?"

Danielson smiled. The second part of his mission had been for Siegal to realize this fact. "I've been waiting a long time for you to say that. You work on developing your New World monkey lab, and I will plan your reunion. It shouldn't take much to get BF and Sally to attend a warm-weather conference. I'll lure Jerry Ravid, your old boss at Interaction Dynamics, who will jump at the opportunity to reap a large government contract. Simi is so independent and will be tougher, but I'm sure I can figure it out. Is there anything else I can do?"

"I need a research library." Siegal scoured the piles of documents until he found what he was looking for. "This one has a notation about the Biggest Primate Bookstore. Check them out. Here are a couple more references like the ones from the Oregon Regional Primate Research program. And this one on primates commonly used in research discussing the breeding of squirrel monkeys. That's enough for a start."

"I'll have as many resource books as I can get on the next supply plane."

"One more thing. Can you get me a plane ticket and accommodations from here to Cape Town? If we are going to make this island as natural as possible for our simian friends, then I want to see firsthand how the Monkey Town Primate Center was built along with learning any pitfalls."

Danielson stood and saluted. "Roger that, Dr. Siegal. A charter plane will fly you to Miami in the next couple of days." He looked toward the beach. "Time to go. My taxi has already landed."

Danielson was off in minutes.

Siegal watched as the plane disappeared into the morning air. He glanced down on the sand where the plane was parked and noticed something on the ground. He walked over and saw a carton of large newsprint, the kind lecturers used for demonstrations before someone invented PowerPoint. Siegal always pinned these sheets to a wall when formulating his best research ideas back at City University.

"You overconfident son of a bitch. You knew I was going to be talked into this monkey lab. You had this dropped off. You son of a bitch. I love you."

Siegal lugged the boxes into the second bedroom/office.

SIEGAL'S THOUGHTS WANDERED BUT MOSTLY focused on Simi Block. Time and distance dulled his memory, but not his passion for her. He would have asked her to marry him if the terrorists had not gotten in the way.

The shanty office was furnished with a folding table for a desk, two folding chairs, an old file cabinet left by a previous tenant, and several boxes, one containing his favorite working tools—felt markers and masking tape. He tore three sheets off one tablet and taped them to one wall. The next task was to get an ODL from the refrigerator. He was ready for work.

Siegal took a long drink, uncapped his felt pen, and started. On the first sheet, he drew a white rat with a black stripe down its back.

"Hello, Tigger. We're back."

FOUR

SIMI'S SENSES SLOWLY RETURNED AS she emerged from her drugged state. She listened for any sound that would give her any clue about her surroundings.

Nothing.

Am I alone? "Hello? Can anyone hear me?"

Unfamiliar smells filled her nostrils. The strongest was the dankness of stale air.

I remember getting into a limousine en route to the airport for my trip to Paris. Then someone forced a cloth over my face. I smelled something sweet. I felt a spinning motion in space.

Am I dead? In a place between heaven and hell? Or where?

She inched her legs from side to side. Then she forced her arms to move ... fingers ... then neck.

Nothing feels bruised or broken. No pain. I'm not dead. And I'm free of any tethers. Straining to get up and not yet fully awake, she fell back on the small cot she had been lying on.

She suddenly remembered being eight years old and having her tonsils out. *That sweet smell. Ether. Whoever did this to me used ether to put me to sleep. A younger person would have used a more modern form of knockout chemicals.*

She opened her eyes. There were no windows telling whether it was night or day. A forty-watt bulb hanging from the ceiling provided the only illumination.

It appears I am in a small basement. Along the walls were barrels and open racks containing several bottles. *A wine cellar. Have I been flown to France? Why didn't they wait till I flew there on my own and save all the trouble?*

A voice startled her. "Dr. Block, be calm. Do not panic. You have been through a divorce, put yourself through graduate school, and become a respected professional in your field. You can get through this too."

Her mind was clearer now. Most of the anesthetic had worn off. Simi listened for anything that would tell her more. Except for the voice, there were no other sounds.

Simi squinted at her calendar watch. It was morning, the day after she was attacked in front of her apartment.

I couldn't have been taken to France. There was not enough time to fly me there. But the wine bottles ... lots of them. I could be in wine country somewhere in the United States. My guess is I'm still in California.

The voice emanating from a speaker next to the light bulb continued. "I am sorry for your inconvenience, Dr. Block. You must be hungry. I will have some breakfast sent to you."

The voice was calm, almost peaceful, with a slight accent. She tried to place it.

Most likely Japanese.

"Who are you? Where am I? What do you want from me?"

"Patience, Dr. Block, all your questions will be answered in good time. You may want to refresh yourself. There are facilities in the corner. By now, you have surmised we are watching you through a surveillance camera. It will be turned off to assure your privacy for the next twenty minutes. Take care of everything you need to do during that time. Your luggage has been returned and placed at the foot of your cot should you care to change clothes or put on makeup. The only item you will find missing is your cell phone. I am sure you can understand why."

Except for the voice, there was a deafening silence. No ambient traffic noise, not even songs of birds to tell whether she was in a city or in the country.

Without warning, the overhead light blinked off. She heard a door open and the shuffling of a person wearing soft shoes. She smelled the aroma of warm food. Simi thought about overpowering her captor using the Israeli fighting technique krav maga she learned at one of Cal-Berkeley's night classes. Instead, she chose to remain seated.

When the door closed and the light was turned on, a food tray lay on a table next to a ladder-back chair in the center of her enclosure.

Hunger overcame her fear. After inhaling the last morsel, she returned her look up to the ceiling. "Are you still there?"

"Yes, I am, Dr. Block. Is there anything I can do to make you more comfortable?"

"You can damn well let me out of here."

"I am afraid I cannot do that. My employer would not care for that. If you agree to be cooperative, in time you will earn more freedom. I promise."

Shouting, Simi said, "Why would I cooperate with you?"

"You don't have to raise your voice. Our sound system is quite adequate."

She took a deep breath to relax, trying to lower her voice, but it mostly just quivered. "Why would I want to cooperate with you? Are you holding me for ransom or just planning to kill me once I tell you what you want to know? Either way, there's nothing to gain by keeping me here under duress."

"That sounds much better. It is neither money nor killing you that interests us. You see, Dr. Block, we did not exactly kidnap you. It is more like we borrowed you for a while."

"If I don't arrive as scheduled in Paris ..." She paused. "Oh, hold on. I get it. The trip to France was nothing but a ruse. Are you the one who planned my abduction?"

"I admit it was my plan that brought you here. You are a unique person, Dr. Block, and we wish to solicit your help."

"Help? Why didn't you ask me in the normal way?"

"It would be more accurate if I said we need your expertise. I doubt you would agree if you knew why my employer is seeking it."

Simi stood up and arched toward the ceiling speaker. "You're getting nothing from me. And torture won't help either. I am a very independent woman. You'll have to feed me indefinitely, starve me, or finally kill me. You will never get what I don't want to do unless you drug me or the like."

"Dr. Block, we have no intention of harming you in any way. Physical torture is not my style. And as for drugging, it is a dangerous alternative. I would only use that as a last resort. I doubt very much I will need to do that."

"Then you must be aliens. I guarantee my body is not worth exploiting."

The voice laughed softly. "We are not aliens. We are humans just like you. Within required restrictions, we will try to make your stay as comfortable as possible. There are magazines and a current daily newspaper under the table where your food tray is. We will talk later."

"Why do you keep saying we. How many of you are there?"

Silence.

"Wait. Don't go away."

More silence.

So now I get the silent treatment. I can't let this get to me. I must be getting brainwashed. I just have to remember who I am, and I will be all right.

"Hello," she called. "Hello. You bastards. Tell me what you want from me."

Only a single light bulb and the beating of her own heart were there to keep her company in the quiet confines.

Lunch was served in the same manner as breakfast. The red light on the ceiling camera turned off, giving a new twenty minutes to refresh herself. Then the small light was turned off again, putting the space into darkness. The door opened, and the same man as before walked in, laid the food tray on the table, and took away the tray from the previous meal.

"Thank you," said Simi, hoping to get some verbal response that she could use to get a sense of one of her captors.

No reply.

Silence is one thing. Being purposely shunned feels worse—much worse. I'm being brainwashed by isolation. It's comforting to know that whoever is doing this wants me alive.

She searched her mind for any knowledge about brainwashing. One event came into her head. An American POW in Korea was kept in a pit without human interaction for several years. When he was finally rescued, army psychiatrists were surprised how he was so mentally sharp. The soldier explained how he imagined building his dream house. His mental powers were so precise that after being released from the army, he actually built his imagined dream house without the benefit of blueprints.

Well, girl, you just have to put your mind to work. I could design and sew some new clothes if only I could sew. Or write a book—a thriller, complete with a kidnapping. That would be nice, but right now, I don't know how it ends. I wonder how long before my brain goes spongy? I need to find out as much as I can before this happens. There must be some logic in all this.

The lingering effects of the ether coupled with boredom moved her to sleep. The lunch tray was gone when she woke. A dinner tray was in its place. Four hours had passed, and she was no better off.

I can't be wasting my time sleeping. I have never exercised before—no time like the present to start. Simi tried unsuccessfully to touch her toes. She laughed. *I'll try again after dinner. At least I still have a sense of humor.*

She picked up the newspaper left during breakfast. *USA TODAY*. She looked at the calendar on her watch. It was the same date as the newspaper. It confirmed her first sense that she was still in the United States.

What do I know about my confinement? I am almost sure this place is a wine cellar somewhere in northern California, maybe on some vineyard. She examined the bottles on the wine racks. *They are not from a single vineyard. The bottles display an assortment of labels, both domestic and imported. I am probably being held in a private villa or estate. Now a magazine label can give me more clues about my location and even my abductor.*

Simi walked over to the wine rack and sat down on a stool she found there. "Hello. Can you see me? I know you can hear me. Are you going to talk or continue to give me the silent treatment?"

The voice in the ceiling startled her. "Are you ready to join us, Dr. Block?"

She decided to play her own silent treatment game and did not respond.

"Are you all right?" came the voice after more than a minute of silence.

Good. They can't see me behind this wine rack. If I want privacy, I can sit back here and wait. They will have to reset the cameras. That means taking me out of this room first.

"Congratulations, Dr. Block. You discovered our blind spot. We will, however, have that taken care of by tomorrow."

Then silence.

It was almost a shock how pleasant even a few words were; now to be painfully aware of the silence again.

SIMI AWAKENED THE NEXT MORNING and noticed bits of wire insulation on the floor. She was positive they were not there before. The surveillance cameras had been realigned while she slept.

They must have put something in my dinner. They eliminated a chance to get out of this place. My only privacy now is when I request to use the bathroom.

Simi smiled, realizing a new clue. Her captors are all males, modest, and proper.

FIVE

SIEGAL'S INTERNATIONAL FLIGHT LANDED IN the Cape Town South African air terminal. He was escorted to a waiting prop plane that flew him to a much older and smaller, non-air-conditioned terminal used almost exclusively by bush pilots. There were no security barriers common in larger terminals. The streets around the complex were crowded with people milling about, seemingly with no place to go but in a hurry to get there. It was more how he expected South Africa should appear based on old Tarzan movies of the dark continent. The air reeked of sweat and animal dung, a change from his fresh island air. He fought off gagging.

Still, this small airport had an international flavor. He overheard conversations in European and Asian languages; all interspersed with what he assumed were languages from various African tribes. Here and there, Siegal detected some English voices, but not American.

Just inside the terminal's baggage area stood a tall, thin young man. He was perched on a box to see over the heads of the myriad onlookers.

Siegal judged him to be in his late teens. He called Siegal's name and waved a hand-painted placard over his head.

WELCOME DOCTARI SIEGAL

Siegal called out a hello, relieved to know there were arrangements made for his arrival. The young man motioned for them to meet at the end of the passport immigration area.

"Good morning, Doctari Siegal." The youth spoke in a flawless British accent. "I am Phillipe. I trust you had an uneventful flight."

"Yes. Thank you, Phillipe. My flight was very smooth. I look forward to experiencing Monkey Town." Siegal found himself exaggerating his words as if speaking to someone hard of hearing.

Phillipe smiled a toothy grin. "Do not worry. I understand English perfectly. Now, if you will, please follow me. I will get your luggage. My Land Rover is parked nearby."

Siegal found the scene outside the terminal to be equally hectic. The air was full of unfamiliar sounds from animals of every variety. And smells, even stronger than the ones inside the terminal, pervaded his nostrils. People, animals, and vehicles ranging from Vespas to six-wheelers filled every available ground space. From a hermit's existence on a small island to this. Siegal summarized it as disciplined chaos.

THE EARLY MORNING TEMPERATURE WAS already approaching one hundred degrees. Siegal wiped the sweat from under his arms. The heat was more intense than on his tropical island.

Phillipe smiled as he watched his passenger show considerable discomfort. He handed Siegal a chilled bottle of water. Then he loaded Siegal's luggage into the back seat, and the two started off.

Motorized traffic soon thinned once the pair reached the edge of the terminal. Now the roads were filled with two-wheeled carts and people balancing bundles on their backs and heads. The hot weather didn't seem to bother any of the natives as they moved along.

"Monkey Town is about twenty kilometers. The road gets a little bumpy. I'll stop if your stomach gets too upset."

"I'm fine, Phillipe. I envisioned deep ruts and gullies *or no roads at all.*"

"Oh, this part is smooth and easy to navigate, Doctari. Soon we will be into the forest where streams run over the roads. You must have faith the water is not too deep. During the dry season, these streams dry up, so there is really no need to build bridges. We are in luck. It is the dry season right now."

Siegal asked, "And during the rainy season?"

"During the monsoons, we keep scuba gear in the truck in case the streams are too deep," grinned Phillipe. "Is there anything you want to know before we get to Monkey Town?"

"I noticed the windows of your Land Rover are covered with heavy chain link."

"Most of the animals are quite used to humans and prefer to keep their distance. But, on occasion, we accidentally drive too close and startle them. You cannot blame them for attacking and protecting themselves. The auto is an incursion into their personal territory. So rather than shoot them, we just try to fend them off."

Siegal gaped wide-eyed at the ever-changing landscape. The open plains spread as far as the eye could see, with zebras and gnus grazing peacefully. Nearby in the low brush, lions stalked them for an opening to complete their hunt. At the next moment, they were driving into a rain forest so dense one could not see past the next turn. Phillipe never used the brake pedal. He drove the straightaways and curves with equal abandon. The whole experience felt more surreal than any photographs and paintings Siegal had ever seen.

"Am I driving too fast?"

"Not at all," said Siegal, holding tight to the support bar in front of him. "I assume there are just as many bumps in the road whether we go fast or slow. Going fast shortens the ride."

At the point when Siegal wondered if they would reach the center before his stomach gave out, they slowed as the front entrance of the preserve emerged through the brush. Phillipe honked his horn, and another young African opened the gate. Siegal noted the sign across the top of the fence constructed from native wood with hand-carved letters.

Welcome
MONKEY TOWN PRIMATE CENTER

Phillipe waved to the gatekeeper and drove to a small cabin next to a hut with a similar hand-carved sign.

Center Office

"This is the VIP house where you will be staying." Phillipe looked up toward the sun and said, "We eat dinner at noon, about an hour from now. Your place is at the head table with the center director, Ro Golden. Everyone here calls her Missy Ro. Do not let the informality fool you. She has her PhD from Texas A&M in veterinary science. Her last position was at the Berlin Zoo, where she was the curator of primate care for ten years. Oh, and she does not like her credentials thrown about."

"What sort of dress is appropriate for dinner?"

"Please do not go entirely native," said Philippe with a toothy grin. "We would not want to embarrass the center's employees who are all members of different bush tribes around here. They are not used to seeing a naked white ape. I suggest a casual shirt and shorts. And be sure never to walk around barefoot. There are many unusual things on the ground that your Western circulatory system cannot tolerate. We only want to treat sick animals and not visitors. We provided some sandals in your room." Phillipe carried Siegal's luggage into the hut, once more showing off his wide grin, and left.

SIX

EXACTLY AT NOON, A TRIANGLE rang announcing dinner. Siegal stepped out of his hut and followed the other visitors walking across the clearing to the mess tent.

About forty guests gathered around long tables in groups of six to eight. Several were families with children. Siegal was the only American. Still, he experienced no language barriers. He was amazed how the support staff was so multilingual.

"This way, Doctari." A native in a white hospital coat ushered him to a small round table for six. Phillipe was already seated.

"This is your place for the remainder of your stay with us," said Phillipe, pointing to an empty chair. "Missy Ro will be in soon." He stood up. "Let me lead you through the buffet line. There are some foods foreign to your taste, but let me assure you, it is all edible and very well prepared by our four-star chef."

Each entrée looked like the pictures of meals shown in expensive safari advertisements Siegal read about on the plane coming over.

"This, Doctari, is roasted zebra. It may taste a little gamey at first, but it is very lean and high in protein. Just ask any lion how good it tastes. These tubers are much like your domestic yams. Also, take some salad. It is made from the local plants found around the center. The flowers in it are also edible and give a sweet honey flavor. This is the same vegetation our monkeys eat."

Siegal followed Phillipe through the line. He sampled some of everything.

"You are welcome to return if you want more. Noontime dinner is our large meal of the day. Supper will be served for those still hungry and is usually leftovers."

Siegal filled his tray and returned to his place at the round table. He was joined by Dr. Ro Golden along with three other staff members. Phillipe stood and waited till Missy Ro and her staff sat down.

Missy Ro gave the impression of a sweet grandmother, but there was no doubt she could manage a hard day's work as much as her younger employees. Even in this backward environment, she maintained her personal appearance. Her hair was dyed a warm auburn to hide early graying. Her face makeup was simple but perfect.

Dr. Golden tapped her glass for attention and offered the introductions. "This is Dr. Bob, our head veterinarian, Jose is our tour guide coordinator, and Maria is my right hand and assistant director. I could never run this place without any of them but especially Maria. And, of course, you already met Phillipe. He used to come here every day patiently watching. We used to find odd jobs so we could rationalize feeding him. Sometimes he would carry luggage for the guests and run errands as a gopher. We finally had to hire him as an employee purely from guilt. Everybody, this is Dr. Ross Siegal, a renowned behavioral psychologist, who is here to learn how we do things."

Siegal interrupted. "Please, just call me Ross."

Dr. Golden slapped him softly on the shoulder. "Then Ross it is."

She gave a short prayer, and everyone began their meals. Siegal watched the order in which they ate and followed suit.

"How is the meal, Ross?" asked Dr. Golden. "I'm sorry we don't have Pizza Hut delivery for you."

"Everything is very good; If I stay here too long, I will be fat as a ..."

"Hippopotamus?" grinned Phillipe.

"As a hippopotamus," Siegal smiled back.

"Don't worry about that. You will be getting plenty of exercise while you are here. My understanding is that you want as much hands-on experience as possible. That means real labor and not just observing. There is always plenty to do. I have assigned Phillipe as your personal guide. One day he hopes to get a scholarship to my alma mater as soon as he finishes his education at the local church school. One day we expect to call him Doctari Phillipe."

The rest of the meal was eaten in silence aside from occasional anecdotes of the day's events. Staff worked hard from the first light and relished the peace and quiet of the luncheon meal. Ross relished the opportunity to savor all the new flavors and even went back to the line for more ground water buffalo.

Everyone in the room, including those at the round table, cleaned their own dishes and stacked them by the kitchen window. The compound was handled in the most Spartan manner as most of the staff had more than one job responsibility and little time to pamper guests.

"You may wander the compound to work off your lunch,' suggested Phillipe. "You cannot get lost as long as you don't go through any closed gates. It is a good idea that you stay inside your hut when it starts to get dark. There are many biting things out there that awaken at dusk."

"You mean like flies and mosquitos?"

"Yes, those. But there are some four-legged hunters that get past our security entrances. We would hate to lose you in just one day."

"Thanks for the warning. I don't want to lose me either."

Both grinned.

SEVEN

ONE LAP AROUND THE COMPOUND and Siegal realized how fatigued he was from his trip halfway around the world, coupled with the bumpy twenty kilometers ride to the center plus the imposing tropical heat. He retired to his one-room hut.

On his bed, he discovered a typed Monkeygram:

We hope you enjoy your stay with us. We have attempted to make your visit as comfortable as possible. Please remember you are now in a third-world country, and many of the comforts you are used to at home have been left far behind.

Much of our foods are brought in. A large variety of fresh meat, fowl, and fish are provided daily by our skilled hunters who live around the compound. We eat what they bring in. Therefore, there will be no published menus. If you have special dietary restrictions, you need to discuss these in detail with the assistant director and master chef.

All meals are buffet style.

Breakfast: served at 7:30 sharp

Dinner: served from 12:00 noon to 1:00

Supper: served from 6:00 to 7:30

Refreshments and snack food are at the cabana: open from 8:00 am to sunset.

Special tours outside the fencing are provided upon request and designed to maintain the full safety of our guests. Use the signup sheet provided on your table at each meal.

The Prehensile Monkey gift shop is open daily from 9:30 to 5:30. Free cassette tapes for loan explain the different animal and plant life in the area. They are provided in English, French, Chinese, and German.

YOUR ROOM IS NOT AIRTIGHT. MANY SMALL CREATURES OFTEN MAKE UNANNOUNCED VISITS. ALWAYS SHAKE OUT YOUR SHOES IN THE MORNING AND WHENEVER YOU TAKE THEM OFF. IT IS ALSO A VERY GOOD IDEA TO SHAKE OUT YOUR CLOTHES BEFORE PUTTING THEM ON.

A second page was addressed specifically to Dr. Siegal:

Missy Ro wishes to meet with you as soon as you finish breakfast. She apologizes in advance for missing breakfast. Her duties require her to be elsewhere.

Have a pleasant stay with us.

Maria

This certainly isn't Kansas, thought Siegal looking around his hut constructed entirely of native woods, bark, and vines. Two window openings covered with mosquito netting served to cross ventilate the hut. Each had a shutter that could be closed during the monsoon season. The shower, sink, and lavatory were in one corner with a privacy curtain. Furnishings included a bed, desk and chair, a bookcase with some selected reading, and a TV with a VCR.

"Everything a person could ask for." Siegal selected a book and lay down. In minutes he was asleep. He missed supper.

THE SUN STREAMING IN THE window nudged Siegal awake. He quickly washed his face, pulled on some clothes, and raced to the mess tent to grab some breakfast before the buffet closed. Refreshed, he went directly to the main building for his meeting with Missy Ro.

"Good morning, Ross," greeted Maria. "Missy Ro is at her desk. She asks that you go in. Would you like some tea?"

"No, thank you. I just had breakfast." He saw the open door and went in.

Missy Ro looked up. "Good morning, Ross."

"And to you, Dr. Ro."

"People here call me Missy Ro or just plain Ro—either works well for me." Her comments were warm and genuine, but her voice was all business. "Running this operation is no simple matter." She changed the subject. "By the way, your reputation for psychological skills precedes you. I have followed your understanding of rat behavior. Your good friend Tom Danielson tells me you plan to start a new world monkey facility in the Caribbean. I like the idea and want to help all I can."

"I certainly don't plan to make it a tourist place. I live the life of a hermit. I don't want to play nursemaid to a bunch of tourists. From what I've already observed, you have done a marvelous job making this place work protecting the animal life and, at the same time, offering your guests a fine educational experience. Tom assured me I won't have to worry about keeping my budget in the black."

She smiled. "You don't have to apologize. I didn't figure you for being the monkey entrepreneur of the Americas."

"Tom seems to be aware of what I need before I do. And he knows just how to get me to do it."

"Is he usually right?"

"He's always right. My life on the island was making me lazy, and Tom felt I needed to get back on the horse and do some kind of research."

"Why not continue the research you did before? You were pushing the envelope pretty far in those days at the university."

"He thought, and maybe I did, too, that I need a change, like researching higher on the animal scale."

"And you think the answer is learning about simian behavior."

"They are closer to humans. The problem is I don't know zip about monkeys and how to manage them."

"If you have a nice population balance and the correct environment, they pretty much take care of themselves. Where I think too many researchers fail is when they try to domesticate their subjects and habituate their wild instincts. They don't get honest results. Monkeys learn very quickly to forget their normal instincts and become dependent on their human caretakers. The one exception I allow here is our compound pet, Garra, who you will meet whether you want to or not. She is really like an employee helping our guests become comfortable with our wildlife."

"I am anxious to start. When will I begin?"

"You began after you expressed a willingness to be here. Your coming here, by the way, was my suggestion to Tom. I want you to spend the morning as a tourist and wander the observation paths. You can pick up a tape recorder at the Prehensile Monkey and get an idea of our different kinds of animal life. Morning is the best time for a novice observer because our friends are most active before the heat of the day. After lunch, Phillipe will start putting you to work."

Energized, Siegal said his goodbyes and went directly to the gift shop. Besides the recorder, he was given a booklet giving facts about Monkey Town, pictures of several monkey types, a map of the covered trails, and a digital camera.

"Very clever," said Siegal to himself. "The entire area, all the buildings, tents, and open spaces are located within wire tunnels to keep the more curious monkeys and dangerous predators away from the guests. The netting over the trees will not be needed on my island. The sea around me will serve the same purpose. I need to take lots of pictures so Tom can use them as construction aids."

Before Siegel realized how much time had passed, the triangle rang for lunch. He rushed back, anticipating he would need all his strength to keep up with what Phillipe had in mind.

AFTER LUNCH, SIEGAL RETURNED TO his hut to take care of personal needs. When he reemerged, Phillipe was outside waiting for him.

"Are you ready to begin, Doctari?"

Without waiting for an answer, he led Siegal to a locked gate. "Take this clipboard and paper. Today we are taking a population count. Make five columns. The first is for the distinct species we find. The next three are to inventory males, females, and immature young. The last column is for you to note anything unusual. It is important to make sure there is an appropriate number of males to females and if the females are producing young. Too large a family and there is sure to be group conflict, and that would mean problems for us here at the center.

"What happens if the numbers are not in line?"

"If there are too many mature males, there can be deadly battles. This would not look good for our human guests to witness. If there are too few babies, we have to assume the alpha male is not doing his job, and we have to encourage a new leader."

"What are your alternatives when you have too many in one family?

"There are always zoos looking for healthy animals to restock their inventories." Phillipe put his index finger to his lips. "Quiet now. We are no longer in the safety of the wire tunnels. These animals are completely wild and may react if they feel threatened. This can be true if the males consider you a threat to them with their females. Jealousy in monkeys can be deadly."

Census taking was Phillipe's way to teach Siegal to spot elusive monkeys in the trees. The many asides Phillipe gave Siegal were like a college professor teaching his honor student.

The afternoon flew by. Phillipe had so much to offer, and Siegal felt he had so little time to absorb it all.

MISSY RO CHOSE TO BE at dinner that evening along with the rest of her staff. "Well, Ross," she asked, "how was your day?"

"Phillipe is a wonderful guide and teacher. The more I learned, the more motivated I became. I can see so many ways they are like humans, or is it the other way around? Laboratory animals' feelings are so masked it is hard to get honest base behavior. Free-range monkeys are so wonderfully honest they really whet my interest."

"Don't be fooled. Our monkeys can be just as devious. You will get to know this once you get to know them."

The group at the table laughed at Siegal's naiveté.

"Are you going to adopt a group of monkeys to experiment with?" asked Dr. Bob.

"Absolutely. I studied rats for years. Studying monkey behavior and their comparative relationship with humans is like jumping light years into the field. I can hardly wait to get started. There is one thing. I have concerns about their health care. Can I visit with you tomorrow in your clinic?"

"Your timing is perfect. We have a couple of kids—I mean monkeys. Of course. You can see how we handle them. Although we keep it quiet, we are always evaluating our population for HIV."

"How long do you plan to stay with us?" asked Jose. "I'm sure Missy Ro would not mind for you to be a guest as long as you like."

"I think two more days will be all I can absorb at one time. However, I would like to be invited back."

"Anything you would like to do is fine with us here," responded Missy Ro. "We can always use an extra unpaid hand."

Dinner ended, and Siegal returned to his hut. He wanted to view the videotapes left for him before getting too tired. His last act before falling asleep was to email the pictures from his camera to Danielson.

TWO DAYS PASSED. WITH FOND farewells to Missy Ro and especially Phillipe, Siegal headed back to Miami and his own little island. He was excited to begin work on his private monkey island and to have a grand reunion with his friends.

EIGHT

SIEGAL'S STOMACH TOLD HIM HE was hungry, but the long trip back to his island left him too fatigued to think about eating. He thought only of his comfortable bed and the cool ocean breezes lulling him to sleep. He smiled, knowing he didn't have to worry about any creepy crawly things from the African jungle. As he walked back to the house, he saw wisps of smoke from the outdoor grill. Warm food smells filled his nostrils.

"Hey, Ross. Want a cold ODL? There are hot dogs and fried potatoes cooking. Thought you might appreciate some old-fashioned American cuisine for a change instead of snake stew and elephant ear soup."

"Tom? What in all hell's name brings you out?"

"I got all your pictures. But I'm curious to know how you felt about your trip. Waiting for an invitation from you might take at least a month. Are we still in the monkey business?"

"More than I ever imagined. Let me unpack my smelly clothes. The stench of the African jungle is unlike anything you can imagine."

"Unpack later. Eat while the food is hot. I hate dogs charred beyond recognition."

The two sat on the porch, talking as fast as they ate. In the space of four days, Siegal had transformed from a naïve sightseer to a degreed master in monkey engineering. Even so, there were still quite a few questions left unanswered before starting up a free-range lab.

"I need to set up my observation area."

"I'm way ahead of you. The pictures you forwarded and the pamphlet of Monkey Town Center provided a good start. I've contacted my Seabee buddies to build everything for you. Those fellows can build anything. They ordered construction materials which should be arriving shortly."

After a lengthy discussion regarding the size and configurations of the tunnel system, Siegal brought up what was really on his mind. "And the other matter."

"You mean your reunion party? You must have some jet lag. We'll talk tomorrow."

THE TWO SPENT THE NEXT day pretending to fish but mostly talking business.

"Tom, did you look at my wall charts while waiting for me to get home?"

"I did. Were there any secrets?"

"Not from you, to be sure. The first two items are office equipment and resource materials. I need your help procuring them. Can you do that?"

"Did that already. Deliveries should start next week. Is that too soon?"

"That's a hell of a lot better service than I ever had at the university," grinned Siegal, scratching the balding spot at the back of his head.

"This is not academic work, you know. The office equipment is easy. I plan to work on your professional library when I get back to the States. As for contacting experts, you'll want to do that on your own.

"Amazing. You know what I am thinking and are miles ahead of me. How in the hell do you do it?"

"Let's just say it is how I became chief of staff at the White House."

Siegal shook his head in wonderment.

Danielson looked at his watch. "Sorry, good buddy. Have to go. I made arrangements for the plane to pick me up around noon. I hate to leave this island paradise. It grows on you. But meetings are meetings, and you can't keep CEOs waiting. They pay our bills."

THE DRONE OF DANIELSON'S PLANE taking him back to the mainland was still audible as Siegal ran into his office. It had been over a year since he felt so energized. He couldn't wait to get going.

He looked at his rat drawing on the wall. "Well, Tigger, we're in business again."

He thought back to when the real live Tigger was his lab's pet at City University. He was named by Simi and Sally, then his research assistants, because of an unusual black stripe down the middle of his back. Tigger became the favorite rat because of his unusual ability to learn tasks. He seemed to have the ability to communicate information to the other lab rats.

Living as a hermit in the mountain chalet in the Colorado Rockies, Siegal had drawn Tigger's image and taped it to the wall of his work area. It became his companion for sanity. He smiled at his latest drawing of Tigger and patted it affectionately on the butt.

Siegal went to the refrigerator. His normal behavior was to get a beer and then two or three more until he became too alcohol saturated to be effective as a scientist. His past life left too much time on his hands. Being inebriated for long periods mattered little then. But, this time, he reached into the refrigerator for some ice and instant tea. He was surprised. It seemed to taste even better than beer. He filled his glass and returned to his office and cartoon friend.

Siegal lifted his glass. "Welcome to our new life, Tigger."

HE LOOKED AT HIS FRIEND. "We have to decide which monkey species we want on our island, Tigger. One of the things I learned in Africa is that all monkey species have their own diets. Most monkeys do not thrive on changes very well, either in habitat or diet. They can develop all kinds of psychological problems.

Siegal poured another glass of iced tea.

"Okay, super rat, let's decide. There are fifty-three New World species divided into two groups: Callithricidae and Cebidae. The Callithricidae consists of tamarins and marmosets. They are the more primitive. The Cebidae includes squirrel, spider, woolly, and capuchin monkeys. They may have families as large as five hundred. Which species suits us best? We have enough variety of flora for their diets right here to satisfy most of them. Come on, Tigger. Help me focus."

Siegal stated at his cartoon companion. A pamphlet on spider monkeys fell on the floor. "Thank you, Tigger, for giving me a sign." He picked up the pamphlet and read:

Spider monkeys are fifteen to twenty-five inches long, minus their tails. *Good size.*

Spider monkeys have a large brain by comparison to other New World monkeys.

Higher functioning. Good.

Spider monkeys live in units as small as two to eight individuals, with the main band numbering from fifteen to thirty. Life expectancy is about twenty-five years.

Perfect.

"Spider monkeys it is."

Siegal cut out a picture of a spider monkey and pinned it next to Tigger. He emailed Danielson to tell him he wanted five or six spider monkeys, three males, and two or three females.

There came a reply almost immediately. "I will get started on it right this minute. I am guessing it will take about a month to find your suitable group and then work through the animal societies to give assurance of good care and no abusive experiments."

NINE

ONE MONTH SEEMED AN ETERNITY for Siegal. He was so ready to begin his monkey research. It allowed him to recall the wonderful times he had with his two graduate students. One being the brilliant Sally Ryan, who received her doctorate at age twenty-seven and married Dr. Bill Feinberg, knows as BF, a psychologist at City University. They were two of Siegal's few friends. And, of course, Simi Block, his one true love, also attained her doctorate under his guidance. She accepted a position in the Cal-Berkeley psychology department. The reunion would bring all of them together again; at least, that is what he planned.

Siegal's cell phone rang, taking him out of his thoughts. Only Danielson knew his number. The only exceptions were robocalls which Siegal immediately blocked.

"Hey, good buddy. I've got some good news and not-so-good news."

"First, the good news."

"Drs. William Feinberg and Sally Ryan-Feinberg accepted our invitations. Jerry Ravid is also coming to our reunion."

"You left out one person."

"That's the not-so-good news. A return message from Cal-Berkeley indicated she was attending a conference in Paris and not expected to return until after spring break."

Siegal was disappointed. Having two of his favorite university friends and Ravid were better than none. The person he wanted most was not available.

"Make it happen, Tom. I'll do something about Simi afterward."

TEN

TWO WEEKS PASSED, AND CONSTRUCTION on Siegal's island was complete. The spider monkeys were scheduled at the end of the month. This was the day of the grand reunion.

The guests arrived on the same plane. None of them guessed the real reason for their trip. Danielson alone greeted them upon landing—a ploy to extend the mystery.

"Welcome to Little Deadman's Cay, the gem of the Atlantic. I hope you all enjoy your two days on the island," said Danielson, doing his best to imitate Tattoo from the old television series *Fantasy Island*. This was not easy. Tattoo was less than four feet tall, and Danielson stood six feet four.

The guests saw the fencing making the locale appear more like a POW camp than an island paradise.

Sally spoke first. "What kind of hellhole is this?"

"Not to worry, Sally." Danielson waved his hand. "Everything will be made clear in a few moments. Accommodations are a bit Spartan, but I think all of you will be quite comfortable." He opened the wire gate into the inner grounds.

A lone person sat on the porch. The sun was low and obscured everyone's vision. "Come sit. Join me for a drink before dinner. I believe the brand of choice for the two of you is ODL. Jerry, what can I get you? Scotch?"

"Ross, is that you?" exclaimed BF. "Aren't you supposed to be dead? What the hell?"

Siegal laughed. "Welcome to Little Deadman's Cay. It's an appropriate name for my home, don't you think? Come, sit. I have lots to tell you and a lot more apologies to offer."

There were hugs all around, including a long one from Jerry Ravid, who seldom let his emotions out so openly. So much for needing apologies.

"Dinner is on the grill," announced Siegal.

"Wait a damn minute," demanded Ravid, pointing fingers at both Siegal and Danielson. "I've been endorsing special projects blindly for some time. Are you now telling me I was really setting up consultancies for you, Ross?"

Siegal smiled. "Yup. I needed the work. We couldn't tell you for my own security as well as yours."

Danielson excused himself to get the drinks from the refrigerator.

Siegal began, "It began a long time ago. I was splitting time between being a professor at City University and working for Interaction Dynamics. The ..."

BF stopped him in mid-thought. "Wait a minute. Am I going crazy? You're drinking iced tea."

Siegal laughed. "Part of my story had to do with me working alone and drinking too much booze. I was becoming an alcoholic. Since starting a new research project, I've decided to get healthy."

The change quieted everyone. Their friend was either very serious or completely insane. Or maybe both. They toasted his sobriety.

He continued. "It was Tom who guided most everything that happened to me from my last year at City University until now, including why I am alive today."

Danielson nodded humbly. "All I did was feed you a bit of stimulus, as you say in psychology. You were the one who made the proper responses."

Siegal continued. "At that time, Tom was a very influential person in Washington. It seemed that there was an extremely serious international threat. It was decided that our government needed a certain type of behavioral profiler to help understand a specific terrorist mastermind."

Sally surmised, "So the mysterious trips you used to take to Washington were all related to that threat?"

"Exactly. I still can't tell you very much about what I was doing. Most of it is classified."

"What I want to know is, did you get the bastards?" asked Sally.

Danielson clenched his fist in triumph. "Yes, thanks to our good buddy here. We got our rat terrorist and his entire pack."

"Hot damn," exclaimed Sally as she danced around the group. "Ross, Ross, he's our man. If he can't do it, nobody can."

Everyone laughed.

"Can you tell us where you disappeared to?" asked Ravid.

"The Feds had a chalet in the mountains just outside of Central City. After getting rid of the terrorists, I discovered my life was again in danger from one of the governments I worked for. One of those politicos, who has to remain nameless, wanted to use the terrorist's secret weaponry for his own motives."

Danielson added, "Whether it was Ross's intuitive sense or his superior skill at ferreting out seemingly insignificant clues, we discovered the turncoat. This knowledge signed Ross's death warrant. Just minutes before the chalet was set to be firebombed with Ross in it."

Siegal broke in, "Tom came to my rescue. It was made to appear I had been killed, including leaving a John Doe corpse in my place. To make a long story a whole lot shorter, I ended up here on this island."

Danielson turned the filets over a final time. "We're having *fruit de mer*. Ross and I spent all morning catching some fine-looking sea bass. I hope you're hungry."

Siegal ushered the group into the yard, where the table from the second bedroom was set with assorted fruits and vegetables. Danielson followed with a platter of fish filets.

Danielson said, "Help yourself. Don't be shy about seconds." There were many more questions, but none really mattered. Their man was alive.

"I am sure you are wondering what this wire construction is all about," said Siegal, after assuring himself that all his guests had their fill. "It seems that Tom here wants me doing research again. This enclosure is to make sure I can't escape."

"That's not true," interrupted Danielson.

"Actually, I was getting stir-crazy living alone and not ready to go back to civilization."

Sally blurted, "I get it. You're going to start a camp and study incarcerated convicts."

"Not even close. The wire network is more to keep me and the other observers enclosed and allows what I will be studying to roam free."

"What are you studying?" asked BF. "I don't see anything."

"Monkeys," said Siegal. "Let's take a walk."

"Monkeys?" they chimed in unison.

"Free-range monkeys. Why not? I developed many theories while understanding rats and comparing them to humans. I now want to study higher forms of animals. Tom and I felt monkeys can offer all sorts of new information."

BF asked, "So, where are they?"

Danielson answered. "They are coming. We had to ensure none were disease carriers. And animal rights groups are always on the backs of researchers. We have to assure them our animals will be treated with great care and not subject to adverse situations or stimuli."

"What's with the wire network around your living area?" asked BF

Siegal explained, "I visited a unique monkey zoo in South Africa. The monkeys there are free to roam, and the observers are caged, so to speak. These tunnels we are walking through serve two purposes. First, it keeps the monkeys from accidentally hurting observers. Secondly, the separation allows the monkeys to move freely and not be spoiled by human interaction."

"And?" Ravid asked.

"And, I wanted you, my best friends, to be the first to find out about me being alive and what I am doing. I'm only sorry Simi isn't here to share this event."

"By the way," asked BF, "where is she?"

"Her office at Cal-Berkeley explained she was at a conference in Paris and wouldn't return until after spring break." Siegal's voice broke at the thought. "I plan to reach out to her next week."

The group sensed his anguish. Simi and Ross were a very tight couple. Everyone felt they would marry after her graduation. Before this could happen, Siegal was reported dead, and Simi went west to create her own life.

Sally felt a need to change the mood. "How can we be of service?"

"Good question. I don't have a plan. You can help me decide what to research."

Danielson looked at his watch. "It's getting late, and all of you had a long ride getting here. If you are up for it, we can get into a session in the morning. That gives us the afternoon to lay on the beach, swim, or fish before we have to leave."

Sally and BF slept in the main bedroom: Jerry claimed the couch in the office. Danielson and Siegal laid out sleeping bags on the porch.

MORNING CAME, AND SIEGAL PROVIDED an island breakfast of fried akee and breadfruit along with fruit from his garden. Then it was back to work.

"Just like old times," said BF.

Siegal began, "Yesterday was a day to get all of you in the mood to work your magic. I first plied you with a four-star banquet followed by a night of royal splendor. I'm sorry, I don't have indoor plumbing yet. Our union is still on strike."

He turned to his sheets on the wall. "As you know, my favorite style of studying a new problem is to brainstorm."

He handed out copies of his plan:

MONKEY ISLAND EXPERIMENTAL PLAN

Spider monkeys are the best-suited species. They are New World who adapt well to the flora of this island. Adults are about three feet long. Family groups contain two or more females. Populations generally are under twenty in number. Their brain size is larger than most other New World monkeys, Therefore, they may possess more humanlike intelligence. The intention is to study them in the most natural setting possible.

Siegal added, "The initial population will not know each other unless, by chance, they came from the same zoo. So, pour a fresh cup of coffee. I'll refill my tea. And we can get started on my new life's work."

They offered ideas faster than he could write. An hour later, the walls were covered with ideas. They scanned the list, culled the least obvious, and kept the better ones.

Ravid scratched his chin in a mock professional manner. "Well, Dr. Siegal, it appears you have enough ideas to keep an entire cadre of scientists busy for a long time."

"I'm not planning to vary any living situation. Everything that happens will be free range. I can study several kinds of behaviors concurrently. I have a unique opportunity to explore a monkey culture from its very onset. Not like Jane Goodall, who spent her time with clans already established."

BF summed it up. "Then it seems you already have your research design. It is very exciting. I wish I could be here. It's a shame Sally and I have professional obligations at our own university."

Sally jumped in. "But we'll come if you want."

"I believe the two of you need to be out there where all the action is. You'd dry up on this island. I wouldn't expect you to throw your careers away and join me. But I do have plans for all of you. This morning proves my idea. Most of the time I can do this work on my own. I know, however, I will need periodic support from you as problems arise—on a professional fee basis, of course."

"Are we forgetting Simi?" asked Sally.

Each time her name came up, the group stopped whatever they were doing. Simi was being missed and not just by Siegal.

"I plan to see her right after she returns from Paris. I hope the shock of my exaggerated death won't be too much for her. I just think a face-to-face visit is better than any mail or phone call."

Danielson looked at his watch and frowned. "We worked right through the afternoon. I radioed the plane while you were brainstorming. It should be landing in two hours. Enjoy some time on the beach."

The plane landed on schedule and loaded its passengers. The island was again left to Dr. Ross Siegal, hermit, psychological researcher, with a plan for his future.

ELEVEN

DANIELSON BOOKED SIEGAL'S FLIGHT TO Oakland. Upon arrival, Siegal collected his luggage and went directly to a car rental agency. A reserved BMW convertible waited.

The car's GPS directed him to the Berkeley campus with only a few correction commands. By the time Siegal arrived at the Institute for Human Development, it was after five, and the offices were closed for the day. Both tired and hungry, he located a motel just off campus that advertised dining.

The first thing he did, even before going to the bathroom, was dial Simi's apartment phone. He couldn't wait. The phone clicked to a recorded message.

Disappointed, he replaced the phone back on its base, unpacked, and went downstairs to eat.

Following dinner, he tried to call again. He got the same recorded message. He laid down on the bed in frustration. He awoke about midnight still in his street clothes. He undressed but tossed and turned the remainder of the night. His mind kept rehearsing what he would say when he and Simi reconnected, and he wondered if they still had the same emotions for each other?

He intended to arrive at the Institute of Human Development at eight-thirty. Instead, he got lost in more dead ends before locating the correct building. It was after nine when he climbed the flagstone steps and entered.

A SECRETARY/RECEPTIONIST SITTING AT THE front desk asked, "Can I help you, sir?"

"Yes, please. I am Dr. Ross Siegal. I was Dr. Block's major advisor when she was a graduate student at the University of Denver. I was hoping to surprise her with a visit. Is she in?"

"I'm sorry, Dr. Siegal, she's not returned from her meeting in Paris."

"Can you tell me when she is expected, Miss …?"

"Lampert."

"Lampert," repeated Siegal.

"I don't have any more information. Maybe you should talk with our director? Her office is down the hall. I can let her know you wish to speak with her regarding Dr. Block."

Siegal thanked her and proceeded down the hall. He was in awe of the modern architecture as he remembered the older buildings at City University. He knocked on the half-opened door.

"Come in, Dr. Siegal. It is an honor meeting someone of your stature."

Siegal entered. "It's Ross, please."

The director stepped out from behind her desk. "I'm Lori Bauer. Can I offer you something to drink?"

"Iced tea would be perfect if you have some."

"No problem. I'll ask my receptionist to make some up. We often have visiting dignitaries, and Raeanne is used to bringing whatever they want. I consider your visit a special honor. Simi has spoken highly of you. Except, I thought she said you had died in a mountain fire some time ago."

"I almost did. I was very lucky. I felt the only way to break the news was to show up in person."

"The shock of discovering you alive is bound to be difficult no matter how you try to sugarcoat it." She paused. "I'm sorry your planned meeting will have to wait a little longer. As you know, she is attending a symposium in Paris where she is the guest speaker. Then we received a letter from the sponsors asking permission for her to remain for an additional week to complete the project's unfinished business. Simi has developed a terrific support staff here at the Institute of Human Development, so we felt it was in the best interest of both her career and our department to give her this extra time. If you would have announced your plans to us in advance, we could have informed you."

"I apologize for my shortsightedness, but I wasn't sure I would be coming at this time until just a few days ago. When do you think she'll be back?"

"My best guess is Monday. Do your responsibilities allow you to stay over the weekend? We can show you around our facility this morning, and then maybe you can enjoy some of the sights in San Francisco."

"I would enjoy a tour. After that, I hear Fisherman's Wharf is a great place to visit. And I've only seen pictures of Muir Woods."

Dr. Bauer checked her iPad. "My schedule leaves me free for most of the morning. I can show you around personally."

She began her voice-assisted tour as a well-oiled guide with a memorized script she so often used when selling their programs to wealthy foundations. "It is a surprise to most people that IHD has been around for some time. It was officially organized as a research unit at the University of California in 1927." She stopped and smiled. "We are always open to exploring new areas if you are interested. We would enjoy having you as an emeritus researcher."

"No, thank you, Lori. Any exploration now is strictly a hobby."

"If you ever change your mind, we always have discretionary funds for leaders such as yourself."

The tour continued, reaching a suite of offices labeled Sociobiological Effects on Behavior. The name under the title was Samantha Block, PhD, Department Director.

"I could spend days telling you about most departments in IHD, but this is one area I know less about. It is Simi's unique creation. She started here in one of the other departments as an assistant professor. One day she presented the board with a research plan that encompassed an entirely unique combination of disciplines. The board was impressed and agreed to support her idea for one year. Her findings were impressive enough to warrant continued support. I'm surprised you haven't heard of her reputation since the two of you were so close before your ..."

"Disappearance? The fact is my visit today will be our first contact in almost three years. During that time, I stopped reading any research journals related to psychology. I was too burned out to care."

"I can understand." Then noticing the time on the hall clock, she said, "I have a meeting in ten minutes. I will introduce you to Dr. Alisa Land-man, Simi's assistant director, and leave you in her care."

They entered a suite, a large room with multiple carrels, each equipped with Wi-Fi connections. Its orderly appearance gave a sterile impression. Siegal thought how different this was compared to his crowded lab at City University and his messy bedroom office on the island.

"I half expected to see a lab full of animals and people in white lab coats. This place looks more like a library."

The two walked over to one of the carrels. A stylish and pleasant appearing young lady was working on a computer. She wore casual slacks and no lab coat.

"This is Dr. Alisa Landman. Alisa, this is Dr. Ross Siegal."

Alisa immediately stopped, winding a wisp of hair behind her ear, and said, "You are the famous Dr. Ross Siegal that Simi talks about. What an honor it is to meet you. Say, aren't you supposed to be ...?"

"Dead? I guess, like Mark Twain, the rumor of my demise is a bit premature."

"I can see that, Dr. Siegal," smiled Alisa showing a wry sense of humor.

"I'm retired and feel more comfortable just having you call me Ross."

Alisa stumbled to her feet and nodded. "It's fine with me. We don't use titles much around here anyway. I am so glad to meet you. You're like an icon in this office. Whenever there's a procedural question, Simi would always say, 'I wonder how Ross would handle it?' And, you know, it always worked out like it was supposed to."

"You're in good hands, Ross," said Dr. Bauer. "If there is anything else you want, let Raeanne know. In the meantime, enjoy yourself, and we can get together for dinner when Simi returns." With a businesslike handshake, she left for her meeting.

"Where do you want to start?" asked Alisa.

"You can tell me more about what you all are doing here in this office of sociobi …"

"Sociobiology. I'll try. First, let me tell you that I've read almost everything you published and think you're as good as it gets in this stodgy old field. There isn't much going on today. It's Friday. Most of our activities are down for the weekend. Many of the staff are already checked out, getting their last licks of spring hang gliding. The area on the west end of the campus has some of the world's best updrafts. So, I can't show you much in progress. Any question so far?"

"Okay. Psychology 101. What is sociobiology?"

Alisa took a deep breath. "The field of study started with investigations of social insects like ants and bees. It changed to studying diverse social groups of higher functioning animals. Sometimes programs around the world have taken what we consider wrong turns and have done some selective breeding, emphasizing the more aggressive behaviors like fighting chickens and dogs."

"It's always been that way. Opportunists have taken some exciting information and turned it into negative energy," responded Siegal.

"In this lab, we have moved off the study of many lower animal forms to understanding the whys and wherefores of humans. We have incorporated the disciplines of ethology, biopsychology, psychoneuro-immunology, and the study of superorganisms."

Siegal put up his hands. "Slow down. I can get a feel for biopsychology; I even know that ethology means animal behavior."

"Sorry," said Alisa. She pointed to the near wall. "These charts and posters here help explain the different disciplines. We put them up for tours from students and individuals who wish to endow what we do. They may be too simple for your knowledge base, but they do a great job explaining."

"No offense intended, but I do better by reading about it at my own pace. Do you have any books or papers on these areas that I can borrow? I can spend the weekend reading."

"No offense felt. In fact, I'm relieved. I wasn't sure how to explain the terms to you. When Simi comes back on Monday, she can give you more details."

She collected several books and publications, packed them in a box, and gave them to Siegal.

"I was looking for an excuse to avoid sightseeing. Playing tourist is not my favorite pastime. I can hide in my motel room and read."

"You can take a shortcut to the parking lot," she said, opening the door and pointing to an exit sign just outside the lab office." She offered her hand to shake. Siegal reciprocated and left.

The science of sociobiology was new to Siegal. The thrill of learning how his protégé had progressed since her graduation was a super energy toxin.

By Sunday night he had poured over every word Dr. Landman had given him.

ON MONDAY, SIEGAL CAREFULLY AVOIDED all dead ends and arrived precisely at eight-thirty when the IHD opened.

Siegal greeted Raeanne with a good morning.

"The same to you, Dr. Siegal. Did you have a pleasant weekend?"

"I did."

"How was Fisherman's Wharf?"

"Actually, I didn't go anywhere, thanks to Dr. Landman." He held up the box she gave him. "I immersed myself for the entire weekend learning about sociobiology." Siegal acted impatiently. "I can't wait to see Dr. Block. Is she in yet?"

Raeanne was apologetic. "Not yet, sir. Dr. Bauer is in. Should I tell her you are here?"

"Please."

Raeanne buzzed her director. "She will see you now. Shall I bring in some iced tea for you?"

Siegal shook his head as he fast-walked down the hall.

The door to Dr. Bauer's office was open. Siegal knocked and walked in.

"Morning, Ross. Simi has not yet arrived. I'm sure Raeanne told you that. She's usually one of the first here in the morning. I can try calling her apartment. Should I let her know you are here?"

"No. I want our first meeting in person before she learns from someone else."

Dr. Bauer checked her phone file and punched in some numbers. The phone in Simi's apartment rang several times. The same message Siegal heard before was repeated.

"That's strange," said Dr. Bauer. "Simi is certainly a type A personality. When she is not where we expect her to be, she always lets us know."

"That's how I remember her, too," agreed Siegal. "I think I'll wander your campus a little to help pass the time. I'll check back later."

Siegal hung around the Cal-Berkeley campus for the rest of the day, checking back every hour or so to see if there were any messages. There were none. He then drove to Simi's apartment and rang the doorbell. No response. The building superintendent pointed to her car parked exactly where she left it weeks ago.

Siegal had thoughts that worried him. *I know she's a big girl and can take care of herself. Maybe it is just paranoia leftover from my adventure at the chalet.* He took a deep breath. *She must have stayed in France an extra day to sightsee or shop. I'll give her one more day and then ....*

Tuesday came and passed. There was still no hint of why she was delayed.

He dialed a familiar number.

"HELLO, TOM? I CAN'T THINK there's any reason to panic, but Simi didn't return afterthe conference. And she's two days overdue."

Danielson had learned a long time ago to trust Siegal's intuition. "You think something's wrong?"

"You know Simi. She would have called regarding any changes in plans. Only she didn't tell her apartment super or anyone at the institute. It isn't like her."

"I'll do some checking. Can you stay there for another day or two?"

"You bet. I don't have any place to be unless our monkeys arrive early. That's the only thing that would cause me to return to the island."

"Then it's settled. You stay there. Do you think Dr. Bauer can get you a key to her apartment? You can look around and check her mail to get any clues. I'll get back to you very soon. I promise."

Siegal was always amazed at the connections Danielson had. As a team, he was the theoretical brain, and Danielson handled the technical where-with-all to get things done stat.

"I just have a feeling," concluded Danielson.

TWELVE

"GOOD EVENING, DR. SUNADA. I am checking the progress of our master plan. Also, how is our guest Dr. Block progressing?"

"Good. Everything is moving well on my side of the ledger. My house-guest is here and well. I have begun my brainwashing sessions. I believe I will succeed. Although, it may take slightly longer for her to become helpful. She is very strong-willed and can counter most of my normal strategies."

"You know, I am very wealthy with earnings from my criminal law practice and astute involvement in the stock market. I can make her very rich if that can be an extra incentive."

"I do not believe money can entice her. When I get her to help, it will be because she wants to participate. It will be to help me, not you."

"Whatever it takes. As you know, I don't want to be identified with any of the actions. I must remain invisible."

"I understand. How is your part of the master plan going?"

"I just returned from the doctor. The news is not good. My nerve deterioration is irreversible. My prognosis is an agonizing death. I want the people who did this to feel the pain I am experiencing now. I understand why your skills in motivation are not adequate to control an entire group of like-minded individuals and that we need your houseguest to make the plan succeed. In the meantime, I am gathering these like-minded individuals in preparation. I only hope there is enough time before I am too ill."

"If the rate of your deterioration does not speed up, I believe we have time. I will continue to do my part and hasten my houseguest's will to assist."

THE SINGLE LIGHT BULB IN the ceiling remained on 24/7 except when food was delivered, negating any chance Simi had to see any of her captors. The red light on the surveillance camera was the one part of her environment she controlled when she wanted personal privacy. Simi knew someone was watching her every move even though the voice overhead remained mute.

She touched herself to see if it all was real. *I'm losing track of my days. Did I forget to put a counting scratch on the wine rack today?*

She had walked, crawled, touched, and smelled every inch of her finite world down to memorizing the three small and two larger nicks on the wooden wine rack shelves. Every piece of chipped paint on the walls and cracks in the concrete floor were indelibly inked in her photographic brain.

Boredom, her enemy, was the first step in the brainwashing process. And she had no way to stop it. Not even slow it down.

Well, it damn well won't happen to me. I must get out of here. Somehow escape. My captors control everything. No, not everything. I control the red light whenever I need privacy. Even the slightest change in my behavior could be important and maybe throw them off guard.

On this day of captivity, she pretended to forget asking to have the surveillance camera turned off. Instead, she went through her entire routine in full view of her captors. It was a total departure in character. Even when she and Siegal were intimate, she remained modest while taking care of bodily functions.

After breakfast, the voice of her captor returned. "Dr. Block, are you all right?"

"Yes, I'm fine. Why do you ask?" She pretended not to understand the purpose of the question.

"Dr. Block, did you forget something this morning?"

She looked toward the ceiling. "I don't think so."

"You forgot about asking us to turn off the surveillance camera."

Simi made her voice sound childlike. "I feel you have not tried to harm me in any way. I just felt you would want to know more about me. I want to share everything about me." She hoped her responses would give her kidnappers a beginning toward hostage acceptance, toward Stockholm syndrome.

"Would you like a short period of personal attention?"

"What?"

"Someone to talk with."

"Yes. Oh please. Yes."

"Does this mean you are ready to help us?"

"I don't know if I can because I don't know what you want from me." She paused. "But I would like to see you."

"That can be arranged, Dr. Block. I will visit with you in your chamber this afternoon after lunch."

IT WAS AFTER FOUR O'CLOCK when the overhead light was turned off. The door opened, and the sound of a single pair of footsteps, different from the ones that delivered meals, entered.

Simi turned. "Why don't you turn on the light? You promised me a personal visit."

"I promised you some personal contact, and here I am."

The voice of the ceiling speaker was now in the same room. It was the first time since her capture that she heard a human sound not coming from the overhead speaker.

"But I can't see you." She pretended to cry. "Is this the sort of contact you offer?"

"Sit down, Dr. Block. I am your keeper and also your protector. However, the light stays off until you demonstrate a willingness to help. What would you like to talk about?"

"I've been thinking about where I am. Will you tell me if I'm correct?"

"That depends, Dr. Block."

The voice, Simi guessed, was definitely Japanese and coupled with its formality, was hypnotic. She wasn't sure if she could maintain her façade. She began with a noninvasive question.

"You are keeping me in some sort of wine cellar. Is that correct?"

"Come now, Dr. Block. That question is so beneath you."

"Okay. I'm in a wine cellar. At first, I thought this place was somewhere in the wine country. Then I noticed the bottles were more of a collection with many different labels. So I think this is a wine cellar in a private residence."

"That is more like you, Dr. Block. To be more specific, this is my private residence."

The use of her name in almost every sentence unsettled her. It clouded her effort to battle wits with her captor.

"Now," she added, "I am not in just any house, but either a villa or an estate."

"Again, very astute. I like to think of my home as a villa. What else can you gather?"

"I think all my captors are men. Correct?"

"Yes. Go on."

"I think from your accent you are foreign-born—Japanese, I think."

"Too many questions, for now, Dr. Block. You must take baby steps before giant ones. You will learn everything in good time. Our visit is up for this day." The footsteps started to retreat.

Simi's voice raised, showing desperation. "Wait. Don't go. Tell me what you want from me?"

"Tomorrow, I may give you more time. Relax. It is for your Zen."

She repeated, "You still haven't told me what you want."

"There is always tomorrow, Dr. Block."

The footsteps moved toward the door and exited. The light in the ceiling turned on.

Am I just pretending to make my abductors feel they are winning? Or am I really softening? How much of my soul am I willing to cede for more moments of personal contact?

THIRTEEN

IT WAS MIDNIGHT WHEN THE phone rang in Siegal's motel room.

"Ross?" It was Danielson. "I want to make sure you were there, so I called late."

"Did you find anything?"

"It seems someone used Simi's plane ticket and traveled to France. Then using her passport, they checked into the hotel. From there, the trail grew cold. I didn't find any scheduled conference in or around Paris at that time having anything related to human motivational systems. We do know Simi cashed her advance per diem check in Denver, so there is evidence of an actual shadow organizational structure. Either she wanted to disappear, or someone else did. I believe the latter."

"Someone wanted her to disappear?" repeated Siegal.

"The perpetrator went to great lengths to keep her absence from being discovered. This was no random event."

"Then you don't think she actually took the trip at all?"

"All the clues point to that fact. It means she's probably still here in the States," concluded Danielson.

"Good. Then it shouldn't be too hard to find her. We have already eliminated about 80 percent of the world," responded Siegal sarcastically.

"There are plenty of closets to hide her in—if she's alive."

"Don't say that, Tom. Don't even guess it. She's alive. She must be."

"I agree, good buddy. My experience in such matters tells me if they wanted to kill her, they would not have gone to such extremes. They want something from her. Something she knows. They need her alive."

"I can stay a couple more days and talk with people at the institute. It must be related to something she is working on."

"Keep a stiff upper lip, Ross. We'll find her, and she'll be just fine. I promise.

FOURTEEN

"HELLO? SIR? ARE WE TALKING?"

Block's questions were acknowledged with silence. The short visit the day before had weakened her resolve. She began to feel panic—not of physical harm, but to her psyche.

Have my captors won me over so fast ... so easily? I feel I'm losing my will to resist. If I knew why I was here, I could fight it.

Simi busied her mind by studying her confinement in even more detail than before. She noticed the wood shelving holding the wine bottles and the door frame were both soft and spongy.

My space is infested with termites. I could force the door open and escape during the night. But to where? I'm not in an urban area, or I would have heard traffic noises. I could be miles away from any help. So far, there has been no attempt to harm me. I am better off biding my time till I learn more about my predicament. The termite door is always an option.

It was late afternoon when the familiar voice returned over the speaker. "Dr. Block, I have a surprise for you. I hope it will not be too much of a shock. You just have to cooperate."

"Sure. What have I to lose?" She surprised herself with how easy it was to agree.

Within minutes the overhead light was turned off, and the door to her prison opened. She heard the same footsteps as yesterday approach.

"Turn away from me, Dr. Block. I must blindfold you. You will be able to take it off soon.

Block turned. The blindfold was put on, and she was led out of her prison. In moments, she was met with a rush of warm, fresh air. Bright sunlight permeated around her blindfold. Her guide helped her sit down on a canvas chair.

"Keep your hands folded, Dr. Block. I will tell you when to take off your blindfold. Your eyes must remain closed for a moment or two until you get used to the sunlight."

After a time, the voice instructed her to take off the blindfold. Simi reached up to her face and removed the soft cloth covering her eyes. As instructed, she waited to let her eyes acclimate to the brightness she felt through her eyelids. Slowly, she opened them. The light was blinding after being kept in a windowless room for the past several days.

The new space, a small courtyard, was no larger than her cell. The surface was flagstone with wildflowers growing between the cracks. It was impossible for Simi to get a sense of direction because the ten-foot walls blocked any view beyond her confinement. On a table in front of her was a pitcher of lemonade and a glass full of ice cubes.

"Have a drink, Dr. Block. You are not used to the heat of the sun and should take care not to become dehydrated. There is more sugar on the table if it is not sweet enough. Don't bother turning around. I am talking inside my house, through a window."

She poured a glass and took a sip. "It's perfect. Won't you join me, whoever you are? There is enough for both of us."

"All in good time, Dr. Block. First, I want to reintroduce you to some freedom. We will have the opportunity to meet later."

She looked toward the window, but the speaker's face was hidden by an opaque curtain. "I very much want to meet you now. I want to know more about you." She then said, hoping to be convincing, "I feel you are quite intelligent and also successful in your field. I think we can establish a degree of professional friendship. I want to know more about your philosophy. You, I guess, are very much aware of mine. So, what harm would there be to see your face? Would I recognize it? You have been in the news. Am I right?"

"You ask many questions, Dr. Block. Yes, my deeds, not my name, have been in the news at different times, only it's not been recent. I doubt very much you would recognize me from photographs. The sun is hot. Drink more of your lemonade. Your visit today is almost over."

The increase of freedom outside her dark prison, even for a few minutes, made Simi want much more. She was weakening. She couldn't help it.

"Your name. Tell me your name," she pleaded.

"In due time, Dr. Block. You have to be patient."

I'm being played. How much of this mental teasing can I endure before becoming a willing slave? I know it will only be a matter of time before I'm completely won over.

"Your outing is over, Dr. Block. It is time to replace your blindfold."

Simi complied and sat, waiting for someone to take her hand. She was then led back into the building and into her wine cellar prison. The next two days passed without any voice or new freedoms. Simi Block was losing the battle, and there had not even been a war.

What harm would it be to find out what they want from me? I can always listen and then either refuse to help or give information. "Hello. Can you hear me? I would like to share a glass of lemonade with you."

Another day passed in silence. "Please," she begged. "I need to talk with you. I need human contact."

In minutes, the ceiling light went out, the door opened, and a set of footsteps came into the room.

"Turn around so I can put this blindfold on you."

Simi passively obeyed.

SUN GAZETTE

The business world is about to have a changing of the guard. Investors have always followed the leads of investment experts like Warren Buffett. However, a new guru has emerged. His name is William Getsen III. He is known as Wily Willie to his competitors. While Buffet and others are buying precious commodities, Getsen is acquiring over-the-counter pharmaceutical stocks. His investment profits are rumored to be many times his purchase prices. Despite efforts by this editor to learn his secrets, he has refused all my requests for an interview. I will continue to pursue my effort to learn more about this mysterious newcomer and share my information with you, my readers.

FIFTEEN

WHAT A REVERSAL, THOUGHT SIEGAL. *First, it was me who planned to tell Simi I was alive and had been secretly hiding. Now it was Simi who disappeared with no explanation. Ironic.*

Siegal stood at the open window of his motel room and yelled for the entire world to hear. "It's not fair. My very own Simi vanished for no reason. There are no notes. Not at her office, not on Facebook, and not on Twitter. It is not fucking fair."

If anyone could find her, Siegal knew it was Tom Danielson. His connections never failed to amaze him. Siegal would have to be patient.

"I guess I will go back home and wait."

THE WEEKLY SUPPLY PLANE DROPPED off the usual collection of supplies. Along with the replenishments were two invoices from zoos in the States. Siegal was about to become a foster parent to ten spider monkeys. The invoices indicated his monkeys would arrive by sea, accompanied by one handler hired to ease the transition onto the island and remain as necessary. Siegal was relieved thinking of the monstrous task of managing his herd, troop, clan, or whatever one calls a bunch of monkeys.

The day before their arrival, Siegal paced the perimeter of Little Deadman's Cay, making sure all was in place. He felt the same nervousness as any expectant father.

THE SPIDER MONKEYS ARRIVED ON a flatbed barge towed by an inboard boat. Each was in individual cages except for two mothers with their young hanging on their backs. Their combined chatter was enough to waken any skeletons left over from days when pirates frequented Little Deadman's Cay.

The man riding on the barge with the monkeys called out when in range. "Hello, Doctari Siegal."

"Phillipe, is that you? Or are you his twin brother?"

Displaying his trademark grin, Phillipe said, "It's me, Doctari. I will explain as soon as we get these creatures on land. One thing, for sure, they do not like the water. Two of them got seasick and vomited."

"Better you than me to take care of them," replied Siegal.

"Shall we release them right away? I suggest no. I think maybe it is better if we let them relax from their trip first."

"Good idea, Phillipe. That'll give me a chance to photograph and put paint markings on their backs, so they can be recognized once they're released.

"Oh, no need to do all that. You will be able to recognize them very soon by their different personalities."

"It's just the scientist in me that wants to keep very detailed records. While the monkeys are settling down, I'll show you where you can unpack."

"Oh, yes. Then we can take a walk around the island. It looks very familiar, very much like Monkey Town."

Siegal laughed. "I didn't want to fix something that wasn't broken. This free-range habitat is perfect for spider monkeys. And there is plenty of space for growth."

THE NEXT DAY AFTER RELEASING the monkeys, Siegal and Phillipe took positions around the enclosure, making sure the new guests were on friendly terms with each other.

"I think you have a good mix of females to males for your research, Doctari. We have two mature males and one adolescent. Two of the females have one infant each. The remaining female should make for some very interesting interactions with the males."

"I left the population breakdown to Danielson."

"And he left that decision to me and Missy Ro," smiled Phillipe.

Siegal smiled back. "That Danielson, he never misses a trick. Now tell me, dear friend, I thought you were saving up for veterinarian school?"

"Mr. Danielson found out about me and my desire to pursue a career with animals. He located a very fine veterinary school in southern Florida that allows me to take much of my coursework by correspondence. Working for you is considered an independent study. He also set up a grant where I get paid, so I can send some money back to my family in Africa. But it is up to you, Doctari. If you do not want me here, the whole deal is off."

"Are you kidding? You're my perfect choice."

The monkeys were also a perfect choice. Their arrival got Siegal back to doing his research, a boon for his mental health. Even more important, it kept his mind from the constant worry about Simi while Danielson did his detective magic.

By the next morning, the effects of travel had disappeared. The three males started to vie for leadership. Their screams and feigned actions were aggressive but kept well below anything leading to injury. For reasons only monkeys know, one male emerged as the alpha figure.

"We should give him a name. Oh, I know. Let us call him Hannibal. His trip across the water is like General Hannibal crossing the Alps," suggested Phillipe.

"I like it," agreed Siegal. "Hannibal it is."

AFTER SEVERAL DAYS, SIEGAL ADMITTED in frustration, "I don't see anything happening. I thought my research would be more exciting."

"Do not let this peace and quiet fool you, Doctari. There are many subtle changes going on every day. Notice how one of the males, the one we named Brutus, is already edging closer to one of the females. Hannibal does not seem to be paying attention. But do not let that fool you for one little bit. He knows that sooner or later, there will be a move by Brutus. Hannibal will have to accept the challenge. If Brutus is successful in mating, the two will have to form a new troop or he will become the alpha male of this group."

"Are we getting ready for a regal exchange of power? Will we be losing a monkey?"

"I do not think so. Brutus still feels Hannibal is the alpha monkey. My guess is there will be some screeching and running about the trees for a while. And then everything will return to normal. In about one hundred and forty days, Leah will become a mother. Hannibal will pretend he is the father, and peace will be maintained."

"I don't think I could ever be observant as you. I look around and see ten assorted monkeys that now have several assorted names. So far as I can tell, nothing has happened that is of research interest to me. In an inkling, you tell me things I should be aware of. Tonight I will graph out the layout of the enclosure. I want to be aware of the exact space each one needs and which areas are common to the others."

"I think you would be more observant if your mind was not so preoccupied. Have you had any news?"

"Tom says things are moving forward, but nothing definite. I just have to be patient. And that is the hardest thing for me."

"Maybe you need more monkeys to study. We have plenty of space."

"As long as you keep teaching me what I'm looking at, I could conquer a hundred spider monkeys and maybe a few dozen howlers thrown into the mix as well."

Siegal texted Danielson to order a new group of seven spider monkeys, three males and four females but no babies. He added they should each be from different sources to avoid any previous relationships.

"The waiting part of field research is different from laboratory study where the investigator is in control of the action," explained Siegal to Phillipe. "It gives us time to learn more of each other."

"There is one part of your life you keep avoiding. Tell me about Doctari Block. She was one of your graduate students at City University. Yes?"

"She was much more than that. She was my heart and soul. I intended to marry her."

"What stopped you? I do not think anything could ever stop you from what you set your mind to."

"Things changed when I met Danielson and became involved in his plans."

"I would like to hear."

Siegal debated how to begin. "Circumstances forced me to move my office away from City University to a secluded chalet in the Colorado Rocky Mountains. I became a part-time hermit. Every so often, I returned to Denver and spent a few wonderful hours with Simi. These times were only quick fixes. I couldn't tell her what I was doing for fear of putting her in as much danger as I was experiencing. Anyway, she earned her doctorate and moved to California while I was in exile. There, she became an associate professor with the Institute of Human Development at Cal-Berkeley. For a period of time, I was forced to hide from some people who were out to kill me. After a time, the danger passed, and I decided to have a reunion on this island. Everyone came but Simi."

"When she did not accept your invitation, why did you not just go out there and see her?"

A wave of emotion pierced Siegal's body. He wept. "I did, and she appears to be missing."

"That is not a good thing. Do you think any harm has come to her?"

"Danielson thinks she may have been abducted. Those who did it went to considerable planning to hide what actually happened, making everyone believe she was out of the country. He feels strongly that she knows something that somebody wants very badly."

"Kidnapping. That is very bad."

"And we don't know where she is or why they want her."

"I think you should be in California right now looking for her ... asking questions ... anything."

"As Danielson put it simply, 'That isn't my job.' He sent me home. I think to keep me out from under his feet."

"Then I agree with Mr. Danielson. You are better off here."

"I know.

He'll let me know when anything breaks. I had hoped to hear news from him by now. I have to put my trust in his ability to find her."

SIXTEEN

"GOOD EVENING, DR. SUNADA. I hope you are progressing. I just received a report from my doctor, and the news is not good for me. My nerve deterioration is moving faster. You must speed up your process."

"I will do what I can, sir. I will try a more direct method. It sometimes works, but the risk for failure is high if I do it too soon."

"Take the risk. I have nothing to lose."

SIMI WAS INSTRUCTED TO REMOVE her blindfold on her second visit to the patio. She blinked, adjusting to the bright sunlight.

Something is different. A second glass is on the table next to the lemonade.

"Do you mind if I join you, Dr. Block?"

She turned to see a slightly built, short Asian man.

"I guessed you to be older, eighty at least. The use of ether instead of more popular drugs to subdue me when I was kidnapped suggested this. You look to be no more than sixty."

"Ninety-five years old would be the correct guess."

Simi searched her photographic memory. She broke into a slight smile. "You seem familiar. I've seen your picture in one of my old psychology books. You are Su ..."

"Sunada. Dr. Akio Sunada. Akio means bright child."

"A perfect first name. You are considered the father of modern motivational psychology."

Sunada sat down across from Simi. "That was so long ago. Many of my theories were thought of as being too radical and never useful to understanding humans until the book *Hidden Persuaders* was published in the 1950s."

"Were you involved in World War II?"

"Yes. I am Japanese and was very loyal to the cause fostered by our leader, Emperor Hirohito."

Simi filled both glasses with lemonade. "I want to hear about you. Let me confess something first. Having you call me doctor all the time has unnerved me. Is that part of your motivational plan?"

"You are correct." He sipped from his glass. "It is normal from my Asian upbringing to address a person by their titles. It is also part of my plan to win you over."

They bowed heads in mutual respect.

The open air of the patio empowered Simi to take control of the situation, unlike the dark cellar where her only power was when she needed to have privacy.

I can reverse the captive captor relationship here for a time. "Tell me about your amazing career."

"Ha. You are very good at motivational techniques, Dr. Block. I was fortunate to have attended Yale University and received my PhD by the age of twenty-four. Success was thrust on me by the Japanese government, and they bestowed upon me the title, Most Superior Psychologist, and created an official position to go along with the title."

Sunada sat silent for a few seconds, recalling the reality of his deeds. He blotted tears from his eyes with his napkin.

Simi could see he felt both proud of his accomplishments and saddened by his success. And he is forcing me to do his bidding now.

"It was my responsibility to guide youths into my schemes. They flocked in overwhelming numbers to become kamikaze pilots against American warships. I gave them red scarves as rewards to wear for special identity. They were the first modern-day suicide terrorists."

"I thought I knew about every study in behavior management," Simi said. "It is not surprising that your name was left out of the history books of World War II. Every American thought those kamikaze pilots carried out their acts as a form of religious patriotism. It never dawned on anyone that a motivational program was the basis. Did it ever bother you that your methods were sending brave young men to their deaths?"

"As I said before, I was a proud patriot. Remember, I was young and hated the United States, as did most Japanese citizens. The exchange of a small airplane and a single pilot seemed a very good tradeoff if an American warship was disabled or sunk. One person and a single airplane to kill hundreds of American sailors and destroy an expensive warship was a very efficient method to wage war. Would you not agree?"

Simi nodded. "Body bombs by radical Islam are just the same. One death and a very inexpensive explosive device in a crowd with many casualties was originally your idea?"

Sunada nodded.

Her effort to gain control seemed to be working. The question remained in her mind: Was she in control, or was this part of Sunada's more aggressive plan?

She pressed the conversation further. "Then you indirectly developed sophisticated methods in brainwashing techniques." It was more a statement than a question, meant to set up the next part of her plan.

"I see where you are taking me, Dr. Block. Let me explain. An anonymous person made a most unusual request. One I am unqualified to fulfill. I recommended your name as a person who had the knowledge to help because you possess a skill I cannot offer. It is my responsibility to encourage you to help."

"Who is this person?"

"Even if I wanted to tell you, I cannot. I do not know a name. It is not so uncommon in my shadow profession to be contracted by individuals who prefer anonymity. As I told you before, I command a lot of money doing what I do. This villa is expensive, and services to do my bidding take a massive budget. You may have noticed in the cellar where you stay a trophy collection of wines. Perhaps you would like to share a bottle with me sometime."

"Tell me what this person wants to do."

"He wants to control a population to do his bidding. I can move one person at a time in a direct manner. Your techniques of sociobiology controls groups to perform in predictable ways."

"At least you can tell me why I am so important to your employer's plan."

"You, Dr. Block, are developing an emerging behavioral science completely new to the field. How would you rate yourself in terms of expertise as compared to others who are just now beginning to understand it?"

"I guess I am close to being on the leading edge."

"You are too modest. You are the leading edge. It is too complicated for my old mind. This person who contracted me cannot wait for someone to learn what you already know. So, it is my responsibility to urge your cooperation."

"Are you suggesting I was kidnapped by you to help control others?"

"Yes. My employer wishes to remain anonymous. The true reason for using you is to provide this human shield that cannot be invaded."

Simi could feel her plan to escape was almost within reach. She carefully worded her next thought. "You almost had me, Dr. Sunada. In fact, I am not sure if you haven't actually won me over. I have used every trick I knew to fight your brainwashing technology. If you have more tricks up your sleeve, I will end up totally in your power."

"Dr. Block, I can tell you I have no more tricks up my sleeve. I feel dishonored for what I have been doing to you."

Simi could not imagine she was the focus of an elaborate kidnapping plot. And, in front of her was the father of her field apologizing for being part of the scheme.

"Tell me in your words, Dr. Block, what makes psychophysiology work so effectively."

The challenge to share her knowledge with the father of motivational psychology was almost too much for Simi to imagine. Just thirty minutes earlier, imprisoned in her cell, she had hatched a plan pretending to come under the influence of Sunada. She wanted him to believe he had won the battle of wits.

"We can do this together. You tell me what your employer wants to do, and I can guide you. Do you have a computer here at the villa? I can access my office files to help us succeed."

SEVENTEEN

IT WAS SUNDAY, A DAY off on Little Deadman's Cay. Not that it was different from most any other days on the island, but a day off just the same.

Siegal had just hooked what appeared to be a large grouper and was about to pull it in when his cell phone rang. Two choices, lose his prize catch or succumb to the call. The third choice was to hand his pole to Phillipe, whose line was hopelessly limp. He chose the latter and pressed talk on his cell.

"Ross, I have exciting news."

"Your timing is less than perfect, Tom. I'm just about to bring in the world's largest catch. Your news better be great."

"It's about Simi. I suppose it can wait for more important matters."

Siegal's voice broke. "Don't fuck around with me. Did you find her? Is she okay?"

"Hold on to your zipper if you're even wearing pants."

"You know birthday suits don't come with zippers."

"Here's the scoop. Someone outside the institute accessed Simi's files six times this past week. Whoever did it had the fourteen-digit password. The person connected without a trial and error technique. My gut tells me it was Simi herself who logged on."

"Why would you think that?"

"A hacker would have downloaded the entire file at one time once they got in. Either she did it willingly or was forced to by her abductors. Either way, it is a damn good bet she's alive and well."

Phillipe was still attempting to bring in the great fish. Siegal didn't care. "What's your take?" he asked.

"She would never give up her files willingly unless she's a Stockholm syndrome victim or ..."

"Not Simi," argued Siegal. "She has a strong mental constitution. I'm sure she could counteract that kind of pressure."

"Don't be so sure. I've been involved in many operations, some of which include prisoner interrogations. Even the most reticent prisoners have opened up under certain conditions."

"You think Simi caved?"

"I don't think she was taken over completely. I think she made excuses to revisit her computer several times on purpose."

"You mean hoping her hacks were monitored? Did you do that?"

"Child's play. It's normal procedure in the spy business."

"Wow, That's my Simi."

"The signal is coming from a villa north of San Francisco in Marin County. I'm sending a strike force to extract her. Do you want to be in on the fun?"

"What do you think?"

"Thought so. I ordered a plane to pick you up. It should be there early tomorrow morning. Can Phillipe handle everything on the island for a couple of days?"

"Are you kidding? He knows more about managing monkeys than I do."

"Then I'll see you in California, Ross."

Phillipe, listening to the call, had just beached the grouper. "Doctari, did you forget? The new batch of monkeys will be delivered tomorrow as well."

"Damn. We can't leave our new charges in Miami for two extra days. Who knows what will happen to them? I hate to lay all the responsibility on you."

"Not to worry. Everything will be fine here. I will accept delivery. Your new monkeys will be waiting patiently for your return."

Danielson continued the conversation. "Do you have any theory, no matter how out in left field it is, why anyone would want Simi?"

"I know she's combining several disciplines into a new field of psychological study. That could be it. Hold on. I'll run up to the shack and get some of her material." Siegal ran up to his office, taking his cell with him. "Here is one paper on ethology. It's how a species acts to protect itself from extinction. She also delved into something called biopsychology."

"What the hell is that?"

"It combines behaviors with one's mental processes. While ethology studies ways animals behave in their natural habitat, biopsychology adds in a certain pharmacological manipulation of the organism. It explains why identical twins act differently from each other."

"Very interesting, professor. It's far too complicated for a government man. What else, as if that isn't complicated enough."

"There is more. Simi's assistant gave me a document on psychoneuro-immunology. Researchers call it the 'faith factor.' It involves the effects of stress on the endocrine and immune systems. It gets into fight or flight to perceived dangers and the evolutionary process that assures the survival of a species if appropriate choices are made. The discipline covers the creation of religion as a mechanism for survival. The combination of all these areas has evolved into her study she calls sociobiology. It's a stretch, but maybe someone wants to protect themselves against the world and needs Simi's know-how to do it."

"It's all bullshit to me. Your girlfriend's come a long way since being one of your graduate students."

"It means that if sociobiology is the behavioral science of the future, then my level of Skinnerian behavioral psychology puts me in the class of the dinosaurs."

"Don't sell yourself short, Ross. You have been retired for a couple of years, but it wouldn't take long for you to get back up to speed. Do you think her knowledge makes her wanted enough to be kidnapped?"

"Don't know. It's certainly logical. I need to put my mind to it. I'll let you know when anything floats to the top. Remember, I'm depending on you to get her out."

Danielson ended the conversation with, "My men are the best."

Siegal returned to the beach to see Phillipe holding the monster grouper over his head. Phillipe could see the worried look on Siegal's face. "It will be okay, Doctari. You just have to trust your good friend."

"He's never disappointed me yet." He looked at Phillipe struggle with his catch, "Nice fish."

SUN GAZETTE

The American public remains split on the management of the Middle East. Big business interests dependent on oil are urging the president to consider a modulated approach toward Arab nations.

In other business news, an unusual tide of interest continues for over-the-counter tech stocks, causing an unprecedented rise. There is unusual interest in pharmaceutical stock, causing fluctuation in stock values for no apparent reason.

EIGHTEEN

SIEGAL STARED OUT THE WINDOW of his chartered plane, a Cessna Citation M2. Below the wing, he saw the Golden Gate Bridge, Anaconda Building, and Alcatraz as the plane descended across the bay toward a private landing strip near Oakland. He attempted to enjoy the scenery while his mind was filled with thoughts of seeing Simi.

The pilot made a perfect three-point landing on a small airfield five minutes north of the city and guided his craft to a stop near an aluminum corrugated outbuilding. Siegal stepped out and was greeted by a uniformed guard who ushered him to a soft chair inside the building.

"Mr. Danielson is still a few minutes out, sir. He will be landing shortly."

Siegal said, "I think my eyes have turned a permanent shade of yellow. Is there a ...?"

The guard pointed to the door with the hand-painted word 'toilet' in the corner of the one-room building.

About ten minutes later, Danielson and five other men, all equipped in full commando gear, emerged from a twin-engine turbojet. Siegal went out to greet them.

"Glad you're here, good buddy," called Danielson.

"Wouldn't have missed this one for the world."

"You remember Lieutenant Ben Goldberg?" Danielson pointed to the large man next to him. "Only you knew him as Sergeant then."

"How could I forget my sole protector and only live contact during my hermit days at the Colorado mountain chalet. It's nice to see you again, Ben. I feel more confident with you around."

"It's very good to see you again, sir."

Danielson wiped the sweat from his forehead. "It's hot out here. Let's go inside, and I'll review the raid plans."

DANIELSON OPENED A TUBE AND took out several aerial photographs and laid them on a metal folding table in the center of the room. "These two satellite photos show our target villa. The first covers an area of approximately five kilometers across. This second one is a close-up of the villa and a few meters surrounding it. The terrain is flat with not much cover. Our drop-off point will be here," he said, pointing to a spot just behind a low hill about a kilometer from the villa. "It's the closest spot where we can't be seen from the villa. Logistics require us to initiate our attack after dark to give us the most protection."

He unrolled several more photos. "These infrared shots were taken by drones at low altitude to show temperature differences inside the villa at different times of day and night. We determined there have never been more than three human markers inside. This dimly-lit figure here, I feel, is Dr. Simi Block. I think she's being held in some protected area, possibly a cellar. One of these images is her abductor. I'm not sure about the third."

Siegal looked on. "Seems too easy. What am I missing?"

"It won't be quite that simple." Danielson unrolled another surveillance photo. "This identifies an intricate electronic detection system around the perimeter to warn of anyone or anything approaching. Although unlikely, we must assume the whole place may have been mined with explosives. At the very least, Simi's location could be wired. One small misstep and not only us but everyone inside become history."

"Would the kidnapper kill Simi after going to all the trouble to get her?" asked Siegal.

Danielson nodded. "They've had Simi a long time. We have to assume they have gotten what they wanted, making her dispensable."

"Holy crap. I hope not. She is not dispensable," blurted Siegal.

"Do you think we can disarm their warning system, sir?" asked Goldberg.

"I'm sure it's in the villa, making that next to impossible. We have to be on them so fast they will not have a chance to use it."

Siegal displayed a knowing smile. "I know you, Tom. You always have a plan."

"Don't laugh. It's a little bit out in left field. I set the odds at less than fifty-fifty. The way I see it, our sense of urgency gives us no alternative."

Danielson called to the uniformed officer who had left the room. "Bring in the crates I sent yesterday. Lieutenant Goldberg, have your men help him."

The back door opened. An awful smell of feces and urine permeated the room.

Siegal held his nose, fighting the urge to vomit. "Those crates smell worse than my rat labs at the university. Leave the poor creatures outside."

Danielson laughed. "Soldiers, take the critters back outside for the squeamish among us. Put them on the shady side of the building. They need to be healthy and active for their part of the plan."

Siegal frowned and scratched his balding spot. "What is this plan of yours?"

"In one crate are some jackrabbits. The other crate holds two coyotes that haven't been fed since yesterday. When the attack team is in the air, the rabbits will be released toward the villa. Then the coyotes will be released to chase them, setting off the motion detectors. If it works, the attention will be off my men."

Siegal sat in disbelief. "That's it? That's your plan? All that activity will alert the two inside. They'll see us coming. Any kind of arousal could put Simi's life in danger. I hope there's more to your plan than putting your hopes on some mangy animals."

"I do have a plan B, but it's riskier. I'll let you in on it if we need to use it. My men have been trained specifically for just such a surreptitious exercise. They're the best." Danielson put his hand on Siegal's shoulder. "You have to trust me on this one." He turned to the assault team. "Everyone, relax and have something to eat. It will be a long night. We lift off at twenty-two hundred."

The assault team crouched along the building walls drinking coffee and swapping war stories. They acted relaxed; some slept. When the assault time arrived, they would be ready as killers or be killed. That was their orders.

AT TWENTY-TWO HUNDRED, THE SOUND of an approaching helicopter broke the evening stillness. It landed just outside the metal building. Casual talk ceased. The men loaded the craft with their equipment and the animal crates. In minutes they were aloft for the thirty-minute flight to the target area.

Danielson laid out the final parts of the assault during the flight. "Here is how the raid plays out. We will make our first touch about two hundred meters from the villa behind a small rock outcropping. Ross, you and Ben will be dropped off along with the animals. The rest of us will proceed to a spot nearer the villa to parachute in. I will be in radio contact with the two of you about when to release first the rabbits and then the coyotes. By the time you release the coyotes, we will be hitting the silk and in a long free fall; we don't want to take a chance of the helicopter getting too close and setting off any sound detectors. Ross, be sure to tell those damn rabbits to head toward the villa, or we'll be out there hung up to dry." It was meant as a joke, but nobody laughed.

Goldberg said in his most serious voice and with a half smile, "We'll work on it, sir. I will show them a picture of the villa so they know which way to go."

It was the first time Siegal had heard Goldberg say anything humorous. He looked at the brave men who were about to go into combat. He sensed they did not know if this engagement would leave any of them alive or dead. He only knew they would do what was necessary to ensure success and bring Simi out safely.

THE PILOT GAVE THE FINAL orders. "We are one minute to drop point one. After I drop off the raiding party, the chopper will go back and retrieve Siegal and Lieutenant Goldberg. The raiding party and I will hover near the rear of the villa at fifteen hundred meters and wait for the infrared signal from me.

Danielson completed the orders. "If you don't get my signal from the ground by twenty-three hundred, you get the hell out of there. Are there any questions?"

Minutes later, the helicopter landed with a soft thump.

"First stop," quipped Danielson like a tour guide. "Wild animal store. Please watch your step."

Siegal and Goldberg stepped off. The raiding party helped off-load the animal crates. The one with the coyotes was hard to manage. The animals were hungry, and the smell of rabbits moved them to a frenzy.

The helicopter blades quickened, lifting the assault team. It was soon out of sight in the blackness of the moonless night.

THE NEW MOON MADE THE villa almost invisible from the air as the helicopter approached the drop site to release the assault team. The only light visible in the darkness came from an upstairs window of the villa.

Danielson put on his night vision binoculars. "I see two individuals on the second floor. That confirms Simi is tucked safely below. That simplifies our plan. Nobody is guarding her."

Five minutes later, a call from the pilot told Siegal and Goldberg the team had left the helicopter and were free-falling toward the villa. Danielson radioed the pair. "Time for you to do your animal act. Over and out."

"That's a roger," responded Goldberg.

Goldberg aimed the rabbit crate opening toward the villa and released them. Siegal stood behind the crate, urging them in the correct direction. By some miracle, the rabbits headed toward the villa. The plan was working so far.

"Now for the coyotes," whispered Siegal as the two men moved the coyote crate next to the now-empty rabbit crate.

Goldberg lifted the cage door. "It's up to Mother Nature."

The coyotes looked around cautiously at first, stepped outside their confinement, and snarled at the two men who were attempting to shoo them in the direction of the rabbits. Realizing they were no longer being kept away from their next meal, the coyotes perked up their ears and gave a yelp of freedom. In moments they were in full pursuit of the jackrabbits.

"Aha," yelled Siegal and gave Goldberg a high five.

The rabbits began evasive maneuvers to escape their hunters. They appeared disoriented and began circling back in the opposite direction, toward the two men and away from the villa.

The animals were still too far away for the warning detectors. The diversion was not working.

Siegal jumped up from his hiding place. "Do as I do, Ben."

He ran toward the animals waving his hands and screeching taunts aping his Hannibal Clan. Goldberg followed in kind. Both the jackrabbits and coyotes stopped in their tracks. Then reversed their direction and headed back toward the villa with Siegal and Goldberg in hot pursuit. Skip Danielson's plan B. Siegal's improvised plan C was working. Siegal and Goldberg were now the chasers of both sets of animals.

NINETEEN

UNAWARE OF THE ACTIVITY OUTSIDE the villa, Sunada and his servant were in the upstairs bedroom doing their nightly observance of deep meditation. A buzzer on the wall stirred them back to the moment. They eyed the security monitor adjacent to the buzzer and first saw the jackrabbits being chased by the coyotes. Then Siegal and Goldberg crossed into the detection system's line of sight. Danielson's surprise raid had been compromised.

Sunada turned to his servant. "It is only a matter of time before whoever is out there discovers we have no true defense. I am too old to be captured. I choose to control my fate. It is time I repay humanity for all my evil deeds of the past. Turn on the perimeter lights and the warning siren. That will slow our attackers and give us sufficient time to prepare."

His servant nodded and rose from his lotus position. He walked to the control panel on the wall and pressed the yellow alarm button. The villa grounds became flooded in artificial daylight. A siren shattered the night's stillness.

No words were needed to communicate the next few minutes' activities. The servant walked to an enameled chest in the closet and retrieved a white linen coat with a matching sash and laid them on the small ceremonial mat where Sunada was sitting moments before. Dr. Sunada undressed and cleansed himself in his bathroom. By the time Sunada had returned, his servant had placed a large white pillow next to the mat. Next to the pillow, he laid a long sword. The servant, now dressed all in white, held out the sterile white jacket. Sunada put it on. The servant placed a second pillow in the corner of the room and placed another sword next to it.

DANIELSON AND HIS RAIDERS WERE still fifty feet above the ground when the lights went on. They unlocked the safeties on their assault weapons and pointed them at the ground, searching for any movement signaling a counterattack.

Upon landing, Danielson whispered, "Careful, the area may be booby-trapped." He studied his map to determine their exact location. It was just outside the wall surrounding the patio where Simi and her captor sat and talked.

One raider tested the door to the patio with the stock of his assault rifle. The door was neither wired nor locked. The assault team, prepared for an ambush, slipped inside. Danielson pointed to the light in the upstairs window. He motioned his team to attack that room, and he would locate the door to the cellar where he felt Simi was kept.

The next barrier was the door to the villa. They approached it with the same caution. Finding no barriers, they entered in attack mode. Danielson edged toward the left, which he guessed was the way to the cellar, while the others made their way along the hall toward the stairs leading to the second floor.

The assault team edged up the stairs. Their nerves tightened. The lead commando whispered, "Either the enemy is stupid, or we're walking into a trap."

At the top of the stairs were several closed doors. A slit of light showed along the bottom of one. They gathered on either side of the door. One hard shove and the door fell open.

They gasped.

In the center of the room was a body. Dr. Sunada lay in a pool of blood, impaled by the sword his servant had ceremonially held for him. The manservant, still kneeling on a second pillow, had forced a second blade deep into Sunada's midsection. He looked up with unseeing eyes at the assault team and, almost melting, collapsed silently on his side. The battle-hardened raiders, who had seen almost everything in their careers, stood frozen at the horrific scene. Unable to move. Unable to speak.

THE WINE CELLAR WAS WELL insulated from the rest of the villa. With no windows to see out of, Simi was unaware of the raid. She had just drifted off into one of her normal catnaps, the kind that makes isolation tolerable.

The sound of unfamiliar footsteps outside her prison aroused her. They were heavier, not the soft steps of Dr. Sunada or his servant who delivered her meals.

A new person? Who? The latch being unlocked unnerved her. Everything was different. The light in the center of the room remained on. The door opened slowly and deliberately.

What do they want of me at this late hour? Is this the end—my final chapter?

"Dr. Block?" asked a whispered voice.

She mustered a bit of courage. "Who's there? Whoever you are, I'm not giving up without a fight." She grabbed a wine bottle from the rack and broke off the end.

"Don't be afraid, Dr. Block. I'm Tom Danielson."

Simi recognized the name Siegal had mentioned years ago. "Who?"

"Tom Danielson. I've come to get you out of here. Are you okay?"

Simi's mind raced. At first, she thought this was another ploy by Sunada.

"I'm fine. Just give me a moment to gather my wits," she said, stalling for time to think. "How did you find me? Where is Dr. Sunada? Is this some other brainwashing trick of his?"

"This is no trick."

Just then, the commandos, with their guns in attack mode, burst into the cellar. She wasn't sure what to believe at this moment.

"Put your guns down," ordered Danielson. "Everything here is under control. Is the rest of the house secure?"

One of the men whispered something into Danielson's ear. Danielson, shocked at what he heard, wiped his forehead.

"Gentlemen, help Dr. Block gather her things and take her to the extraction point. I'll meet you there."

IN MINUTES, THE HELICOPTER WITH the full commando party and Simi took off and proceeded to the first drop-off point. As the helicopter landed, Siegal stepped out and was lit by the chopper's landing lights.

"Ross? Is that really you or another part of this dream I'm conjuring?"

"It's me," said Siegal attempting to act casual.

"You bastard. You fucking bastard," screamed Simi. "You led me to believe you were dead all this time. Two years of silence. Not even a fucking letter to let me know you still were alive and cared for me. And now, as calmly as can be, you walk back into my life. I don't know whether to cry from happiness or rage."

Simi was surprised at her own outburst of anger. Abandoned by her husband, she decided to pursue a college education, choosing psychology as her major field of study. It was there she fell in love with Ross Siegal. When it was reported to her that he was dead at the hands of a secret enemy, she became absorbed in her own career at Cal-Berkeley. Her mind was in turmoil. In the space of only a few moments, her life was turned inside out. Her inner strength, the one that protected her from Sunada's brainwashing techniques, was challenged again.

She blurted, "I don't ever want to speak with you again. I can no longer trust you to be open with me. In my mind, you are better off dead."

As she began walking away from the encounter, Danielson stopped her. "Do not put all the blame on Ross. I'm the one who's at fault for keeping his being alive a secret from you. I'll explain later. Now let's get out of here. Goldberg, you and your men stay behind. I'll call a cleanup crew to go over the villa and collect any information of value. "

"What about Dr. Sunada? Isn't he coming with us?" asked Simi.

A troubled frown from Danielson gave her the answer. In the short period of time, the bond between Simi and Sunada had become more than captive and captor. In Simi's mind, it was another abandonment by a man she trusted.

"With your permission, Dr. Block," said Danielson, "I will notify the Institute of Human Development and tell them you are fine, but we need you for a few days of debriefing."

"I guess that's all right. I suppose I need some time to readjust before going back to work."

BACK AT THE LANDING STRIP, Siegal, Simi, and Danielson boarded the Cessna, whose engines were already warming for takeoff.

Simi asked, "Where are we going?"

Danielson answered, "To a little piece of paradise created especially for Ross. There we can put this all together. There are a lot of questions of exactly what they wanted of you and who is at the center of it all."

It had been a long night and a long flight from the Pacific Ocean to the Atlantic. Simi and Danielson fell asleep from all that took place. Siegal was too worked up to relax. He decided to call Phillipe and check on the monkey arrivals.

TWENTY

"HELLO. IF THIS IS A call for Dr. Siegal, he cannot come to the phone right now. Can you leave a message?"

"Phillipe, it's me, Ross."

"Oh, Doctari. I am so glad you called. How did everything go?"

"It is all good. The raid was a success. Dr. Block is safe and back with us. We're in the air on the way home. I know it's early morning, but I need to know how our shipment went."

"It is not too early for me. It is almost dawn this far east. Our monkeys are about to rise. I chose to sleep on the observation deck and see how they react to their new surroundings."

"Then everything is well?"

"It was scary for a while. Just after you left, a tropical storm came and lasted the entire day. Our monkeys were housed in cages on board a flat-bed ark towed by an inboard craft. The captain was prepared and had each of their cages covered by waterproof tarps. So, our charges managed to stay dry. Still, they were shaking from the ordeal. I fed them some fresh fruit which calmed them a bit. I am glad they all came from zoos and were used to humans providing food, or we could have lost some of them. I named them the Storm Clan in honor of their auspicious arrival. You can rename them something more appropriate when you return."

"The name sounds perfect. I can't wait to get home."

"Are you coming alone, Doctari?"

"Good question. Simi is on the plane and is invited to stay with us. Right now, she is angry at me for not letting her know I was alive. Hopefully, time will heal." He changed the subject. "How is the Hannibal Clan taking to their new neighbors?"

"Doctari, it will be very interesting for a while. Hannibal and his cohorts immediately challenged our newcomers. They crowded the edge of their southern territory, taunting the Storm Clan, who retreated to the far edge of the range we set apart for them. Thank goodness the Seabees placed an electric coil along the top of the divider fence, or the Hannibal Clan would have overrun the defenseless Storm Clan, slaughtering all the males and stealing the females. All in all, everything is well." He yawned, "Time to take a nap."

TWENTY-ONE

IT WAS EARLY DAWN BY the time the small plane approached Little Deadman's Cay. The pilot turned on the bulkhead lights.

"Heads up, everyone," he said. "Dr. Siegal, you're home." Still on autopilot, he handed out refreshing wet wipes and retrieved a thermos of mango juice from the storage bin and poured each a paper cupful.

Simi rubbed her eyes and looked out her window as the plane descended toward Little Deadman's Cay, preparing for a sandy beach landing. "Where are we?" she asked. "All I see is water and this dot of land."

Siegal smiled, "It's my private island paradise—sort of a gift from Tom."

"The beach is too short for a normal landing," informed the pilot. "Be prepared for a bumpy landing." As he approached, he feathered the engine to just above stall speed. At the extreme tip of the beach, he cut the engines and nosed the plane up slightly to increase drag. He dropped to let the wet sand beach at the water's edge slow the plane's speed. Then he taxied to a safe stop.

After a near-perfect landing, the pilot retrieved Simi's clothes, items that were not for the tropics but for French spring weather. Danielson and Siegal gathered their own packs and headed toward the shanty. A puzzled Simi followed.

Simi, still angry, spied the wire mesh structures. "Aha. You intend to keep me a prisoner until I forgive you, Dr. Big Shit! It's not okay to let your friends think you are dead."

Siegal searched his mind for a response. He had no answer. She had a right to be angry. They all sat down on the porch. Danielson sat between them. Each waited for the other to speak.

Siegal excused himself and returned with some iced tea and four glasses. The pilot drank his and begged his leave. The three watched the final tinge of the sunrise and listened to the diminishing sound of the jet as it left their airspace.

It was Simi who broke the silence. "I want to hear the unabridged story. And this better be good."

Siegal began. "It all started when Tom wrangled me into becoming part of a unique group including several high-level world leaders. We tracked down a terrorist who planned to use a lethal virus to bring fear to the free world. Once the threat was over, I discovered one of our so-called allies had turned rogue and put out a contract on my life. He wanted to keep some of the virus for the same ends as the terrorist. I determined this danger before he could put his plan into action. I barely escaped with my skin. This brought me here on this island, feigning my death to protect me and all of my friends."

Danielson added, "Thank goodness the danger is over, and Ross is now able to move about freely as he chooses."

Simi blurted, "Why couldn't you trust me? I would have run away with you anywhere. All you had to do was ask." Her words came out like dialogue from a paperback novel, followed by uncontrolled tears. "Tell me something to make me believe in you again."

Siegal said, "You know me. I always go it alone when things get hairy. Trust me; it was very hairy for a while. Those people play for keeps."

"Are you still in some kind of funny business?"

"No. I swear it."

"It still boils down to the fact that you just didn't trust me. You didn't think I was strong enough to handle it."

Siegal reached over and touched her on the arm. "That's not true." He retracted his hand. "Well, maybe, it is a little." He rubbed his balding spot. "I feared for your life more than mine. I don't know if I made the correct decision, but at the time, I thought it was for the best."

He said all he could to ease the tension. It was up to Simi to make the next move.

In silent forgiveness, Simi leaned over and kissed him on the cheek and then gently on the lips.

It wasn't the first time in the past two years living on the island that a woman kissed him. He had several experiences in Nassau. But her advances were not of the one-night stand variety he experienced during his Nassau trips. He could feel the layers of acting like a hermit peeling off. He began feeling almost human.

"I want to hate you. I had finally put you out of my mind. It all reminds me of my husband leaving me to run off with our apartment doorman. I didn't want another rejection. We're not spring chickens anymore. I just wish I didn't love you so much. Is there more to your story?"

"A few weeks ago, I invited you, Sally, BF, and Jerry Ravid to my island to have one big tell-all session. You were the only one missing. I was led to believe you were at a conference in France. I decided to see you in person, timing my visit to California with the end of your meeting. When you didn't return as planned, I became worried and asked Tom to look into it."

"You mean you have been looking for me almost as long as I was missing?"

"Pretty much. Tom looked into that conference and discovered it never existed. We concluded something had happened to you. I felt useless and returned home. Tom continued the chase."

"You know most of the rest. You hoped and correctly so that we would keep a trace on your computer,' said Danielson. "The rest was simple investigative work."

"How did you know it was me who contacted my office?" she asked.

"An unknown hacker would have downloaded the files in one shot. The hacking was done in such an orderly manner we concluded it had to be somebody who knew what to look for. That, Simi, had to be you."

"When Sunada told me why he needed me, I suggested we work together, but I pretended to need materials from my files. I don't know why he went along so easily. All I know is that it worked. In fact, I was so excited to be working with the father of motivational psychology. I really liked him."

Danielson opened his laptop to take notes. "What can you tell us about Dr. Sunada?"

"Dr. Sunada developed techniques of nonabusive brainwashing." She continued, describing Sunada's obsession with money. "He was contracted to deal with me. These contracts afforded him the good life, as his villa will attest. When you audit his wine cellar, you will understand his taste for expensive toys."

"Then what?" asked Danielson.

"I just took a risk someone would see my hack into the lab files. If it didn't work, then I probably would be part of his employer's scheme, whatever that is. I knew it was wrong. It was like I wanted to be his equal. He shared his life, and I shared my knowledge. I couldn't help myself. No, that's not true. I didn't want to help myself."

Danielson typed as fast as he could to keep up with Simi. "Then we were lucky we found you out. So, what exactly did you feed him aside from giving him your file information?"

"Not much, I think. Most of what he got had already been published in one journal or another. Your attack came before I could offer him the know-how to do things that assured his employer's success. Is this what you want from me?"

"Just tell me and let me be the judge."

Simi continued mostly rambling. Danielson's eyes lit up as she added, "One of our goals was attempting to understand certain alogical actions of humans in different situations."

"Alogical?" asked Danielson.

"Not logical. It seems that individuals or groups of individuals change their expected behaviors without any physiological or psychological reason. We know something causes the change but don't know what. Our premise is that everything in nature has a logical and completely predictable pathway."

"Don't you believe in the chaos theory?" Danielson asked.

"It's more understanding than just knowing. The person who contracted with Sunada thinks what you understand is important."

Siegal asked, "Who would be interested in Simi's knowledge? Are we looking for another terrorist?"

"I don't think so," Danielson said. "Most terrorist leaders are skilled in this instinctively." He closed his laptop. Then he leaned over and touched Simi's shoulder. "We didn't tell you until you had time to unwind, but you need to know Dr. Sunada took his own life with the aid of his servant who followed in kind."

Simi paled from the information. Tears filled her eyes. "I assumed they were killed when your men attacked the villa. I guess I shouldn't be surprised. You see, he told me about his unholy love for wealth. I believe he truly hated what he was doing to me."

"How did Dr. Sunada set up the kidnapping?" asked Danielson.

Simi jumped out of her chair, upsetting her tea. "He only carried out orders of the contract. He used ether to immobilize me so that I wouldn't be harmed."

Siegal concluded, "Tom, it appears the elaborate scheme was the work of someone else. Sunada was only a cog in the whole plan."

Danielson nodded in agreement. He looked at his watch. "It's after midnight. Time to hit the sack. I can sleep here on the porch."

"Simi, you can have my bed. I'll sleep out here with Tom." Siegal said. "I'm more used to it.

She blushed. "If you don't mind, Ross, I'm willing to share your bed. It's been a long time, and I don't want to lose you again. Just don't expect too much."

The three gave a group hug. There was much to talk about tomorrow. Siegal still had to explain about his monkey island and introduce Simi to Phillipe, who was watching over their monkeys from the observation platform.

Danielson had a lot to think about. The case was not over. His new mission was set: finding the 'who' and 'why.' With Sunada dead, he was out of clues.

PART TWO

Stock Market Noise
The motivation for investors to trade based on fake news rather than fact, a very large part of what moves the markets in either negative or plus territories.

Fischer Black, "Noise," *The Journal of Finance,* vol. XLI, no. 3, 1993, pp 529-543.

TWENTY-TWO

LITTLE DEADMAN'S CAY, WITH ITS calm, sandy beaches and far away from California's active environment, should have been a relaxing time for Simi. It should have been that way, Then ...

Screech.

She jerked out of her sleep. "What kind of a hellhole am I in? First mysterious wire fencing. Then those inhuman sounds. Is this really the Island of Doctor Moreau? And you're the crazy doctor incarnate?"

Siegal, still drowsy with jet lag, rolled over and, without thinking, said in a casual tone, "Oh, that's just the Hannibal Clan threatening the Storm Clan. Go back to sleep. It's too early for us to get up."

Simi had avoided any eye contact with Siegal on the plane trip, which gave him no opportunity to forewarn her about his recent activities. And now, hearing for the first time about some Hannibal and Storm Clans, whatever thoughts Simi had of extra few winks were swept away.

The noise from the spider monkeys woke Danielson as well. Within the hour, the three of them were on the porch having some fresh fruit and chai tea.

A young black man came through the doorway carrying a tray overloaded with eggs and toasted breadfruit. He took the fourth seat at the table.

"You are just full of surprises," said Simi.

Siegal smiled at the puzzled look on Simi's face. "Let me introduce my island companion. This is Phillipe. I first met him at the monkey preserve while I was in South Africa learning how to manage monkeys. He was still in a church high school and working at the preserve till graduation when he hoped to go to college and become a veterinarian. He arrived here on the same boat carrying the Hannibal Clan monkeys. His experience at the preserve has been an invaluable resource for me here while working toward his veterinary degree from a southern Florida university. Again, all this is through the courtesy of Tom. Phillipe, this is Dr. Simi Block."

"I'm very impressed. I must say, a large island laboratory and a student intern to boot certainly wear well on you." She gave him a soft nudge.

Danielson winked at both. "Did you two have a pleasant night? Sleep, I mean?"

"The best. I really haven't slept that well since before Simi turned up missing."

Simi blushed, eager to change the subject. "Breakfast is delicious. Thank you, Phillipe."

In the daylight, Simi saw the expansive wire network surrounding them was not just along the beach. "I know this is not really the island of Doctor Moreau. Bring me up to speed. Where exactly is this island?"

"We're about two hundred and fifty nautical miles southeast of Nassau. Except for meat, dairy products, and certain seasonings, the island is self-sufficient. Fresh fruits, vegetables, and a variety of fish abound."

"And this screeching I keep hearing? Sounds like a pack of wild monkeys."

"More accurately, two," said Danielson. "You can blame me for them being here. After staying on this island with nothing to keep Ross mentally active, I suggested he turn this utopia into a free-range animal lab."

"That explains the wire fencing," concluded Simi. "Tell me, are the monkeys caged, or are we?"

"A little of both," answered Siegal. "The idea of observing behaviors in higher-level mammals instead of contriving experiments seemed intriguing. This island, surrounded by the ocean as a natural barrier, offers a perfect setting for a free-range laboratory. The wire network keeps the monkeys and us apart. We try to simulate their natural living conditions. Walkways and observation areas are designed for watching without bothering their normal activities."

"Very interesting."

"Ready for a tour?" asked Siegal.

"Only if it's okay with the monkeys," joked Simi.

Siegal explained the layout as they walked through a wire tunnel to the observatory platform. "This north part of the island houses my first group of spider monkeys. We named their leader Hannibal and his family the Hannibal Clan. Their yelling, arm-waving, and throwing sticks are to taunt our newer troop, the Storm Clan, that arrived the same day I went to California hoping to rescue you. We had a wire barrier placed between them to avoid any unnecessary bloodshed."

"Then the Hannibal Clan is rightfully angry when you took much of their territory away," said Simi. "Given half a chance, they would kill the newcomers. So, why don't they just climb over the fence barrier and do it?"

Siegal answered. "We're very modern here. When we had the fence built, we added some solar panels to passively electrify the top wires."

"I get it. It's just like the avoidance studies at the university. Our lab rats refused to cross the charged grids, even if it meant starving themselves."

The tour ended at noon. As they returned to the shanty, the smell of fresh fish frying on the grill filled their nostrils.

"Enjoy your tour?" quizzed Danielson. "I hope you worked up an appetite. The fish were literally fighting to get on our hooks this morning."

Simi sniffed. "Smells wonderful."

"Nothing better than fresh fruit of the sea mixed with fruits of the tree." Phillipe smiled at the rhyme he had been saving to spring on any guest to the island.

Danielson gave directions while Phillipe tossed a salad from their garden. "Take a seat, you two. Ross, you pour the drinks. The grilled potatoes are just about ready. Get your bibs on and dig in before it gets cold." Lunch was topped off with cut-up mangos and bananas.

Danielson turned to Simi. "Did you get all your questions answered?"

"There are still some gaps. For the past two years, I have been lucky to do some fantastic scientific research. Then I was thrown into the middle of some mysterious intrigue. And now, I've emerged to learn that my lover boy was never dead and has been living here with his man Friday along with a bunch of wild monkeys. Does this mean I have to change my name to Jane? I wish I could stay here with you, Ross, except my obligations at Cal-Berkeley do not magically disappear."

"Maybe I can arrange that you can stay here at least for the summer," Danielson said. "I've talked with Dr. Bauer, and she agreed you need a rest. She was especially agreeable when I suggested there was a large contribution possible to the institute."

Siegal said, "Sounds very similar to the financing that originally lured me to sign onto our last project."

Danielson gave a Phillipe-like grin. "You may be right."

"That doesn't seem fair to my staff."

"Not to worry. I also talked with Dr. Landman. She told me there are no new projects needing your attention until fall. And the two of you can communicate daily by phone, email, and Zoom. Of course, you are the boss, and it is your lab. It's up to you to decide."

Simi thought for a moment. "Alisa is a great assistant, and I trust her. And, since we can be in constant communication, and I'm only a few hours away if there is an emergency. It can work. I guess I'm here for the summer."

"Good," said Danielson. "This island is secure and unknown to most of the world. There are lots of questions we need to work on. We know your skills were needed, but we don't know to what ends. And we don't have a clue as to the perpetrator. All we can figure is that there is some serious money directing the show. Simi, I need to go over everything about your kidnapping again. There must be a clue Sunada dropped that you overlooked the first time we talked."

Siegal and Phillipe excused themselves to leave Danielson and Simi alone.

DANIELSON OPENED HIS LAPTOP AND reviewed what he already knew. "Think hard, Simi. Did Dr. Sunada ever mention his employer?

Simi scanned her photographic memory. "All I remember is he said he did talk with someone by phone regarding me."

"Good. We can trace those things. Do you know whether his employer was American or foreign?"

"I can't say for sure, but I felt his employer was American by the way he worded his questions to me."

"Did you ever see any emails?"

"I was never allowed in the main part of the villa except to contact my lab files. Sorry."

"Don't be. For now, we can concentrate on an American."

Simi grimaced in frustration. "How does that help? There are over 375million people in the US"

"We can eliminate those that aren't wealthy, leaving the top 2 percent." What sort of criminal are you looking for?"

"It's too early to tell. No doubt, a white-collar type of some kind." Danielson gave her a supportive hug. We'll get whoever it is. There are always clues to trap even the craftiest criminals."

Simi rose from her chair. "I need to walk off lunch. It was her polite way of excusing herself in order to use the chemical bathroom. "Tom, I'm not a fan of roughing it. Can I cut my visit short whenever I choose?"

"You're a guest resident here and free to come and go as you wish."

"Do you mean I can leave this island if I want to?" She had to know if she was still a prisoner but under a different warden.

"You can leave with me on the plane today. But for your own security, I'd rather you wouldn't. Anything I can do to make your stay more pleasant, just tell me."

"Then, if I'm staying, what can you do to modernize the toilet facilities?"

"No sooner asked than done," said Danielson. He reached in his pocket for his cell phone and texted his Seabee friends who did the fence construction. Then he made another call. "Are you clear? Good. I want your crew to go over the villa in California. I want everything and anything that ties Sunada with his contractor. Check any electronic and paper trails. Look for any checks or receipts. He had to be paid by someone from somewhere. Don't miss a flyspeck. Is that clear, Jamie?"

SUN GAZETTE

Financial section: Gossip centers on William Getsen III. His meteoric rise from obscurity in the market has made him the King Midas, whose touch makes record upsides swoons in stock values. Rumors say he plans to leave his CEO position at Investments Central and form his own corporation. Financial leaders, already used to following his lead, have expressed concerns about his leaving. As always, Getsen has refused all requested interviews.

TWENTY-THREE

A WOMAN ON LITTLE DEADMAN'S Cay magically changed how two bachelors led their lives. Dirty clothes were strewn about wherever they were discarded prior to Simi's arrival. It was a dead heat as to whether the monkeys or the men were more primal.

Siegal and Phillipe thought they had created every combination of fish and local produce. Simi proved to be even more inventive. The adage two's company and three's a crowd did not hold true with this trio.

"What kind of psychology are you doing at Cal-Berkeley?" asked Phillipe one day during lunch.

"It's called sociobiology. You and Ross are doing field observations and explaining what you see in terms of stimulus/response actions. You know, classic behavioral psychology. But there are many behaviors you cannot explain simply by observing."

Phillipe grinned. "Oh, I have read of that in my college courses. It is called Gestalt psychology. When animal behavior is not explainable, in Gestalt terms, it is because the whole is greater than the sum of its parts."

Siegal broke in. "Simi, don't tell me you have gone over to the dark side and forsaken what I have always professed?"

"Don't be completely insane. It still fits your ideas. If it is not explainable, it is because we don't have all the facts. Sociobiology is the next step in behavioral science. It takes in all that is previously unknown and brings that information into the equation."

"Then that can explain why the Storm Clan acts so different from the normal monkey behaviors as exhibited by the Hannibal Clan," concluded Phillipe.

Simi continued. "Biologically, they are the same in all respects. But no Storm Clan male has succeeded in becoming the alpha male. In this rare instance, it is not the strongest males determining the outcome. For some reason, the Storm Clan females have rejected any of their male counterparts as worthy to father their young. The clues are there. We just have to look more closely to get our answer."

IT WAS A FRUSTRATING AFTERNOON on the observation deck. Siegal watched and saw nothing. Simi had nothing to add.

Phillipe just smiled. "Two very smart Doctaris and one poor native boy. You haven't seen the obvious. In a normal group, you would want to see how the males behave. It is very rare, but I have heard of females taking power. If you look very carefully, you will see the females groom one particular lady. I suggest this prime female will lead the pack. As time passes, maybe in a day or two, I predict she will select a male to foster her offspring."

Siegal suggested, "We haven't had a chance to name any members of the Storm Clan. I think it is appropriate to call her Cleopatra. And, when we determine, I mean when Cleopatra determines her alpha male, we'll call him Caesar. Simi, do you have any thoughts on why this occurred?"

"Monkeys are a strong social group," said Simi. "When they came to this island, they had no leader. None of the males were strong enough to take on the responsibility. So, it became logical that the strongest member of the group had to be chosen, and it turned out to be a female. Survival is the strongest drive of any species. End of story."

Siegal enjoyed his former student displaying her knowledge. "Here is another question for you. The Hannibal Clan knows they are so much stronger than the Storm Clan. Why do they bother to taunt them when they offer no threat?"

"Not now. But once they become organized with a leader, the threat becomes real."

Phillipe gave his toothy grin. "Monkeys behave so much like humans. Or vice versa."

"When the changes become a regular event, a species will change either by getting stronger or become extinct," added Simi.

"This is sociobiology?" asked Phillipe.

"At least part of it. It's been going on for thousands of years in the animal kingdom and translates to understanding what seems like aberrant behavior. So, you see, everything that goes on is logical."

"You get a belated A for that explanation," said Siegal.

Phillipe grinned, "Two Doctaris in one place. I don't know if I can stand it."

FOLLOWING THEIR NORMAL ROUTINE FOR each day, the trio gathered their video equipment and walked to the observation platform. They videotaped and made diagrams of how their animals moved about.

Phillipe, the most observant when it came to studying wild animals, was the first to sense a change. "Doctaris, are my eyes playing tricks on me, or are things happening down there?"

"What? It all appears the same to me," answered Siegal.

Phillipe pointed to the Hannibal Clan side. "See, Hannibal sits a little further back from the fence today."

Siegal rewound the videotape from the previous few days and ran the results. "I see what you are suggesting. Do you think it is just an accident?"

"I don't think so, Doctari. Monkeys are creatures with very strong habits. Hannibal has changed his posture. I think he is not looking directly at the Storm Clan. One more thing. He is hunching slightly to one side instead of sitting erect as in the past, a much less imposing stance."

"I never thought about noting eye contact. We need to review our video downloads for the past few days. Simi, do you make anything of Phillipe's observations?"

"Recent rains leaving puddles can be the culprit. Old Hannibal may just be looking for a more comfortable place to sit. If he continues this new posture, then we are seeing something very important taking place. Behaviors don't change without motivation. If we eliminate all outside causes, then we may be observing Hannibal sensing his loss of power."

Siegal asked Simi. "Do you theorize his behavior is internal within his clan or because of the Storm's presence?"

Simi said, "I haven't been here long enough to make an analysis of the situation. Time will tell."

PHILLIPE'S OBSERVATIONS OF HANNIBAL DROVE new energy into the trio's curiosity. Several days of charting showed Brutus now sitting in second place near Hannibal.

Simi concluded, "We're experiencing a nonviolent beginning in the change of power. My guess is Hannibal, the old warrior, is not about to step down graciously. It's just like the downfall of General Hannibal of old. How prophetic of you guys to name this alpha monkey Hannibal."

"Then you expect a physical conflict, Doctari Simi."

"There is always a battle."

Phillipe added. "If Hannibal wins, nothing changes. If Brutus wins, Hannibal will fade into the pack and take a position behind the females. It's likely that Brutus will kill any of Hannibal's children."

"It's all very complicated. I liked it better when we simply studied rats in a maze," said Siegal.

"You forgot, Ross. It got very complicated with family traits at the university."

"Wait till later. When I get you alone, I'll teach you about animal behavior," joked Siegal.

"Whoa, Doctaris. I think this is when I say, 'time to retire.'"

"Good idea," said Simi. "I want to be fresh and focus more on the Storm Clan. I'm sure something is happening across the fence to cause Hannibal's reactions. Any change in the Storm Clan, no matter how slight, will cause a change in the Hannibal Clan. Any increase in strength in one group means a perceived weakness in the other."

"It's still early enough for me," said Siegal. "I want to check in with Danielson to see if he has made any progress in learning about Sunada and his employer."

TWENTY-FOUR

AT THE UPPER END OF Marin County, twenty miles north of San Francisco, Danielson's handpicked investigators, he called them his headhunters, approached Akio Sunada's villa. The leader, Jamie, and her three associates, Doug, Kevin, and Tim, were often used by Danielson whenever a job required utmost discretion. And the need for the team to be there required utmost discretion.

The headhunters rented an SUV and checked into a nearby motel. Then they drove the ten miles to Sunada's villa. By midmorning, they reached the target location and parked under a nearby shade tree. It was summer, and the weather was unusually hot for northern California. They walked once around the perimeter before entering the premises.

Jamie studied the furniture and artwork. "Take note, guys: a regular bachelor pad."

"What are we looking for?" asked Doug.

"We need to find anything that can tie this Sunada with his last employer. So far, nobody knows anything except that Sunada was hired by an individual with very deep pockets to kidnap Ross Siegal's girlfriend.

Our job out here is discovery. The man said the events at this villa happened to Ross Siegal, making it personal for him. And that makes it personal for us too."

"Do we know why she was kidnapped?" asked Kevin.

Jamie shook her head. "The word I got is that she may have had special knowledge they want. Mr. Danielson wasn't specific, as usual."

"Where do we start?" asked Tim.

"We do it like they do on television. We walk the grid to get a feeling of the house. Then we go room to room."

The villa smelled musty, having been closed since the rescue. Professional cleaners had removed the bodies and taken out most of the bloodstains from the bedroom where Sunada and his servant killed themselves, but the odor of death was still present. After the tour, they met in the great room and put together their plan.

Jamie began. "The wine cellar is where Dr. Block was held. Tim, you begin there. Make sure to inventory and take photos of everything."

"I'm on it."

"Doug, I want you to search the study. There ought to be some records or correspondence that would give us a clue. Kevin, you're our computer expert. See what you can find on Sunada's PC and cell phone. I'll check out the bedrooms upstairs. Remember, take lots of notes and pictures. Collect anything we can take with us."

They worked till sunset, skipping lunch. It was hunger that brought them back together.

Jamie said, "We need to go back to our motel to shower and find a place to eat. An army works better when clean and with a full belly. When we put our findings together, we're bound to get some clues."

They loaded the things they had collected in the SUV. Kevin drove while the others closed their eyes and napped. He parked in front of a diner around the corner from their rooms.

Doug swallowed his last bite of hamburger. "Now I need that shower."

"Good idea for all of us," said Jamie. "We'll meet in my room, say in thirty minutes."

THE HEADHUNTERS, REENERGIZED FROM THEIR cooling showers and fresh clothes, gathered in Jamie's room. She, laptop in hand to take notes, sat at the round table by the window, and the rest found comfortable places on the bed and an overstuffed day couch.

"Who wants to go first?" she asked.

"I will," said Tim. He connected his digital camera to the room TV. "Okay. There are two rooms in the cellar. I first went where Dr. Block was kept. Along the walls are wooden racks filled with bottles of wine. I counted over two hundred bottles. As little as I know about wine, I did recognize a few labels. As you see, on the floor are several unopened cases, each containing a single brand and year." He stopped the TV images as he elaborated on the scene. "The shipping labels on them are from various vineyards around the world. Labels on the crates do not indicate whether Sunada bought them or they were given to him. Either way, I would guess the entire collection has to be worth over a million bucks. I conclude Sunada is more a collector than a drinker."

"What else did you find?" asked Jamie.

"There was a cot where Dr. Block slept. A single light bulb in the center of the ceiling lit most of the room. There is a bathroom setup in one corner. The only other furniture is a small table and chair. I also found a surveillance camera and a two-way speaker system in the ceiling."

"Anything else?" urged Kevin.

"Not in the wine room. I found a small storage room next to it." The TV screen aped Tim's report. "Total size was a little less than eight by ten feet. You can see it is disorganized. It appears they just threw anything they didn't want into that room. Something interesting, though. There was one wall where empty freight cartons were neatly stacked. I would guess Sunada and his manservant used those cartons when they moved into the villa."

"Any file boxes?" asked Kevin.

"Nada. Zip."

"That doesn't surprise me," responded Jamie. "Any files are likely in his study."

"I couldn't find anything definitive. You can retrace my steps to see what I missed."

"That would be a waste of time," said Jamie. "If there were any clues, you would have found them. All right, who's next?"

Kevin said, "That would be me. I'm not sure I found much more than Tim. I was looking for an address book for any contact names and struck out there. I did find an old leather binder that had names and numbers. It looks like World War II vintage. None of the numbers had area code prefixes. I doubt he used his phone very often. I conclude Sunada was a loner."

"Yes," quipped Jamie. "Rich and lonely."

"Then I looked through his desk for any current correspondence. Nada. All he had were a couple of health cataloges, and trash mail addressed to owner and occupant. I guess even someone living so far out in the country gets trash mail. I didn't find any postage stamps, so I suspect he didn't send any letters. He probably only communicated by emails and cell phone."

"Did you find any books around to give us a hint of his interests?" asked Jamie.

"He did have a few books, none of which had copyrights later than 1955. His library doesn't reflect he was studying any new theories."

"What do you make of it, Kevin?" asked Jamie, who had already guessed the answer.

"We've never studied a person who is so clean not to leave a paper trail of some kind."

Jamie said, "There is always a trail. We just haven't found it yet."

"I suggest we have some forensic research done on some of the impressions I found on his desk blotter and notepad near the phone," suggested Kevin. "Danielson's specialty lab can do that for us."

"Good idea," said Jamie. "We'll send them along with whatever else we found. Maybe we can get some latent prints off them that belong to someone in the FBI registry."

Doug raised his hand. "Guess I'm next. I was able to recreate some of Dr. Sunada's emails and incoming calls. I may have found a piece of useful information. It seems he was carrying on communications with mainly one person this past year. There were a series of fifteen exchanges beginning about six months ago. The dates are still on the computer, but I couldn't capture any of the text. One message came in as recently as the day before Dr. Block was kidnapped."

Jamie asked, "Were any of the calls from the same location?"

"That's the curious thing. Each of the calls was from a different location. The only thing they had in common was that they seemed to all be from somewhere in the eastern U.S."

"I just had a thought," said Tim. "Our bad guy doesn't know Sunada is dead, and Dr. Block has been freed. I bet there will be at least one more message from him. We can log into Sunada's email or cell phone. If and when a new message comes in, we can troll for its location."

"Great idea," said Jamie. "Can you do that sort of thing?"

"It's no big deal. I suspect he will be asking for an update on the brainwashing. The only problem is that he may still use another location."

"That leaves you, Jamie," said Kevin.

"Okay. I checked out the bedrooms. I checked the servant's room first and came up with a zero except for one dresser drawer that contained several thousand dollars. I suggest Sunada paid him in cash. I was about to come up dry in the master bedroom when I found this shoebox in the corner of the closet. Take a look." She opened the box and revealed two stacks of invoices.

"This first stack contains shipping receipts probably of the wines in the cellar. The second contains transactions from a local bank near where we are staying. All these deposits were made to Dr. Akio Sunada. Each was for similar amounts and showed origination from a single bank. No name was printed on them; only a bar code printed at the bottom."

"Great clue," said Doug. "I'll browse the internet and bank bar codes. It'll be easy."

He opened his laptop and typed a few keys. In moments he displayed a frown.

"Bad news?" asked Tim. "Can't trace the code?"

"Oh, I found the bank. But I don't think it's going to help a whole lot. All the transfers were from a bank in the Caymans."

Jamie said, "As clever as the perp is, I'm not surprised. Maybe some of the wine invoices will give us a clue. Tomorrow we'll go back and collect any other stuff of interest to take back with us. The old address book and shipping receipts should keep us busy for a few days. And, by that time, maybe our mysterious friend will send another communication that we can trace."

By nightfall the next day, the headhunters were on a plane headed home. The evidence was boxed and air freighted to Jamie's apartment. Jamie readied her report for Danielson, asking that the villa remain closed should they need to return.

TWENTY-FIVE

ONE HUNDRED MEN GATHERED AT the Fairmont Empress Hotel in Victoria, Washington. Each was a leader in their own segment of the economy: finance, education, electronics, real estate.

A man barely five feet tall, in his late forties, and wearing a dark pin-striped suit, walked out on stage. He tapped the microphone to test if it was turned on. The noise in the room hushed.

He read from a printed sheet. "Gentlemen, this conference is on its third and concluding day. These past two days, we have provided you with cutting-edge knowledge in making money through creative ways of funding manipulation. All legal, of course." He paused for a laugh. There was none. "If you take what you have learned, every one of you will be more successful compared to your current ways of doing business. I say this with no exception. The secret to positive money management is not just diversification, as many of you have been led to believe. You went into business and were motivated to make money. Lots of it, or you would not have been invited here. You do not have to apologize for your success. Do any of you have any questions? This is the time to speak up."

The room remained silent save for the tapping on laptops by several participants. On this, the final day, there was an air of disappointment. This conference, headed by William Getsen III, was supposed to be special. Why else would they attend? Getsen had not even bothered to make his presence known the entire time.

The man in the pinstriped suit turned the page in his prepared script. "At this juncture, I suppose you wonder about the fee for this conference: ten thousand dollars for hearing such a simple premise. If you leave with what we covered yesterday and the day before, you will gain ten times your fee. This last day is for a select few. It depends completely on the choice you are about to make. What now will be imparted works only if you follow Mr. Getsen's instructions with precision."

The pinstriped suit bowed slightly at the waist and disappeared behind the curtain. Another person now standing at the podium had not been present during the initial two days. This person is why each participant paid ten thousand dollars to attend.

Most attendees had never seen a picture of William Getsen III and only knew of his reputation as a financial wizard. Now he stood before them, medium height, hunched over a bit, and balanced on a cane. His voice was controlled with almost no inflection. Nothing at all was imposing about him, at least not what one would suspect from his reputation in finance. He could walk down most streets and never be noticed.

Getsen skipped any salutation. He minced no words. "Let's get started. If you remember, your specific invitation states that your undivided attention is mandatory. You were to come here alone, leaving wives and lovers at home." He pulled a sheet of names from his inside jacket pocket. "Twenty of you failed to follow this instruction. My assistant is instructing them to leave now. Within the envelope he hands them is the complete refund for the conference. For the twenty now leaving, what you learned can serve you well. However, you do not fit the next part of the program." Getsen offered no 'thank you' or 'good luck' closings.

Twenty industry leaders, not used to being unemotionally discarded, felt this penalty was harsh and unfair. No business competition eliminates individuals without at least one strike. Getsen was a man who had acted against all forms of logic in accumulating excessive wealth. He made his own rules. The twenty exempted, angry and embarrassed, expected some backlash support. Yet, not one person acted to support them. Each of the remaining eighty wondered if they, too, could expect a letter before the day was out.

The room remained stone silent, expecting the next shoe to drop as Getsen continued. "My assistant is now going about the room with a second envelope." Getsen gave a look of remorseless pleasure. "You are about to enter a contract with me. Inside each envelope is ten thousand dollars in bogus Getsen money. In thirty days, I will meet with you to review your success or failure."

One person raised his hand. "What is this silly game you're playing? I came here to learn from you. This has been a waste of my time."

"I never play games. To prove what I say, you, sir, are excused. My assistant will repay your ten thousand dollar fee less two thousand for incidental expenses and collect your Getsen dollars." Then addressing the remaining participants, he said, "This man has not learned anything from me, and I doubt he ever will. Now, are there any more questions?"

The room stayed silent.

"Good. We can go on without further distractions. As I stated before, you each have an envelope with ten thousand dollars. At your discretion, you are free to buy and sell what you wish. I will not intervene in any way. Remember one thing. Each one of you is a leader in your field. I suggest you do not step outside your defined area of expertise. Now I will let each of you ask one question."

There was a murmur in the room. Everyone had questions, but only one dared to ask.

"Ah. We have one person willing to take a risk. Yes, sir, what is your question?"

"I would like a clearer understanding of how this will work."

"A quality question. I want you to buy, sell, and negotiate however you do business in your real marketplace. The only difference is that you will also be trading with me on each of your transactions. Your successes and failures will remain a secret between us. At the end of thirty days, your Getsen bank account will be reevaluated. Those at the top will continue to the next step. Those who are not among the top will still learn enough to consider your fee for this conference as money well invested."

The assistant in the striped suit stood at the rear of the room. "Excuse me, sir. It is near noon. Perhaps you may want to break for lunch."

Getsen nodded. "A good idea. All of you have the opportunity to consider your participation. If you choose to be released, you can have your ten thousand dollars, less, of course, the two thousand in incidental expenses. We will reconvene at one sharp for final instructions. Play it safe or take the risk. The choice is yours."

With those words, William Getsen III turned on his weak legs and disappeared behind the curtain as mysteriously as he appeared.

TWENTY-SIX

"TELL ME WHAT YOU AND your headhunters found, Jamie?"

"Mr. Danielson, Dr. Sunada was quite a man. He had one failing. He needed to succeed all the way or accept anything less as failure. We think he felt considerable guilt while working with Dr. Block. This may have precipitated his suicide, coupled with his sense of imminent capture.

"Knowing that, what does that tell us?"

Jamie said, "We've met this type of individual before. My experience tells me his latest employer may have been the strongest individual personality he had ever been involved with. He pushed Sunada past his comfort limit."

"Are you also suggesting we are looking for a person so self-serving that he hasn't one iota of social guilt?"

"Boss, I think you have him pegged. We're dealing with a villain who preys upon the public with impunity. His power lies in the fact that few are willing to challenge his rules."

"You keep saying his, Jamie."

"I think it is a 'his' unless we are dealing with a wonder woman."

"Go on."

"We learned the wine and the shipping were paid for by the same offshore account that paid Sunada. We're hoping your lab can isolate fingerprints off the wine boxes we're sending, and you can match any known prints in the FBI or CIA files."

"Did you discover any clues why Dr. Block was chosen as the target?"

"It's a poser, Mr. Danielson. The most logical scenario is that Dr. Block has some special knowledge or talent. They could have forced her through torture or drugs. However, there is a better possibility that our villain wanted her ongoing cooperation. So, Dr. Sunada was contracted for his ability to brainwash Dr. Block into agreeing to help."

Danielson asked, "Then you think Dr. Block's specialty in sociobiology is the key."

"We think so."

"Did you find any clue as to where this is going?"

"Not yet, boss. Whatever it is, it must involve a lot of money. That would put our villain in the white-collar world."

"You make sense, as always. Give my thanks to Doug, Kevin, and Tim for their great work."

TWENTY-SEVEN

FEWER THAN FIFTY PEOPLE RETURNED following lunch. At precisely one o'clock, William Getsen III appeared from behind the curtain.

"I see our numbers have dwindled greatly. That is good. This next part of your program is most crucial. There is no room for those not willing to take the full risk. The lectures are over. The rest of the day will be spent on questions and answers. I shall give no information unless a question is asked." He chose his words carefully—no extra adverbs or adjectives.

The participants remained silent, afraid their questions would eliminate them from the conference.

"Remember, you came here to learn my secrets of making more money than you ever thought possible. But, like the turtle, you will never move forward unless you stick your neck out. With that said, begin the questions."

"Are you talking institutional success or personal success?"

"Good starting question. The decision is yours. If you want to carry the burden of your company's success on your own shoulders, then it is your problem. Your only responsibility is always to yourself. You cannot reap the level of success I suggest in any other way. Next question."

"Sir, thirty days seems a very short time to demonstrate one's skill in making money."

"If your plan is well thought out, then two or three days can be an eternity ... your future.

"Mr. Getsen, should our goal be short-term or long-term?"

Getsen scowled at the question but answered it as promised. "If you want long-term success, then I suggest you diversify your holdings. You will become rich and happy. But ... you will never achieve the level I am proposing. Your goal is simple. Your plan must be one quick strike. The risk is great, but the reward is greater. If you or anyone else finds this too uncomfortable, please elect to leave now. No one will think less of you. However, there will be no refund."

Another eight chose to leave, choosing the loss of the conference fee over surrendering their personal integrity.

"Next question."

"What if our action is in direct competition with someone in this room?"

"So what? You can compete and knock your competition out. In which case, one or both of you may lose. Or ... you can join forces if it seems prudent, and both of you can win. I never made much money cooperating with others, but the risk is less. You remaining participants will become invincible."

"You use the word invincible. Are we at war?"

"War?" smiled Getsen. "Yes, war. The world of competition is just another set of words that mean the same thing. You are only as strong as your last conquest. Everyone out there is your enemy. Display a weakness, and like Hannibal, you will be eaten alive."

"If this is a form of war, are there rules of engagement we must follow?"

"This is not a form of war with bullets but of minds. And now I will answer the second part of your question. The only measure of success is whether you have success. If rules of engagement bother you and you demand some sort of fairness, then you do not belong here. The only level of success is your degree of financial gain."

The question and answer session lasted past the dinner hour. Getsen was developing an insider supergroup of financial wizards as he and Sunada planned. The men in the room knew they were changed. Their previous friendships and business relationships were no longer held as inviolate. In thirty days, Old Wily Willie would have his army of followers. More accurately, this would be a super army, stronger than any single one of its members.

"Remember. There will be no prisoners. Only casualties."

Not one remaining delegate questioned Getsen's motivation. They never asked the vital questions: why was he letting them in on his secret, and why was he gathering this army of supporters? The greed of his audience overshadowed their rational thinking.

SUN GAZETTE

This week, the financial world has been set on its ear. Municipal National Bank ordered the downgrading of two major offerings to a level of junk bonds even though there appeared to be backing for both companies. Rumor has it that just prior to the action, Municipal National Bank sold its holdings. There are rumors circulating about the level of insider activity.

We at the *Sun Gazette* are investigating the motivation behind the transaction.

TWENTY-EIGHT

"HURRY, DOCTARIS. IT IS AFTER seven," called Phillipe outside the closed bedroom door.

"I'm up," Siegal called out as Simi giggled at her lover's double meaning.

Simi and Siegal's relationship was progressing back to where they were before Siegal disappeared two years ago. Simi thought back to how cold her marriage was to a man who left her suddenly. It never dawned on her that her husband carried on a double sexual life. She guarded her feelings even when her relationship with Ross became so warm and real. But when Siegal disappeared, she rebuilt a strong emotional shield. She tried to forgive Siegal for not letting her know he was alive. The pain she felt over losing her man was lessening. She was lying next to the only man she really loved. And it felt good.

"Put on the coffee, Phillipe. We'll be ready in ten minutes," Siegal added.

Phillipe grinned. "The coffee is ready, and the breadfruit is getting cold."

Siegal in shorts and Simi, adding a halter, came out to the porch. The weather was calm and warm, normal for late spring. Fresh smells of flowering buds on the fruit trees punctuated by an overnight shower made the promise of another fine day.

"Good morning, Doctaris," said Phillipe with his toothy grin.

"What do you have in mind for us today? You were so excited when you woke us," said Simi.

"Things are changing between the clans. We can go watch just as soon as I clean up to keep the scavenging sea birds from making a mess of our whole house."

"Fill me in on how the Storm Clan got its name, guys."

"They came to us during a big downpour," said Phillipe. "The monkeys were thoroughly drenched by the time we took them off the boat and got them under a shelter. I thought about calling them the Wetback Clan, but Doctari Siegal said that was a derogatory name in this part of the world." Phillipe swept the crumbs off the porch for the always hungry gulls. "Okay, we are ready to observe some very interesting facts. I want to know what you think is happening in psychological terms."

AS THEY WALKED TO THE observation platform, Phillipe set the scene. "Keep in mind how the Hannibal Clan is acting. Old Hannibal is definitely the alpha male. Each member of his troop has a specific placement in their territory. These social behaviors are very different in the Storm Clan. They have a different social hierarchy led by a female."

"Dear, did you get a chance to study any of our notes yet?" asked Siegal.

"Does a zebra have spots?" Simi answered.

"Stripe. Zebras have stripes," retorted Phillipe

"Whatever," she laughed at Phillipe for not catching on that she was joking. "Let me recap. At first, the Storm monkeys stayed as far away as possible from the common fence separating the two groups. They didn't trust the barrier to keep them safe. But this didn't stop them from developing their own society, and your notes explain that one of the females you guys named Cleopatra emerged as their leader. She chose a male, Caesar, as her mate."

Phillipe cleared his throat. "The way to determine who is dominant is to note the amount of time grooming takes place by the other monkeys."

"Is this the only way you can determine dominance?"

"No, there are other ways," continued Phillipe. "The main troop spends time roughhousing with each other, but none roughhouse with either Cleopatra or Caesar. Also, when it is time to nest for the evening, Cleopatra and Caesar have the first choice. The others surround them almost as if they were circling their wagons for protection.

"Seems like nothing much has changed since we humans came down from the trees," said Simi.

"I don't believe humans ever lived in trees," corrected Phillipe.

Simi laughed and continued, "Cleo simply chose the most suitable stud to breed with among the available males. Monkeys must have a single alpha male required by their genetic imprinting to maintain group quality."

"We can discuss that theory during our evening sessions," said Siegal. "For now, we need to be tracking their exact positions within their territory. Like Phillipe said before, when they were first dropped off, they stayed to the far end of their enclosure, away from the Hannibal Clan. It is only after Cleopatra began to show her leadership that they moved closer toward the center of their space.

Simi answered, "Well, with what you explained, these creatures being thrown together without a leader is why they acted in such disarray."

Siegal asked, "Why did a female emerge instead of one of the males?"

Simi, using her sociobiological knowledge, explained, "You missed some subtle efforts of a male to take over, but he was not taken seriously. Who knows why? Historically, women have assumed male roles even to the point of wearing fake beards as Hatshepsut, female Pharaoh of Egypt."

"Why did Cleopatra take on a consort?" asked Phillipe.

She continued, "It's genetic. Call it the nesting trait inborn into generations of females. The queen needs the best possible gene choice because she has only a limited number of eggs to breed her future bloodline. A male can leave his sperm countless times raising the odds that one of his progenies will turn out as a quality future leader."

Siegal leaned back against a tree in wonderment. *All this is coming from one of my graduate students. When did she become so knowledgeable? Whatever I did certainly worked.* Deep inside, he knew she would have done as well without him.

"I remember when anyone would be very happy to specialize in just one form of science," he said. "In just the past couple of minutes, you have drawn your comments from philosophy, history, genetics, right-brain/left-brain, natural selection, sociology, and I'm not sure what else."

"I know," said Simi proudly. "It's exciting to associate all observations to form answers to questions that have plagued us since the beginning of scientific investigation."

"Can you predict future behavior with your super science, Doctari?" asked Phillipe.

"It's not super science. And, yes, we have found in some of our initial research that not only can you predict results with unusually high accuracy, but also by varying certain factors within the equation, you can even control the choice of outcomes."

"I get it," said Phillipe. "While the Storm Clan remained without a leader, the Hannibal Clan felt omnipotent power. As soon as Cleopatra took over, old Hannibal started to feel threatened, even within his own troop."

"Did anyone notice if the threatening taunts got louder or softer as the leadership across the fence became more established?" asked Simi.

"Didn't think to notice," Siegal responded, "We can check volume levels on our videotapes." Siegal put up his hand to halt the conversation. "Wait a minute. Just before we went off on this thought, Phillipe, you said something profound. You said something about controlling the choice of outcomes. Simi was kidnapped to help Sunada and his employer to control specific outcomes. I have to think about it. It may be a very important clue. I want to pass it by Danielson and see what he thinks."

Phillipe felt he was sitting in a class with two master psychologists. "Doctari Block, what else can you tell us about our monkey population?"

Simi continued. "We may be at the crossroads of a complete power shift. The underdogs could be in the process of a takeover. Odds of any success at this moment are low. But I never want to bet the bank on any future outcome."

Siegal added, "This is like a reenactment of Hannibal's underestimating the will of his enemy. It was his downfall."

Phillipe questioned, "Is there a thread between General Hannibal and our Hannibal Clan?"

Simi answered, "There is one. A weaker rival can never take over the stronger unless an internal weakness is discovered and exploited."

"We're talking monkeys here. I appreciate your esoteric theories, but it's just monkeys," challenged Siegal. "What do they know about having strengths and exploiting weaknesses? Are you suggesting that both clans sense this change, and the results will be inevitable?"

"Not always, Ross. It happened enough times, however, to make it statistically significant. The Hannibal Clan is biologically the same as the Storm Clan. The change is sociological. With this change, different behaviors must take place, which affect any interaction with the Storm Clan. The Hannibal Clan gives the appearance of becoming weaker, and the Storm Clan has taken up the aggressive space left by them."

THE NEXT FEW DAYS WERE quiet on the island. The monkeys did their thing, Phillipe studied for one of his veterinary school exams, and the Simi/Ross love affair was back on a fast track. Life was good.

TWENTY-NINE

MARVIN SHAUER EARNED HIS INVITATION to William Getsen's conference by being one of the most successful financial consultants in recent years; continuing his style of offering timely tips to people and corporations assured his success. But the challenge by Getsen was one his competitive nature could not resist.

He turned to his ever-present executive assistant. "Take a letter, Miss Quinlin."

Dear Personal Investor,

For the past several quarters we have experienced unusual movement within several sectors. Many high-tech companies have shown a reluctance to introduce new products. As a result, they have fluctuated down from their previous highs. Undercapitalized companies will be unable to withstand this downturn and could be taken over by more aggressive companies. As a result, we can expect very quick growth in a few specific companies.

I have been following one company in particular, New Technology, part of the Pacific Rim group. Two years ago, it was offered at $23.56.

Last year the stock traded for $224.64 per share. It is currently at $101.88. I predict it will move lower to about $99.00 before reaching resistance. I predict it will then move higher quickly based on its price-earnings ratio to over $200 per share.

Please call me if you wish to participate.

Marvin Shauer, Executive Planning Resources

"Miss Quinlin, send this letter to all my accounts. Oh, and get Price Waterhouse on my private line."

He picked up the phone. "Price Waterhouse. Whom do you wish to speak to?"

"This is Marvin Shauer. I would like to speak with your accounts manager."

There was a short pause accompanied by canned music.

"Good morning, Marvin. How can I help you?"

"Fred, I wish to release all my holdings of New Technology immediately. I will accept the current trading price."

Shauer reached into his desk for two antacid tabs. Then he turned on his computer, made some entries on his spreadsheet, and punched total. At first, he felt a twinge of guilt, but not the normal pain commonly associated with his type A personality.

Under his breath, he said, "Over fifty million in commissions. A tidy sum if I do say so myself. Some of my investors may get stung a little, but that's their risk. In this business, it is always buyers beware. New Technology doesn't stand a chance in this market. This is what Getsen intended for me to do." He then recorded his transaction as instructed in the envelope given to him at the conference. Had he done enough to place him in Wily Willie's good graces? He hoped it would.

SIMILAR SCENARIOS WERE BEING PLAYED out by at least a half dozen investment offices nationwide. Brokers were telling their investors to buy when they should have been telling them to sell. False noise signals are common when commissions drive recommendations more than client satisfaction. Many of these were motivated as a result of attendance at the meeting in Washington state. Copycat investors followed.

THIRTY

ANOTHER PERSON MOTIVATED BY ATTENDING Getsen's meeting was Thomas O'Mally, a real-estate developer in St. Louis. Buy low and sell high was the motto etched at the base of the minuteman statue standing on his desk.

Recent market volatility had been especially kind to him. He was able to increase his fortune by picking up several pieces of property when owners were feeling a cash crunch caused by a Midwestern-driven downturn in grain and animal futures. Many of his new holdings included small farms along the confluence of the Missouri and Mississippi rivers. Now he was challenged by William Getsen III to liquidate his hard assets, and he had only thirty days to make it happen. It meant causing many farmers to lose their livelihood and become hopelessly in debt.

"I need a scotch."

MORNING SUNLIGHT CREPT THROUGH THE window of his tenth-floor office. An empty bottle of Glenfiddich single malt scotch lay on the desk. Thomas O'Mally sat, slumped in a drunken stupor in his executive chair.

"Bring in some coffee and an Alka-Seltzer," muttered O'Mally. "I had to work late."

His personal executive assistant knew it was not that he worked late. Thomas O'Mally was an alcoholic. His work made him that way. His wife left him for just that reason. Still, he maintained sobriety enough of the time to be one of the top ten real estate developers in the nation. His assistant had stayed with him through thick and thin. And many times, his investment mistakes left him very thin.

"Did you figure out your problem?" she asked.

His voice slurred. "As you know, I was out of town for a business conference a few days ago. I have never experienced such a unique presentation."

O'Mally was a lonely man. Even before his divorce, he seldom shared any of his business at home. He had only one real confidant. That was his executive assistant Miss Berry. There had never been any hint of sexual interaction between them, but she was as devoted to him as any person could be. Whenever a particularly difficult problem needed discussion, Miss Berry was there. Her best skill was never offering any solution but acting only as a sounding board.

"This Getsen laid out a challenge to a small number of attendees. He promised fast and enormous wealth if we followed his direction and without suggesting the normal ten steps to success. When I try to think of what he said, I can't put my finger on one damn thing. But it was perfectly clear what I have to do."

Miss Berry handed him his Alka-Seltzer.

O'Mally continued, "He invites you to attend his conference and then ends up not telling you anything at all."

Is this man some sort of con artist?"

"No ... just motivated."

"He challenged us to become equally motived. I'm a very wealthy man, at least on paper. My net worth is over three billion in land and futures. But, if I wanted to buy a car today, I'd have to go to the bank and take out a loan."

"Sir, you don't need him, and you know it."

"It's the challenge that Getsen put out. I can't let it go."

"What must you do?"

"I need to liquidate my hard assets in just two weeks. Are you ready to dig in? We have a hell of a lot of work to do."

She sat down in the chair next to him and opened the laptop she always had handy. "Ready, sir."

"Have my attorneys meet with me this afternoon. Call our publicity department. Have them drop everything, and be in the conference room by ten o'clock. Order in coffee and lunch. It looks like we'll be there most of the day."

Thomas O'Mally finished his coffee and swallowed the rest of his Alka-Seltzer. He knew his profits would impress Getsen and turn millions of dollar assets into ready cash.

No risk, no gain.

Two days later, his plan went public. The *St. Louis Tribune* ran a double-page ad announcing the greatest live property auction ever in the state of Missouri.

LIVE REAL ESTATE AUCTION—
COMPLETE LIQUIDATION
ONE DAY ONLY
ALL SALES FINAL

Individuals interested must present a $500,000 letter of credit or a certified check to be admitted.

All available products will be listed with certified appraisals, color photos, and virtual images. Interested parties will be presented a complete listing on O'Malley's web page or by coming to Thomas O'Malley's offices prior to the auction.

The auction shall begin at two o'clock and continue nonstop until the entire list is exhausted.

Within an hour after the ad was released, phones in the office suite started ringing. A few of the callers were typical curiosity seekers. Most, however, were from eager speculators who knew of his skills at selecting properties at very competitive prices and were hoping for some bargains. Next came the inundation of calls from local television and radio stations.

All staff was delegated to phone duty parroting O'Mally's statements where one could receive preliminary information and how to make reservations for the auction. They were instructed to answer 'no' to any inquiries about making early sales before Friday at two o'clock.

A BUFFET LUNCH WAS SERVED at noon the day of the auction. Qualified investors ate, drank, and discussed strategies. The buffet was cleared. At one forty-five, chairs were rearranged in theater fashion, and the room took on the air of a formal business meeting. The auction began promptly at two.

Except for a thirty-minute break at six o'clock, the buying process went nonstop. By eleven-thirty, that night, every property, save two small homes, was sold. The buyers appeared equally as happy to buy as O'Mally was to sell. The auctioneer's gavel pounded a final three times, declaring the auction was over.

O'MALLY TOOK THE TITLES OF the two unsold properties and signed them over to Miss Berry. "This is my thank you gift. You have been my trusted employee and friend throughout all my real estate years. I won't need you for a while. Sell these or rent them as you wish. It should give you an extra retirement pension. I am now officially out of the real estate business."

She teared up with emotion. "But you're still young. You can't just sit back and let the rest of the world go by. What will you do to stay busy?"

O'Mally patted his bulging briefcase. Inside were checks and drafts totaling more than four billion dollars.

"Don't worry about me. I just made the biggest deal of my life."

SUN GAZETTE

The financial world is in shock today with the news that real estate magnate Thomas O'Mally was found at his desk with a gunshot wound in his head, an apparent suicide. This is the third untimely death of a major industrialist in the past week. There is no obvious way to tie these deaths together. Is this a coincidence? This reporter will be seeking answers.

THIRTY-ONE

IN THE HEART OF SAN Francisco's financial district in the Transamerica's building on the forty-second floor were the offices of B-Tech Industries, Sam Blackman CEO. Richard Brand, investigative financial reporter for the *Sun Gazette*, had set Blackman as his next investigative target.

A receptionist answered the phone. She listened and then buzzed the intercom. "Mr. Blackman, it's that same reporter on the phone. He insists on an interview with you."

"He's been dogging me for over a week now. I suppose I should see him. Find me time tomorrow morning. Please hold all calls for the rest of the afternoon. I have an important matter to take care of."

Sam Blackman leaned back in the brown leather chair he had custom-made to fit his rotund body. He looked around his expansive office. Across the far walls were photos of him with many important world personages. One wall housed a built-in kitchenette complete with dark brown marble counters. In a prominent corner was a tall breakfront to match the wood of his desk. The lighted interior showed off his trophies and awards given to him when he was an All-American linebacker at UCLA. Even the brace he wore after a career-ending leg injury during his senior year was there as a reminder of what he may have become as an NFL professional. Scattered about were collections of paintings from near-famous artists. Several bronze and marble sculptures were tastefully displayed on stands and tables about the room. Everything around him showed the good taste that only a highly paid interior designer could accomplish.

Blackman thought of himself as a self-made man. He had started B-Tech Industries at the height of the dot.com revolution. He prided himself on being the stereotypical athlete who didn't take his business courses at the university seriously and yet beat the odds. It helped, of course, that he inherited three million dollars from his grandmother.

His good luck held through a series of high-risk ventures building his capital to over a billion dollars. He took his company public and two and a half years later became one of the fortune five hundred. He now had six thousand employees in more than twenty countries. To describe Sam Blackman as a financial success was a gross understatement. He earned an annual salary of twenty-seven million plus stock options and other benefits. His personal possessions included real estate, a Learjet, and full ownership of the local professional soccer team.

Blackman attended the financial business conference headed by Wily Willie, more to pit his own business acumen against the current national guru than anything else. He was intrigued by the competition Getsen offered.

Following the conference, he devised a plan he felt could not be derailed. Even an investigative reporter from the *Sun Gazette* flying in from Washington seemed no more than a bothersome gnat. Filled with confidence, he left early to work out at his exclusive club's gym.

AT FIVE MINUTES TO NINE the next morning, Richard Brand entered the suite of Sam Blackman and presented his business card to the receptionist.

"Do you have an appointment?" she asked, pretending not to know who he was. "Please sit down, Mr. Brand. I will let Mr. Blackman know you are here."

She announced Brand's arrival into the mouthpiece hanging from her neck. Then turning to Brand, she said, "He will see you now. Please go in."

Brand was pointed to the end of the hall and directed to Blackman's personal secretary.

"Please go in." The personal secretary gave an unfeeling smile. "He is expecting you."

BLACKMAN PUT DOWN THE LETTER he was reading, stood up from behind his massive desk, and extended his hand as a greeting. His voice, large as his football hands, boomed out with confidence. He set the clear tone that this office was his power stage.

"Good morning, Mr. Brand. You are prompt. I like that in a man. If you're ever out of a job, give me a call. I can always use a time-conscious person around here. Getting people to show up on time is one of our great American weaknesses."

Brand had met the likes of Sam Blackman many times before and was not moved by his approach. He felt comfortable having done his home-work and was well prepared to wade in with both feet.

Blackman continued his performance. "There is coffee, tea, and ice water on my custom wet bar. What can I get for you? I prefer the dark Cuban blends."

Brand nodded. "American roast with a little cream, if you please."

"Coffee with cream it is. Sit down, Mr. Brand. May I call you Richard?"

Richard Brand recognized the classic father/son approach, as he called it. Fouling off the first pitch like a major leaguer, he said, "I prefer Mr. Brand, thank you."

Brand had plated his first power card. He enjoyed taking some of the wind out of Blackman's sails.

Retaking the seat behind his desk, Blackman folded his hands and said, "So, Mr. Brand, what can I do for you? Or should I ask more directly, exactly why are you here? I suppose you are wondering what is happening out here in the Wild West at my company B-Tech Industries. Let me assure you that business is as usual."

Blackman continued his smoke screen effort by leaning back on his chair, exposing his large athletic frame. He knew this usual behavior often made less experienced interviewers wary. It didn't seem to be working on Brand.

"Maybe I should start on page one," said Brand. "I have been tracking your company for the past several months and have come across some issues that have turned on several yellow caution lights. If you care, I would like to discuss them with you."

In defense, Blackman pushed a button on his intercom. "Please check my schedule. How much time do I have before leaving to open the new special needs wing at Children's Hospital?" He stared directly at Brand and said, "B-Tech Industries has created a ten million dollar trust to support their research, and I feel it would be in bad taste to be late. Don't you agree?"

"I understand, Mr. Blackman," parried Brand. "If this interview takes more time than you can spare at the moment, I would certainly be happy to reschedule a follow-up appointment at a more convenient time."

The game of cat and mouse continued. Both men were seasoned warriors at sidestepping issues and putting off their unfriendly adversaries. As much as Blackman tried, Brand could not be taken off his course.

"I still have one hour. Hopefully, we can get through your inquisition in that time," said Blackman.

"Thank you. As I already stated, there are several questions I would like to ask. Of course, you may not be able to answer all of them today, but you have the opportunity to research them, and I can come back next week."

"I assure you I have a complete understanding of everything that is happening within my company. I pride myself that even with six thousand employees, I maintain a strong oversight on them."

Brand smiled. "Good. Then this interview should go quickly. I know this next point may be sensitive." He reached in his briefcase and took out a report. "This document shows what I consider some questionable business practices. While they may not be unlawful, they are at least leaning to the unethical."

"Are you here to interview me or make allegations? If it is the latter, then I believe I should have my attorneys present. Better yet, just leave your questions, and I will respond to them in the next four to six weeks."

"I'm sorry, sir, but my story will not wait four to six weeks. It will not wait for even two weeks. I plan to release the first part in a week, and I want you to have an opportunity to respond before going to press."

Blackman rubbed his hand, his form of agitation. "Okay, what's your first question?"

"It's not actually a question but an observation. Your most recent annual report raises several flags. Specifically, your profit level does not correspond to increases in sales. When this is combined with an overall change in production-related expenses, these leave questions of your management practices."

"I'm not sure I understand. What are you driving at?"

"I think you do understand. You are showing more expenses without increases in sales. On the surface, your company appears to be making money, causing stock values to rise. This creates an untenable price-earnings ratio. This forces your company's stock value to tumble, leaving investors to most likely lose their shirts."

"You're suggesting we are controlling stock values improperly. You are wrong. We are acting according to our approved business plan. The market fluctuations are just the nature of the beast. Let's be honest with each other. People are greed driven. They jump on the bandwagon, then cry foul when things go south."

"I agree with you to some extent. But let me go on. Your six thousand employees all have their retirement funds tied up in your company's stock. My understanding is that they have no choice in how to invest their 401(k)s. If the B-Tech stock should take a strong downturn, these people will lose what they have worked hard for all their years."

Blackman saw his opening. "And if our stock should go up, they will become even richer. I'm not sure you have a point." He glanced at his desk clock. "Hurry, I have to be at the opening shortly."

"Then I'll make it quick. Your annual report shows large profit increases with little to back up the numbers. Now at the same time, while you require your employees to fund their 401(k)s with B-Tech stock, you and your top five executives have been selling large blocks of B-Tech stock for huge profits and placing these funds outside the company. How do you wish to respond to this?"

"I feel there is no better investment for an employee than to invest in his or her own company. It is akin to being a part-owner. Now let me respond to the second part of your accusation. I do not tell my executives when to buy or sell our stock. They, like me, are free to make this decision on their own."

Brand nodded. "It is my understanding that the lower echelons of your company do not have this choice.

"They are offered B-Tech stock at a percentage lower than market value. We are just trying to protect them from uninformed choices."

"I understand. But, your executives appear free to invest as they please. And, selling B-Tech stock when it appears to be in a strong position sounds as if they are acting on insider information."

Blackman, now very agitated, raised his voice. "What is your last point?"

"It is straightforward. How do you rationalize a 125 percent increase in your personal salary when, in fact, your annual balance sheet does not support this raise? Add to that, you also received, along with your five executives, large bonuses. I believe yours alone was in the range of seventy million dollars. And finally, loans you have taken through B-Tech are not part of the annual record. Instead, you did it off the books. It would seem you undermined your company's capital, putting it on the verge of collapse. You would never have to pay back the loans. And I believe I can prove it."

"We're through. I met with you today in good faith, and you are asking questions that slander me. My attorneys will be contacting your little rag, and I am sure not a word of this will ever be printed. Goodbye. You know the way out."

THIRTY-TWO

DANIELSON SAT IN HIS OFFICE. His phone was silent and had been for over three days. As if afraid to stay mute a second longer, it rang.

He read the caller ID. "It's about time. What have you come up with?" he yelled into the mouthpiece.

"This one has us stumped," said Jamie.

"You must have something."

"Okay. We feel confident we are looking for a white-collar criminal living somewhere along the eastern part of the US."

"I guessed that," said an agitated Danielson. "What else?"

"And we know Deep Pockets, as we've dubbed him because of how much investment he has in the caper, funnels all his money out of accounts in the Cayman Islands."

"Not surprised. Tell me something I can hang a body on. It'd be nice if we could get a name."

"We're not there yet. Right now, the wine collection is our strongest lead. We first checked brands, sorting by dollar value. That didn't help. Now we're looking for fingerprints and DNA samples on the bottles."

"And you found what? Get to the point."

"Fingerprints on the bottle have been registered with the FBI as a known felon. The man works for a company that shipped most of the wines. But he's been clean ever since his release from prison. Your call, boss, but we don't think he's connected to Deep Pockets."

"At least you know the shipper."

"And, they were very helpful when we told him we were attempting to investigate Sunada's death, especially after we showed a federal court-ordered search warrant."

"You got a warrant? How?"

"You don't want to know. Anyway, the company made several shipments of wine over this past year to Sunada's villa. They always picked up the wine from the same location, a distributor on the East Coast."

"Now you're getting somewhere. Do you have a record of who ordered the wine?"

"Our perp was very clever. Each time a different purchaser's name was used. I had a handwriting expert study the signatures, and only two people did all the signing."

Danielson clapped his hands. "Then we're not looking for a whole cartel.

"The method of ordering was always the same. It makes us believe there's only one person and the second signature is a subordinate."

"That's not much, but it's more than nothing. How about Sunada's computer?"

"Kevin's been working on it. So far, we have confirmed that all messages to and from Sunada were from within the United States. Language helped us conclude that all incoming emails were from only one person."

"Any take on why Sunada was hired and why he kidnapped Dr. Block?"

"We think he hired Sunada first because he had the reputation of performing certain unscrupulous acts of motivating individuals to do certain things."

Danielson asked, "Then why do you think he or she needed Dr. Block?"

"Her knowledge of sociobiology may be the key to even a different form of people control. Does that make sense?"

"It does. I got a message from Dr. Siegal that says Dr. Block, in her specialty area, could manipulate groups of like-minded people to act in concert with each other. If this is true, then we may know why she was kidnapped, but we still don't know by whom or for what specific purpose. I have a thought, but I want to float it past Dr. Siegal first. It may be a way to smoke our Deep Pockets out into the open. At any rate, I'd like you to report back every day, even if you have nothing new to tell."

Jamie knew this was not a friendly suggestion. "Yes, sir."

THIRTY-THREE

THE WEEKLY SUPPLY PLANE MADE its scheduled stop on Little Deadman's Cay. This day it carried Danielson. Phillipe spied him getting off and had placed a pitcher of lemonade and four glasses on the porch table by the time Danielson reached the house. Siegal and Simi also spotted their visitor and rushed back from their lookout platform.

A huffing Simi received a hug and asked, "What brings you to our tiny island sanctuary?"

"Do I always need a reason?"

"You always have a reason," smirked Siegal as the group settled around the porch table.

"Guilty on all accounts," said Danielson, gulping one glass and pouring another. "I need to probe more with you, Simi." He relayed his conversation with his lead headhunter. "They're sure our perp is only one person. They've nicknamed him Deep Pockets because of his willingness to spend a good deal of money to get what he wants. Simi, you were with his man, Sunada. What's your take?"

Well," she said, "Dr. Sunada and I started to talk a little about his past before you rescued me. But I never got the whole picture. He only developed his techniques to work on one person at a time. I think Deep Pockets wanted more of a mass brainwashing result."

"I got all that."

"I personally think Dr. Sunada could have developed the methodology, but something inside him prevented his accepting the challenge. Deep Pockets wanted more than the good Doctor was willing to give."

"And you were tagged for that purpose?"

"Sounds logical. I was identified as the person with my special knowledge to do it. Dr. Sunada knew I wouldn't do it freely unless I was brainwashed by the competent hands of the one-on-one master."

Siegal added. "That answers the question 'why you?'"

Simi pursed her lips. "Thinking back, he almost had me if you guys hadn't come along. I might have spilled out my entire guts."

"And those guts are?" asked Danielson.

"As you know, I was working on understanding how people can contrive plans to manipulate others and vice-versa. It explains why people are willing to be manipulated by others."

"Now, Mr. Danielson and Doctaris, all you have to figure out is what this person wants to accomplish," Phillipe blurted out, accompanied by his patented wide grin.

"Phillipe said it very succinctly. It's one of the things I am here to discuss. The reason for Simi's kidnapping was easy to understand."

But, not one of the group had the slightest clue about Phillipe's query. All they knew was that they had to find out before it was too late.

Danielson said, "We may be a small step ahead of Deep Pockets. He doesn't know Sunada is dead, and Simi is safely back with us."

"I don't see how that helps us," said Siegal.

"How does this idea sound," said Danielson. "Deep Pockets has depended on Sunada to develop the master plan to carry out his wishes. Without Sunada, our perp has to carry on alone. I believe this man is rich because he is self-absorbed in his own success. I think his confidence in himself, I like to call it ego, makes him think he can do it by himself."

"I think I know what you are getting at," said Simi. "We let out that Sunada is dead. He will have two choices. Either he backs out of his plan, or he is compelled to go it alone."

Siegal concluded, "Our villain cannot quit. It means that much to him. I say to go ahead with your plan."

"Like life or death?" asked Phillipe.

"Maybe not that to that extent," said Danielson.

PHILLIPE STOOD UP. "EXCUSE ME. I need to finish dinner. It will be ready in about one hour. Why don't you take a little walk to work up an appetite?"

"Good idea," said Danielson. "I haven't seen your monkey menagerie for a while. Anything new happening?"

"Not yet," said Siegal. "We have been watching some interesting behavioral differences between the clans. I'll tell you about them as we walk."

The stroll between the palms was a pleasant change from the hustle of Washington, and Danielson enjoyed seeing how his experiment of turning Siegal back into a research scientist was working. With Simi keeping him company, he had never seen his good friend in such a happy mood.

After hearing some of the backstories of the monkey activity, Danielson said, "It's just like you're talking about humans. One clan has a headstrong patriarch and the other a headstrong matriarch. What else?"

"They don't like each other very much," said Siegal. "We plan to find out how much by taking away the barrier fence between them. We've been waiting for the Storms to feel strong enough to fend off the Hannibal Clan."

"We actually scheduled to begin taking away the barrier tonight," said Simi. "You can see what happens for yourself. Don't worry; we're ready to intervene if things get touchy."

Danielson smiled. "I've never seen you psych guys work in real life."

"Okay," declared Siegal. "Tonight, after the monkeys have nested, we change from being passive observers to being active manipulators."

Simi added, "We won't take the whole structure down at once, just a gap large enough for one at a time to pass through. They will have to discover the opening in the morning. I hope it will be peaceful. I'd hate to be in the middle of some garrulous monkeys."

The ringing of the dinner triangle announced Phillipe had finished cooking. It was like Pavlov ringing the bell to make his dog salivate. The trio suddenly became hungry.

During dinner, Phillipe suggested, "Better set your alarms for early. We need to be at the observation platform before they wake. We don't want to miss a thing."

Danielson pushed back his chair and rubbed his full belly. "Your dinner of fresh grouper from the smoker and yellow yams from your garden was great, Phillipe. Better than any Washington chef could match."

"I have an idea," said Siegal. "Tom, you and Phillipe can create the opening. One or two people should not disturb any of our friends."

PHILLIPE PLANNED TO RISE FIRST and assume the duties of an alarm clock. It was still an hour before sunrise, and he knew they had to be at the observation platform before the sun came up and the monkeys awoke. To his surprise, Simi was in the kitchen brewing a pot of fresh coffee, having long before finished her regular morning stretching exercises. He went to rouse Tom and Ross, but they were up as well. They gathered on the porch for some toasted breadfruit and canned yams.

Simi said, "I couldn't sleep much after three. Getting a chance to observe two very different functioning cultures of the same species emerging is monumental. In human timelines, the comparable moment is equivalent to hundreds of years or more. At the institute, we can only observe a sample spot of time." She reminded them, "Don't be surprised if nothing happens today. My research experience suggests that small changes in the environment do not evoke immediate observable changes in behavior."

"Do either of you think there are internal changes taking place?" asked Danielson.

"I was trained by the best observable behaviorist, and maybe old habits are hard to change," said Simi as she gave Siegal a loving nudge. "Still, it would be nice if we had some telemetry to measure changes in heart rate, blood pressure, or hormonal levels."

THE HANNIBAL CLAN WAS THE first to stir. They moved out of their nests and foraged for their morning meal. It seems that not a single member noticed the small opening in the fence.

The Storm Clan had, by now, developed enough group unity to wander their entire range, which led them near the opening. Caesar walked over and gave an uninterested glance at the gap, then moved away. However, as other Storm members wandered toward the opening, Caesar gave a sharp warning cry and chased them away.

The rest of the day remained calm and quiet as Simi had predicted.

SINCE EVERYONE WAS ON THE watch, there was no one to cook.

The group had to settle for a fish salad made of leftover grouper.

"Well," a disappointed Danielson said, "I didn't see anything exciting."

Simi acted miffed at his remark. "We saw a lot today. Neither group pretended excitement. Old Hannibal and his followers had been very aggressive in the past. This could have been their big moment to attack, and they didn't. That's major stuff."

Phillipe said, "I was surprised it was Caesar who chased the clan away from the gap. Cleopatra should have taken the lead."

"It will be interesting to see what happens when we widen the gap."

That night the gap was made larger, and the dynamics between the clans did not change. Only one observable event took place. A young male from the Hannibal Clan sauntered toward the opening and touched the fence. His backward glance toward Hannibal appeared dismissed by the alpha male.

Danielson only yawned. "This excitement is more than I can handle. I have to get back to DC. Duty calls."

SUN GAZETTE

A reliable source reports that the notorious Dr. Akio Sunada took his life this past week. He was known as the father of motivational psychology. During WWII, he was responsible for the development of death squadrons that flew into our naval ships in the Pacific Ocean. His actions were responsible for killing more of our sailors than any single individual of the war. At the time of his death, he lived in a secluded villa north of San Francisco.

Elsewhere in the world

This is Richard Brand, financial reporter for the Sun Gazette. This is the first of a several part investigative series on CEOs who have raised yellow caution flags regarding their unethical and illegal accounting and administrative practices that should be brought to public attention.

Mr. Blackman, founder and CEO of B-Tech Industries, is my first target. I personally interviewed him and offered an opportunity to respond before writing this article.

He is a highly respected individual in his community who underwrote the special needs wing at his local children's hospital and has six thousand employees working within his company. However, even an average accountant can see how he is destroying B-Tech, putting all his employees in peril of losing not only their jobs but their retirement plans. He denied my accusation. Mr. Blackman abruptly ended my interview and refused to answer further questions except through his legal staff.

He challenged my newspaper as well as my own legal right to pursue this investigation. I assure you, this investigation is far from over.

Until the federal government takes oversight and accepts its responsibility, I promise to be your watchdog.

THIRTY-FOUR

THE FOUR HEADHUNTERS, JAMIE, DOUG, Kevin, and Tim, gathered in Danielson's favorite hideaway, the Smoking Musket Restaurant. National News Channel (NNC) showed on one of the many large-screen televisions. The sound was muted. A stream of words scrolling across the bottom told of B-Tech Industries stock tumbling.

Danielson approached their secluded table. He greeted each with a handshake. "Kevin, I trust the bullet you took from our last action has healed."

Keven nodded, patting his wound scar.

"Good. Doug and Tim, you men have been a great part of the team. Don't take any extra bullets to stay even."

It had been a while since Danielson met with the team in person. Their work at Sunada's villa was all done through cell phone communication and secured emails.

"Have the four of you eaten? I, for one, am starved," said Danielson. He waved his hand, and almost magically, a waiter appeared and took their orders.

They ate, talking only of trivial things. It was Danielson's style not to discuss business while eating. As the last of the four-star lunch was consumed, the waiter refilled their coffees, a signal that it was time to get serious.

"Okay, down to business. I called you here because I think you are the best at solving the toughest problems. I remember when I asked you to find the best behavioral profiler. In all the world, you came up with Ross Siegal. You guys were spot on. Then I asked you to infiltrate a terrorist group making noises on the Riviera. You saved a lot of lives. Then, Jamie, I asked you to do the most dangerous thing possible by attaching yourself to one of the mid-level terrorists and help lead us toward their nest in Germany. You were unbelievable. I doubt I would have had such courage to do what you had to do."

"Enough of this sugar coating," interrupted Tim. "What you want is for us to find your needle in a monster haystack: Deep Pockets." "And I think the job may be impossible to achieve," added Danielson. He first reviewed what they already knew.

"One new thing," Jamie said, "in our search of Sunada's messages, we found they were all sent to and from the eastern part of the United States."

"A point for our side," said Danielson. "Do we have clues to this perp's motives?"

Jamie said, "We'll do our best. Experience tells us that Deep Pockets is motivated by the common energy that drives most white-collar criminals."

"You're talking about greed and power over others," added Danielson. "You can bet he's not doing this for the good of humanity I have to go. You all work better when somebody is not looking over your shoulder."

A round of handshakes and Danielson was gone.

Tim said, "We can make frequency graphs with people before these past few years who were in the news. People who have power over others need to be in the public view. Then we see if this person, for any reason, dropped out of the limelight this past year as a form of invisibility."

Kevin added, "And we do this in professional fields where Deep Pockets's actions are respected forms of behavior."

"I get it," added Doug. "If anyone dropped out of the public eye, we can put those names in a probable file. When do we start?"

Jamie said, "It is already late in the day. I suggest we get started first thing tomorrow. We can use my apartment space as the nerve center. Everyone, bring your computers to my place. I'll have the doughnuts and coffee."

THIRTY-FIVE

THE ISLAND TRIO OF SIEGAL, Simi, and Phillipe gradually opened the gap between the two monkey clans to six feet across, enough space for a troop of forty-pound monkeys to scamper through. Yet there was no angry charge by the Hannibal Clan. Only a psychological barrier deterred them. In turn, the Storm Clan showed no outward signs of fear.

"Do you have any thoughts, Doctari?" asked Phillipe.

Simi shook her head.

"Do you mean to say that the great Dr. Block is at a loss for words?" joked Siegal.

Simi saw no humor. Her science mind was busy formulating answers.

The team got excited once when Hannibal ambled toward the opening and stuck his hand through the gap. He cocked his head and waited. When nothing happened, he ambled back to his normal place where he could watch both his clan and the Storms.

That night the entire barrier was removed, and still, nothing transpired between the two clans. This gave the three an opportunity to discuss what happened to Simi at Sunada's villa.

SIEGAL SCRATCHED HIS THINNING HAIR spot. "We've avoided talking about your kidnapping since Danielson left. I have been trying to theorize why they took you and not one of your contemporaries."

"And what did you determine?" asked Phillipe.

"I think it's because she is the best at what she does. And, that is to interrelate all the factors of mammals' sociological and biological elements."

"Why would anyone want to know that information?" continued Phillipe.

Simi said, "It's not just knowledge about how mammals, in general, act. I believe we are talking about the most complicated of all mammals—humans. Anyone in my field can make knowledgeable predictions of an individual or even a group of like individuals. Our villain needs to know how different groups would react to other groups. Then by feeding in controlling factors, he can make a small number of people control the actions of thousands."

Phillipe displayed his wide grin. "You mean like Hannibal, who was beaten by the weaker and outnumbered barbarians."

Simi laughed, surprised Phillipe would know about Hannibal. "A good example."

"I have another question," said Phillipe. "Doctari Siegal, you say in a perfect world, everything is planned? Outcomes are always predictable and never chaotic."

"True. But there are so many variables that alter predictability. Simi's abductor would need the best person on his side to reduce guesswork. And that best person, my dear, is you."

Simi added, "I have an interesting take on Deep Pockets. For one thing, he is extremely intelligent. Further, I think he is a student of history. When we locate this person, we will discover an extensive library on great leaders of the past and in-depth studies of historic battles."

"Finally, a clue not based on anything from Sunada's villa. I'll call Tom and tell him about our discussion. Anything else I should add?"

"I can't make out whether I wanted to help him succeed or whether he needed me to control outsiders from interfering. Personally, I think both."

"I'M LISTENING." DANIELSON NEVER IDENTIFIED himself when answering his cell. Years ago, he had several colored phones installed, each with a different purpose. The red phone was the direct line to the president. Since his apparent retirement from Washington politics, he converted to only using a cell phone that identifies the caller and can be carried anywhere.

"Tom, it's Ross."

"I know, good buddy. How're the monkeys doing?"

"You know, monkeys will be monkeys."

"I know you didn't call to discuss monkeys. What's up?"

Siegal explained Simi's assumption about her abductor.

"Good intel. I'll have my headhunters add it to their profile. It could narrow the list down. Say, did Simi have any feelings about where to focus our search? Is Deep Pockets out there only for greed and power?"

"We talked a little about it. It could be something simple, like a grudge."

"Interesting. I've known many powerful people, and they do hold grudges. We'll talk soon."

THIRTY-SIX

JAMIE ADDRESSED HER TEAM. "WE must figure a way to bring our possible perp list down to a workable number. What do we know or think we know that can help?"

Doug made the first suggestion. "I believe our person is a male judging from the communications with Sunada."

"Mr. Danielson said he thought Deep Pockets was doing business in the Northeast," said Kevin.

Tim, working his calculator, said, "That brings us down to almost fifty million. Remember, the guy is very rich, probably in the top 2 percent. Now I figure we are looking for 1 in 815,000."

Jamie asked, "What if we look for those between the ages of forty and sixty-five?"

Tim said, "We are looking for 26 percent of our population. And if we estimate how many of them hold college degrees, we are down to about one thousand. We can group them into professions that would benefit from the sort of knowledge Dr. Block has. I think politics is one profession for sure."

"Great idea," said Kevin. "How about finance?"

"Petroleum and precious metals," added Doug.

Reenergized, the team came up with twelve categories: politics, economics, mining/exploration, banking/finance, stock market, wholesale/manufacturing, real estate, electronics technology, education, mass communication/social media, law, and medicine.

"Now that's more manageable," said Jamie. "We can eliminate for, the moment, those where greed and power are not very important traits in order to be highly successful. Any suggestions?"

Tim suggested, "Mining/exploration, electronics technology, and education."

Doug added, "Medicine and wholesale/manufacturing,"

Kevin said, "I suppose we can also shelve mass communication for a time as well."

"That leaves us six professions where Deep Pockets' traits would serve him well," concluded Jamie. "We can always go back and add them back, but I think we have a good start."

Tim gave all a round of high fives while adding, "The good thing is that most of these professions have a Who's Who listing and several of their own special publications. There is also a constant flow of information put out by public television. It shouldn't be hard to get names by any single year."

"What filters should be used to cull all the names?" asked Jamie.

Doug said, "That's easy. Eastern US residence, under sixty years old, college educated, high level of wealth, in the news frequently except for the past year when there is almost no publicity about him."

"Each of you, select two and have at it. I think we are on the right track. Remember, highlight any information that points to greed and power over others. Good luck," said Jamie as she busied herself cleaning up breakfast.

Doug asked, "One more thing. Are we striving for a specific number of names?"

"We'll let Danielson figure that out," answered Jamie. "We won't throw out any names but put them on a B list in case we need them later. Nothing gets thrown out completely."

By the time pizza and Pepsi were delivered for dinner, the team had their lists. Some names were duplicated on more than one. This fact didn't slow them down.

"I'll give Danielson a call," said Jamie.

THIRTY-SEVEN

SIEGAL SAT IN HIS MAKESHIFT office, formerly a second bedroom, collating information on his monkey clans. Simi, enjoying the open air of the Caribbean, spent the afternoon tanning on the beach and texting her assistant at the Institute of Human Development. Phillipe was left with the responsibility of observing their charges on his own.

Late that afternoon, they gathered on the porch. Phillipe was excited and could hardly wait for the others to settle.

"Something happen out there today?" asked Siegal.

"Yes, Doctari. Oh yes, very much indeed."

"Are you going to tell us, or do we have to hang you by your thumbs until your nose bleeds?" smiled Simi.

Phillipe began slowly to draw out the suspense. "As you know, for the past week since the barrier was taken down, both clans stayed in their own territory. I have been observing one of the Storm Clan males testing the space between them by stepping a few feet over the invisible barrier. The Hannibal Clan never challenged him. I would have expected some sort of aggression. To my surprise, there was none."

Siegal turned to Simi. "Ahem. Dr. Sociobiologist, is there any significance in that?"

"Actually, yes. We are experiencing what I've described before, the Hannibal paradigm. It has often been observed across species, as with lions and hyenas. One group of animals, let's say the lions, would stake a claim to a prey. The hyenas, at first, are subservient and allow bullying behavior. After a time, the subjected and superior groups reverse roles. The stronger lions can no longer protect their prey, and the hyenas develop a strategy to get part of the kill."

"Like quarterback Tom Brady gave the New England Patriots a football dynasty," grinned Phillipe. "A weaker team hires Brady and changes the dynamics."

"Exactly," Simi smiled back. "They are no longer feared. They are still good, but not unbeatable."

"That's what I am so excited about. The Hannibal paradigm is already happening, I think. I decided to stay at the platform last night. And that was when it happened."

"Out with it," urged Siegal, "or you will be living out there permanently."

"Well, all the monkeys were nested, or so it seemed. I must have dozed off. Some rustling woke me. The male who had been testing the space between the two territories crossed the line and proceeded toward one of the Storm's females. He gently groomed her, and the two consummated their relationship. The female actually encouraged him. The male returned to his territory, and the female followed closely behind."

"What now?" asked Siegal.

"I guess that nothing will happen," said Simi. "The Storm Clan has reversed their role. The takeover was peaceful. If food or land was in play, there might have been a physical confrontation."

"And what about old Hannibal?" asked Phillipe.

"He has little choice. His best chance for survival is to retire to the edge of their territory. He will be tolerated and not bothered unless he attempts a leadership comeback."

"All the fun of watching these monkeys is gone. The best part happened when we were asleep," frowned Siegal. "Damn. We need a vacation. When the supply plane comes tomorrow, the three of us should hop on board. A few days in Nassau will do us all some good. I know some great places." He ran to the beach, chucking off his shorts. "I need a swim. Last one in is an old dried crab."

Simi, in native fashion, stripped off her clothes and followed.

Phillipe, waving his arms and pinching his thumb to his fingers, imitating crab claws, was last.

The monkey clans were at peace. And there was no information from Danielson regarding Simi's abduction. Everything was calm on the surface. The headhunters' research could be the shoe that drops.

THIRTY-EIGHT

A SATISFIED RICHARD BRAND LEANED back in his office chair and gazed at the *Gazette's* latest edition. He crossed his feet across the desk and puffed on an unlit cigar in celebration. His doctor made him quit smoking over ten years ago, but the feel of his lips around a cigar still felt good.

He had just finished uncovering questionable business practices of two major companies. Their executive officers and their close associates were taking unfair advantage of insider information, and he was letting the public know about it. Brand saw his work rivaling former colleagues of another Washington newspaper who wrote about the famous Watergate investigation several years earlier.

On his desk was a stack of mail delivered while meeting with Sperling. He thumbed through it, dividing the missives into two piles. The larger collection went to the shredder. Most from the smaller group were negative comments; some included threats of lawsuits. The threats did not bother Brand because he was supported by the Constitution's First Amendment guaranteeing freedom of the press.

His hands stopped at one handwritten letter:

> Dear Power-Hungry Rabble-Rouser,
>
> I have been following your @#$$&**^$. I am usually too much of a gentleman to use such swearwords. It is obvious you have never been in private business. Competition requires creative solutions. Get your head out of the #$^%^& sand. This country has grown because of our free enterprise system. It is people like you who profess the socialist doctrines that undermine everything. If you don't like it, get the #$&* out!
>
> You need to be silenced! If your own newspaper won't do it, someone else will have to.
>
> GOD BLESS AMERICA and the free enterprise system!!

"My very first actual death threat. Well, I'm not stopping."

A COPYBOY DELIVERED THE AFTERNOON edition to his desk. Brand opened to the business section. One syndicated article in Section D, page three, caught his eye. A sportswear manufacturer reported gains that beat the street estimates by more than 20 percent.

It would have gone unnoticed in an age of strong market trends. *Twenty percent is too much. Omicron Shoes bears watching.*

The financial iceberg he had been investigating was showing more surfaces. Brand's columns were selling newspapers. He needed more help.

After some begging, the editor in chief agreed to give Brand one assistant, Ted Cousins. Cousins, a rawboned man less than a year away from retirement, was filling time at the paper as a gopher until his gold watch party. It wasn't much; still, Brand was happy for a least one support person.

"Ted, can you come to my desk as soon as you are free?"

With nothing pressing, Cousins was there almost before Brand's phone was back in its cradle. He walked in wearing a broad-brimmed ten-gallon hat and a bolo tie sporting the largest turquoise rock Brand had ever seen.

Cousins was raised in Wyoming's cattle country. He had never been to a big city until he went away to college, earning an engineering degree. The idea of sitting behind a drafting table never appealed to him, so he ended up living in DC doing odd jobs as he found them until ending up at the *Sun Gazette*. His talent for sniffing out a good story kept him there for thirty years, always staying in the background and never upsetting any egos of the writing staff.

Following a few introductory greetings, Brand said, "Ted, we need to do some heavy digging in the area of finance. Are you up for it?"

"You betcha." His spoken language showed his upbringing, but his written work was always in the best Queen's English. "Anythin' ta keep me from fallin' asleep."

"Do you know what I've been working on?"

"You mean, do I read your column? You put out some shit-kickin' good stuff. Yessiree."

Brand nodded. "I want to focus on Omicron Shoes. Have you ever heard of them?"

Cousins pointed to his feet. "You betcha. I wear their brand all the time. Except when I'm sleepin'."

"Good," said Brand with a smile, enjoying Cousins's good humor. "As you know, I've been working on stories that show some pretty bad business improprieties. The more I research, the wider the problem. At first, I thought only a few individuals inside a company or two were playing some number's games. The more I investigate, it seems more of a pandemic. I believe many firms may be working together. This investigation will not be simple. These people are experts at hiding things."

"It sounds to me that these outlaws, if not colluding with each other, certainly are all in cahoots with the Devil hisself. When do we start?"

"Yesterday."

SUN GAZETTE

Yesterday, I received an interesting piece of mail. I wish to share it with you since it involves one of our most precious possessions, freedom of the press. This letter is an obvious attempt to challenge my right to print the truth. I swear. My every word has been fact-checked.

You, my readers, and especially the individual who wrote this certain scathing letter I received, deserve to know why I am doing this investigation. There must be oversight when company executives tout their success and have awarded themselves large bonuses when their profit and loss statements do not warrant them.

I challenge the Securities Exchange Commission and the office of the Attorney General to study these practices and bring those unscrupulous CEOs to justice.

Investors beware. Richard Brand

PART THREE

GREED.
There are more than 411 synonyms and only 66 antonyms; an unhealthy juxtaposition for our nonviolent world.

THIRTY-NINE

TOM DANIELSON MET WITH THE headhunters at his favorite Maryland restaurant. "Well, where are we?"

Jamie cut right to the chase. "Did we discover the kidnapper? The answer is no. But we are further along than step one. We made this list of possibles based on the profile information you gave us and grouped them into twelve professional areas, which we shortened to six filtered down using greed and power over others as criteria." She handed the list of names to Danielson.

"And?"

"You didn't give us a deadline. I took this to mean you wanted our work to be completed quickly. We decided against seeing any of these possibles eye to eye."

"I agree with your decision," said Danielson. "In the meantime, I'll share this list with Dr. Block to see if any of the names or categories ring any bells with her."

Danielson studied the list. "I see there are names that appear in more than one profession category."

Jamie continued, "It was curious to us that several of the names appeared twice, in their own discipline and then in the area of stocks and bonds."

Danielson gave a puzzled look. "Explain further."

Doug said, "Our thinking goes this way. Assume Deep Pockets became very rich in his primary profession. He then moved to investing his earnings in a flexible field where he could make even more. Financial markets give this flexibility to multitask. To a lesser degree, some of our successful possibilities ventured into real estate. We think the important variable here is power. Wannabes try to copycat. Sometimes they win, and often they are a day too late and lose. But they still follow the leader. We, the team, guess our kidnapper is rich enough to buy power from some, and he may move others through their personal greed. There may be a large group of people he wants to control. He needs some special kind of knowledge, and that knowledge may be exactly why he needed Dr. Block."

"I am impressed," Danielson said. "This gives me a clue to look into the stock market as a way to determine a name for Deep Pockets.

Jamie said, "For the moment, we are assuming Deep Pockets is on our list and focus on the markets as well, especially if the name is on more than one of the professions as well. We also didn't throw out any names but kept them on B and C lists in case we have to relook at them."

Danielson slapped the table. "Your work is better than I had hoped for. Great job. I have an idea I want to pursue. Take the rest of the day off. Try the apple pie they make in-house. Put on some vanilla nut ice cream. You deserve it."

Doug said, "How does this sound for a strategy? We used a three-tier grouping. As are most probable, Bs are a strong possibility, and C's are pretty much eliminated. And let's hope to keep tier A to fifty names or less."

The meeting was short and to the point. Danielson was in and gone in less than thirty minutes. Finding the kidnapper of Dr. Simi Block for his good friend was paramount. And he wanted the job done fast. He knew micromanaging his team like a mother hen would not get it done any faster.

The headhunters had blocked out the entire afternoon for the meeting with Danielson, and it was just barely past noon. They decided to stay and have lunch courtesy of their boss before proceeding.

FORTY

BRAND, SLEEVES ROLLED HALFWAY UP his arms and an ever-present mug of stale coffee in his hand, sat in the fishbowl conference room at the rear of the open composing area. In front of Brand were old newspaper editions, computer printouts, and notes he had collected for his current research.

Cousins sat opposite him at the worktable with a pile of yellow legal pads and handwritten notes almost as voluminous in front of him. He looked like a character from a cartoon with the windblown facial lines of an old-time cowboy. And, of course, he sported his turquoise-inset sterling silver belt buckle. Everyone called him Ted. It was as if he never had a last name. His unique accent was mostly, but not exactly, western. It was as if he created it to make himself unique. Over time this speech pattern served a useful purpose in his investigations: it kept people who didn't know him off their guard. Every time the date was set for his retirement at the newspaper, a job arose requiring his particular style of fact-finding. And now, five or six years later, it seemed he had a permanent home and would probably die there at the *Gazette*. Cousins never required or even asked for bylines on stories he helped develop. If the rent was paid on his little apartment down the street, he didn't mind being anonymous.

Cousins rose and refilled Brand's mug while taking one for himself. The coffee was black and strong from sitting all day, the reporter's trademark showing strength of resolution. Both toasted each other and took a sip, grimacing as if they were drinking thirty-day-old hooch from the stills of Appalachia.

"Ready to roll on Omicron Shoes?" asked Brand.

"I'm in the saddle with you, sheriff. Where do ya want us to start?"

"How about at the top with the CEO? What do you have on him?"

Cousins rustled through the disarray in front of him. Brand marveled at how he could find anything. But in seconds, he pulled out a yellow tablet and located on the second page what he was looking for.

"Let's see what I have in my little craw. Okey dokey. Company officers. The CEO is a thirty-five-year-old trust fund baby inheriting the firm from his father. It seems a couple of weeks ago, just after announcing record sales and profits, he sold about a billion and a half shoelaces worth of stock options. Rather peculiar, wouldn't ya say?"

"Seems so. Any reason you can find?"

"Scuttlebutt on the street claims he was diversifying. Reports have it that he is buying a partnership in an overseas shipping firm not even related to shoes."

"Interesting."

"Hey, that ain't all. The street says he also took an off-the-books loan for another five mil. This here money is apparently being stored on some waterlogged island bank."

"So much for the good guy image. If the stock goes down, we could be building a beautiful case for some illegal insider trading."

"Ain't illegal and insider redundant words?"

"In this case, yes. What else did you find?"

"I found something kinda interestin' about the company's personnel policies. Seems employees are required to place all their 401(k)s into company stocks. Ain't that a fine kettle of fish? I guess it would be okay as long as Omicron is a profitable concern. But should any setback happen, these folks could take quite a retirement beatin'. I wouldn't want ta be in thar shoes iffen that becomes real. No pun intended."

"Neither would I, old friend."

"Ta back that up, all the brokers who promote their stock are tellin' their blind-eyed clients to keep buyin' it cuz it has enough strength to move up a lot more."

Brand checked his laptop. "It appears they are already over their resistance level of support."

Cousins continued to scan his notes. "Somethin' very curious here … very curious indeed. The accountants inside the firm are contracted employees of the same firm that audits them. Now, why would anyone trust the foxes that guard their own chicken coops?"

"That's it. We're looking at pure fraud."

"Hey, sheriff. I ain't through. They recently asked a bank to issue some bonds for them. Now I normally wouldn't make much of it. That is until I learned that the bank prez hisself had owned lots of Omicron stock but recently sold his shares about the same time the CEO sold his. Deep down in my arthritic hip, I feel that shit is about to rain on the small investors' parade."

Brand tilted his chair and attempted another drink of coffee. "Any one of these events could have been overlooked as normal. But when they're all happening at the same time, it's criminal.

"I've been following several other companies. It seems these kinds of events are happening in a similar fashion on a global basis. Thank you, Ted. Thank you very much. I have a story to write. Do you want a byline?"

"No thanks. I ain't much for notoriety. No threatenin' letters for me."

"Whatever. Just keep up the good work. Our story isn't finished with just exposing Omicron Shoes. We have a lot more to tell. Now let's go down to the canteen and get some decent coffee."

FORTY-ONE

WILLIAM GETSEN, III, OLD WILY Willie, scheduled his meeting for two o'clock Pacific daylight time with a select few CEOs from the original group. Of the thirty-two men who remained at his first conference four weeks ago, only seven were invited back. These seven followed Getsen's directions to the letter: Be in it for yourself and no one else. Strike quick and then get out just as fast. Do whatever you plan to do once and once only. Report gains using Getsen bucks.

Among the seven were Michael Sperling, the Philadelphia financial accounts executive; Sam Blackman of Omicron Shoes; and the Reverend Andrew Jackson of Beloit College.

The clock on the wall indicated fifteen minutes past three. No one, not Getsen, not even the man in the pinstriped suit, approached the dais. Normally these attendees, all type A movers and shakers, would not have waited fifteen minutes for someone so late. Yet, not a soul left the room. Another half-hour passed. Finally, Reverend Jackson declared, "I'm done," and left. The remaining six sat quietly or carried on business using their smartphones, iPads, and laptops. They acted almost too timid, like sheep waiting for the butcher to shock them into eternity.

Another hour passed. Finally, a bellman entered and announced that Mr. Getsen was delayed and asked them to be patient. At five o'clock, two more gave up the wait. The remaining four looked at each other like gladiators in the great arenas of Rome. Just how many of them would be picked. It would be at least one, and now the odds were four to one. Attrition had taken its toll.

At six o'clock, a pair of waiters set a buffet with halibut and filet steak as the main entrees. The men ate with only minimal conversation even though they all knew each other by name or reputation.

The bellman returned twenty minutes later with a television monitor and VCR player. He turned on the power, and the image of William Getsen came into focus:

Gentlemen:

I am unable to meet with you today. I have followed each of you very carefully and predicted that you all would be in this final group.

You were told my plan includes only the most strategic businessmen. The one part of all your personalities that brought you to this point is your blatant disregard for your fellow workers. You need not apologize for this attribute. Or, maybe I should have worded it as this character flaw.

Because of this flaw, I cannot be sure that even I can trust you. Therefore, I will be meeting with each of you separately. One, possibly two, shall be hearing from me. The rest of you are casualties.

Don't be dismayed at how you have been handled. My motivation made you all some of the richest men in your fields.

The television monitor went to black. There were no final salutations or apologies. The bellman returned and wheeled the unit out of the room.

To a man, each had given up their professional and personal lives, life-long friendships, and, more than anything else, their souls. If Getsen had been in the room just then, he would have had his manly parts separated from the rest of his body.

Unbeknown, they had been taken by Wily Willie on a ride to suit his own purposes. Not even in the farthest reaches of their imaginations could they ever have guessed why he set them up. He, through his sub-terfuge, created an invincible shield around himself.

The several men left the room with all degrees of disappointment and changes in their way of investing. On the one hand, they were angered by Getsen. On the other hand, they learned that following his actions in business was a strategy they could not resist. Dr. Sunada's grand plan was working in spite of Getsen having to go it alone.

FORTY-TWO

THERE IS SOMETHING HYPNOTIC ABOUT Caribbean steel drum music. It can make anyone forget their cares, and this was the medicine Siegal, Simi, and Phillipe needed. Phillipe made more than a passing acquaintance with one of Nassau's young ladies at a calypso club and disappeared for most of their three-day holiday. Without Phillipe's presence, Siegal and Simi used the much-needed private time in one of the luxury beach hotels.

"Time to get back to our problems," said Simi.

STEPPING OUT OF THE PLANE back on their private little island, Phillipe commented, "Doctaris, we should check up on our monkeys. I suggest you two pay them a visit while I make the house ready again. The birds always take over as soon as we're out of sight, and I am sure there are some nests along the roof that need removing."

"Good idea," agreed Siegal. Thankful for the quiet of Deadman's Cay contrasted against the activity of Nassau at this height of tourist season, he set a quick pace to their observation platform. Simi felt hurried but kept up with him. By the time they reached the platform, they both calmed, and the power walking pace slowed to a leisure stroll.

They had been gone only three days, but Simi noticed how the monkeys were acting curious about their visitors as if they were there for the first time. The unified clan gathered at the nearest point of their enclosures to do some people watching. Odd how the table had turned.

"Seems we're the testees instead of the testers. What does your sociobiological science tell us about that?" asked Siegal.

"Our clans have developed a comfortable relationship with each other. Our coming back into their environment has created a slight bump. They are examining who we are and if we would further affect their normal way of life."

"These monkeys can fathom that out?"

"Not like we would. Their imprinted genetic history is having them act this way. Very soon, they will forget about us and go about their daily routines."

"Fifteen, sixteen, seventeen," counted Siegal. "Everyone is present and accounted for. Wait on that head count. I think one of the females gave birth to twins. I can't get a good look because mama is hiding them in the bushes to protect them from the males."

Simi checked her laptop. "It tells us that twins are not common. In the wild, a mother may only want to care for one. If so, we will have to take the other, or it won't survive."

As Simi lectured, Siegal rummaged through their knapsacks and heard a clink. "Would you look at this?" pulling out a bottle of wine. "Phillipe must have brought it back from Nassau. And here's some brie and crackers, too."

Simi said, "Look, another of the males from the Storm Clan is making advances on one of the females from the Hannibal Clan.

"Isn't youth wonderful," said Simi. "The two lovers can't keep their hands off each other. First, they're grooming and then ..."

"Making love. It turns me on watching them."

"I remember how we used to act that way," she said.

"That was before I left to work on the government project."

"Are we going to keep talking or what?" urged Simi, taking off her shirt and bra.

The air was warm, and the trees around them provided shade. Phillipe was at the house and would not be interrupting them. They nervously undressed each other as if it was their first time. They had sex at the house and several times in Nassau, but for the first time since they were back together, a special animal warmth came over them like old times. Soon nothing mattered except to be in each other's embrace. Simi moved with every touch of Siegal's hands. And Siegal quivered when Simi reached for him. The platform floor was rough raw lumber. That didn't matter. They were in total Caribbean rapture with sounds of the ocean to monitor their rhythm. Their emotions filled the platform until both were totally spent. Only then did they allow themselves to release their holds. Thanks to those wonderful monkeys, Simi and Siegal finally completed their return to each other.

Siegal broke the silence. "I can't let you go away from me. I made that mistake before."

"But what about my position at Cal-Berkeley?"

In the middle of her question, Siegal kissed her again. Another round of release followed. The dinner triangle rang, startling them back to reality.

"We best be getting back, or Phillipe will be sending out a search party," joked Simi.

They gathered their spent wine bottle and empty food wrappers. Hand in hand, they half walked and half skipped back to the house.

Phillipe smiled his trademark grin when he saw them. "I trust you had a good afternoon observing. Funny, though, there must have been a hot stiff breeze out there. You two seem extra windblown and sweaty. Why don't you take a quick dip in the ocean?"

They smiled back. Without ever saying it, Siegal and Simi vowed never to part again.

SUN GAZETTE

This is Richard Brand, investigative reporter, with my continuing story of publicly held corporations and the less than appropriate actions of their CEOs. Today, I have another story.

I have received many letters admonishing me for my effort. Among these were several death threats. The nature of my reporting attracts such intimidations. I have sent a few to the postal service for prosecution. Most, however, were less intimidating, coming from those disgruntled who lost their fortunes and are seeking me as someone to blame.

Three days ago, I received a different kind of letter. It could best be called a preobituary notice because the next day, this person was dead by his own hands. I chose to write this story as an apology to honest CEOs who realized what they had done. This communication, probably his last, came from an individual who felt his guilt without being tried in a court of law. He tried himself in the toughest court, the one within his own mind. To honor his commitment to admitting the truth, I have omitted both his name and company. It goes as follows:

Dear Mr. Brand,

I am aware you have been investigating my company and me for some time. This company was started by my father. When he retired on a better-than-modest income, I took over and grew this small business to over two billion dollars in sales per year.

Then the business world changed. Profits within our company fell drastically. We were just short of bankruptcy. I inflated our profit picture to raise stock prices and traded much of my stock into more solid arenas to protect our company's assets.

Dumping as much as I did caused my company stock to plummet, and many unwitting investors took major losses. Employees of my company who had purchased stocks for their retirement lost their fortunes as well.

I borrowedmoney from my company without having it recorded on the books. I talked myself into believing I would pay it back, and nobody would be the wiser. In truth, I knew I never would.

I can no longer go on in this manner. I have instructed my attorneys to sell all my hard assets. They have also been instructed to collect any cash assets I have in US and foreign banks. Finally, they are to place all into a trust fund in the name of the company for the purpose of replacing, as much as possible, that which has been lost by our investors and employees.

I have pondered who should administer this trust. I believe you, as a Job among men, must be the executor. My attorneys will draw up the legal documents. I know you will carry out my wishes.

I attended his funeral yesterday and grieved for him. I did not grieve because I was sad he was dead, but because he was a good man and did not deserve such an untimely death.

Readers, I do not plan to relax my effort to clean up the dirty part of big business. I plan to investigate more than just large companies and their CEOs. I plan to expose the courts and government agencies should they fall under my umbrella. I have given myself the responsibility to perform a duty to you, the public, and I will not back down under any pressure.

FORTY-THREE

WISE BEYOND HIS FORTY-PLUS YEARS, he had worked his way through college washing dishes in a sorority house. Richard Brand was proud of what he had accomplished, proud of the respect from his contemporaries, and most proud of his reporting ethics. Brand was at his desk and in deep concentration when his phone rang. There was no CID. That didn't matter. He never refused to accept any call.

"Is this Richard Brand and not some recorded message?"

"Yes. Can I help you?"

"I hope so. My name is Tom Danielson."

Brand sat up in his chair at full attention to the phone. "Is this the same Tom Danielson who used to be the White House chief of staff for our last president?"

"One and the same," answered a very surprised Danielson. "I wasn't aware anyone would remember me from my public days."

"I seem to recall you died in a plane crash somewhere in the South Pacific."

"It's what I wanted the world to think. I had to disappear for a time. That's a whole other story. I'll tell you about it some time off the record."

"This is an honor, Mr. Danielson. Why do you need me?"

"I have a knotty problem, and you may have insights that can help."

"Tit for tat. If I have information for you, you may have something for me."

"Sounds fair. Can you be free for lunch tomorrow?"

"Tomorrow? Let me look." *A call from out of the blue from such an important person as Tom Danielson. There must be a story in this.* "My schedule looks good. Can I bring my research assistant?"

"Absolutely. I also have four colleagues I wish to invite."

"Sounds more like a major conference than a simple lunch. You've tweaked my curiosity. Tell me when and where. We'll be there."

"I know a restaurant in Maryland that offers a little privacy as well as some of the best lunch entrees. I'll fax you a map this afternoon. The reservation is for one thirty. See you there, and thank you."

Brand cradled his phone as Ted came sauntering in with a mug of coffee in one hand and his always handy yellow tablet in the other. "I just had a strange phone call."

"Was it your wife, a girlfriend, or maybe a call from Publisher's Showcase wanting you to write a book on investing?"

"Do you remember the name Tom Danielson?"

Cousins pursed his memory. "Wasn't he killed a couple of years ago? Don't tell me, buckaroo; you got a call from the beyond."

"He's very much alive and wants a meeting with us tomorrow. We're being treated to lunch."

"Never heard of a free lunch. I gets tired of my daily regimen of pb and j. Do you know what it's about?"

"Not an inkling. Anyway, that is tomorrow, and this newspaper works on today's news. Ready to get started on our new target?"

"Let the rodeo begin."

FORTY-FOUR

IT WAS PHILLIPE'S TURN TO command the platform. Siegal and Simi opted to spend the day lying on the beach. However, even the warm Caribbean waters and the calming waves lapping onto the sand failed to relax them.

"I can't get it out of my head," said Siegal. "I get it that you were kidnapped for something to do with your field of research. So why haven't any other experts been kidnapped once you were freed? It must be more specific than just general knowledge. The focus is your research lab. If I were the villain and couldn't get to you, I think I would ..."

"Go after Alisa?"

"Exactly. My guess she could be a valuable asset in his scheme."

"I was thinking the same thing. Then I thought Alisa knows what we've done but is not so creative. She's a fantastic plugger and the best assistant I could ever want. This person has a need for me and no one else—no other expert in sociobiology, not even Alisa. He must have a plan B. I'd not be surprised if Deep Pockets already has his alternative plan well underway. Even to the point that he doesn't even need me anymore."

"I agree. Deep Pockets has the power to accomplish whatever he wishes. But does he have the knowledge to hold onto his gains?"

"Lover, that means we have two questions to answer. First, we need to know what this person's motivation is. And secondly, we have to figure out what frightens him into believing he needs my special thinking to assure his success and keep it."

"Hopefully, Tom can get an answer to the first question. In the meantime, our job is to come up with an answer to the second."

FORTY-FIVE

IT WAS ALMOST LUNCHTIME ACCORDING to the atomic clock on Brand's desk. He called the receptionist to inform her that he and Cousins would be out of the office for most of the day to work on a story. He closed his laptop and emptied his stale cup of coffee into the wastebasket by his desk.

"Ready?"

Cousins said, "You go on ahead. I have to complete my senior duty in the men's room."

Minutes later, Cousins heard a large boom that rattled the building windows. He looked out to see a fireball on a single car and a man lying on the asphalt surface. He zipped his fly and hurried to the scene as fast as his old legs would take him. By the time Cousins reached the area, first responders were already there attending to the victim.

Cousins attempted to identify the car, but it was already too engulfed in flames to recognize. The entire front end was scattered for twenty yards or more. He edged toward the front of the curious crowd and saw a man on the ground covered in blood. One of his arms was at an angle that could only show how broken it was. The man's clothes still smoldered from being on fire. Cousins gasped when he saw Richard Brand lying there, more dead than alive.

The amazing emergency medics stabilized Brand and lifted him into the ambulance. The ambulance, followed by Cousins in a press car, raced in tandem toward Howard University Medical Center.

DANIELSON, NOT A MAN WHO enjoyed waiting when he called a meeting, took out his cell and dialed Brand's number. The phone rang several times and finally clicked to a messaging service. "I'm sorry I can't talk with you ..."

Danielson hung up before the message concluded and dialed the paper's front desk. A woman answered, *"Sun Gazette.* How may I direct your call?"

"I am trying to reach Richard Brand. It is very important. Can you forward this call to him?"

"I am very sorry, sir. Mr. Brand is unable to come to the phone. He had an emergency and is out of the building."

Danielson had been in the people business too long not to know when he was being put off. "This is Tom Danielson, chief of staff to former President Thompson. I need to speak with your editor."

The telephone operator sounded flustered for the first time. "Please hold, Mr. Danielson. I will put you through."

In a few moments, "This is the editor."

"And this is Tom Danielson. I must get in touch with Richard Brand. It is very important for mutual investigations we both are conducting. We were to meet today, and I am sure he would not have missed our appointment."

The editor recognized Danielson's name and chose to explain Brand's absence.

"You say he was in an auto accident—a car bomb explosion?" Stunned by the news, Danielson added, "You say he is alive? He is where? Thank you very much."

Danielson turned to the headhunters. In a subdued voice, said, "Our special guests won't be showing up today. While we've been working one side of the street trying to find the kidnapper. You were making assumptions that he may be in finance; Richard Brand, investigative reporter for the *Sun Gazette,* has been writing a series of articles on malpractice issues in the stock market. In short, it appears he touched an open nerve and has gotten car bombed."

Doug said, "First a kidnapping and now an escalation to attempted murder. It isn't war games we're in. It's war."

"From my experience," commented Jamie, "kidnappers often kill their victims. They usually don't kill anyone else unless to avoid capture. Brand may have gotten too close to something."

Danielson continued, "It does leave questions. If Deep Pockets wanted Dr. Block killed, he would have made some kind of payoff threat or demand. No, he took her for a reason, and it wasn't for money. I don't believe killing his victims was ever in his scenario. I think Brand's attempted assassination was to stop him from opening up a new Pandora's Box. I know Brand's reputation. He would never be stopped through ordinary intimidation. At any rate, this meeting today is over. I have to see Brand at the hospital."

DANIELSON PARKED IN THE HOSPITAL'S VIP lot and entered the waiting room at Howard University Hospital via a private elevator. Several people were sitting on the uncomfortable vinyl couches. By process of elimination, he singled out an older man sitting in the corner.

"Would you by any chance be with Richard Brand?" asked Danielson.

The man tipped his cowboy hat.

"I'm Tom Danielson."

"Most people call me Ted. I've seen your picture lots of times. Say, ain't you dead or ...?"

Danielson forced a smile. "It's a long story. You know I was planning to meet with the two of you for lunch today. Can you tell me what happened?"

"Don't know much. He's in the operatin' room right now fightin' some heavy odds. And he'll beat 'em too, I say. All I know for sure is that there was some kinda explosion in our parkin' lot. When I ran outside, I saw Mr. Brand sprawled out on the pavement. I thought he was dead. Bless them paramedics. It's amazin' how they can do what they do in the open street without all that high-powered equipment. Anyway, they got him stabilized in just a few minutes and brought him here."

"How bad is he?"

"The best I can figger is that he looked worse than he is. There's at least a couple of broken bones and a concussion."

Just then, a doctor came out to give an update. "Are you both friends of the victim?" he asked.

"Yup, we are," answered Cousins.

"He is awake now. One of you at a time can go in there but only for about a minute or two. He is pretty groggy."

"Go ahead," said Cousins. "I'm sticking around fer a while. You probably have lots to do still being dead and all. I'll ketch him later."

Danielson nodded and followed the doctor through a closed curtain to a bed full of tubes. Under all the equipment was a man covered with monitoring devices and special bandages to protect the burned areas on his body.

"Hello, Richard Brand," said Danielson softly.

The body, under all the paraphernalia, moved a little. He turned his head and attempted to open his eyes.

"I sure am glad you are alive," said Danielson. "You must be the luckiest person I know."

Brand managed a slight head nod and mumbled a few words through his scorched lips. "Right now, I don't feel that way. Sorry I missed your luncheon invitation. I've been told that restaurant of yours has a very good chef."

"Forget the lunch. You have a raincheck coming. How did you escape being totally blown up and burnt past recognition?"

"I was getting so many threatening letters; I naturally stayed alert for almost anything." Brand tried to lick his lips but had no saliva. "There was a paper stuck on the windshield warning me to back off my investigative reporting and stating I was out of second chances. That must have been enough to put me on my extra guard. I unlocked my car and stepped in. I hadn't yet put on my seat belt, which probably saved my life. There was a funny click when I started the motor. It was just enough to alert me, and I tried to get out fast. I got the door open when all hell broke loose. That's all I remember until I woke up here in the hospital."

A nurse came in. "Times up. He needs to rest. We'll be moving him to an intensive care room now." She gave Danielson a reassuring touch on the shoulder. "He is coming along very nicely and should be ready for visitors after some more rest. You can come back tomorrow."

As Danielson passed Cousins in the waiting room, he said, "Richard is going to make it just fine. But it looks as if your boss will be out of commission for a while. Maybe you and I can get together. I'll give you a call."

"You betcha. Me and the boss ain't quittin'. This kinda stuff just jerks my chain that much harder."

Danielson traded warm handshakes and left Cousins to watch over his fallen comrade.

Danielson's drive home was more relaxed than the ride to the hospital. He was sure the newspaper would put every ounce of energy into finding the bomber. The DC police would be working on this case as well. He would put his headhunting team on it if needed.

FORTY-SIX

IN A TEN THOUSAND SQUARE foot mansion just north of West Point Academy on the Hudson River, a man sat in his wheelchair reading the latest edition of the New York Times. There was a satisfied look on his face as he read of the car bombing.

"What can I get you for breakfast, sir?" asked a smallish man in a dark pinstriped suit.

"I think some fresh orange juice and one slice of whole wheat toast will do. Thank you, Paul."

"Very good, sir. You seem to be in good humor today."

The man in the wheelchair replied, "I think this will stop those articles this Brand has been writing. The bomber fits right into my plans."

**STOCK MARKET CONTINUES
ON A SKITTISH NOTE**

Historically, the world markets falter each time bad news, no matter how insignificant, comes to light. The day after Sam

Blackman committed suicide, the Dow plunged over two hundred points. Yesterday, when the beat writer for the Sun Gazette was car bombed, the markets reflected the bad news in kind.

"It is time to make my play. What do you think, Paul?"

"I always rely on your good judgment, Mr. Getsen," said Paul as he returned with Getsen's breakfast and set the food tray down on the table next to the wheelchair. "I brought blueberry and cherry marmalade for your toast, sir." He lifted both choices in a double sterling silver serving dish.

Getsen nodded his approval. "I will be at my desk most of the day. Hold all calls."

Getsen reopened the paper to page two and found the continuation of the article on the car bombing.

There are rumors that Richard Brand had been receiving numerous death threats because of his exposés regarding mis-dealing by certain CEOs. Usually, these threats are baseless. However, this time an individual or group followed through with their threat.

"Yes, everything is working out for me. My target is Emphasis because of what they have done to me, and the company will be helpless to stop their demise."

FORTY-SEVEN

"DID YOU SEE THE MORNING news on your phones?" asked Phillipe.

"Are you referring to the drought in California or the article about the Giants taking over first place in baseball?" joked Siegal.

"I am talking about the car bombing in Washington, DC."

"Why do you ask, Phillipe?" queried Simi, who had just come in from a short morning swim.

"It said this writer worked for the *Sun Gazette* and specialized in the area of finance. And, I was just thinking, the headhunters felt Deep Pockets could be involved in finance.

"It's too early in the morning to think about it," responded Siegal. "Odder coincidences have happened."

"I agree," said Simi. "I don't think my kidnapper is the car bomber. It doesn't fit my sociobiological model. Terror bombing and kidnapping are not related activities."

"Does this mean Phillipe and I are about to get another lecture?"

"Don't be obnoxious, dearie. A person or any other animal that has had success in one way would not suddenly change a way of functioning.

Changes in behavior occur after a series of failures. So far, Deep Pockets has not demonstrated any failures that I can tell."

"Does that mean you have figured out what our mystery man ultimately has in mind?" asked Phillipe.

"Not yet. But I am getting close."

"It sounds to me if we are due for a brainstorming session. You both need breakfast energy first. I'll cook up some fried akee and toasted breadfruit."

"No, thank you. I'm getting fat on your cooking and need to go on a diet. Besides, I am anxious to get started," said Simi.

Siegal took the lead. "Remember, brainstorming requires us all to sit without any comments for at least three minutes."

"Ha. Two Doctaris, speechless for the first time that I can remember," grinned Phillipe.

Sim was the first to break the silence. "I was thinking through our speculation of my kidnapping. Sunada was a special kind of interrogator. Right?"

The two men nodded in agreement.

"And there has been no other attempt to harass anyone else associated with me. Not even Alisa. Why?"

"And what have you concluded," asked Siegal.

"He knows I am no longer his prisoner by now. I feel he thinks he is smart enough to do his bidding without me. If we can get into his brain and understand his motivation, we may be able to short circuit his plans."

"There are only a few things that motivate such a man," said Siegal.

"What are they, Doctari?"

Siegal felt good to be asked a psychological question. His behavioral knowledge had taken a back seat since Simi brought her expertise to the island. "I recall Maslow's levels of motivation. He identified five categories. The first two, biological needs and safety, don't fit this person. His need is far beyond them. The third level is belonging coupled with love. I don't believe this person is motivated by love, and we know he's a loner. The top two levels probably are where we'll discover his motivation.

"What are they?" asked Phillipe.

"Level four is the need to be esteemed by others. I don't think he is looking to be appreciated. Being already rich makes me think he is already revered. That leaves self-actualization, which puts him in the top one percent of all people."

"I am still lost," said Phillipe.

Simi responded, "Maslow's five levels of motivation all are directed to positive goals. We're trying to understand a person who may, in fact, have negative goals as we see them. I agree that he is motivated by one of the top two levels. Now, what if we turn from positive motivations to negative ones? For example, instead of getting someone to respect him, he uses his power over people to loath him. That still puts me at a loss why he wants this power in the first place."

"You once said he either wants material gain, meaning greed, or he wants to lord over someone. If you want to listen to this simple monkey manager, I think this person wants to do the 'lord over' thing," concluded Phillipe.

"I think we're all right," said Simi. "That still doesn't put us any closer to the answer."

"Be patient, Doctaris. I am sure it will come to us."

THAT NIGHT, PHILLIPE PLAYED SOME calypso music on his iPad as they sat on the porch to enjoy dinner and the late summer sunset.

"You're very pensive tonight, dear," said Siegal.

"We would not expect such behavior from lower-class animals. This option is only available to us higher functioning critters," said Simi.

"Then we just have to wait until Deep Pockets makes his next move," suggested Siegal. "I only hope it won't be too late."

"When we wait that long, our perp will carry out his plan and vanish." Simi added, "We're on a time clock."

FORTY-EIGHT

SUMMONED TO THE UPSTAIRS CORNER office, Ted Cousins sat uncomfortably in front of a large oak desk. He was seldom rattled. This was one case. Across from him was the editor in chief.

"Relax, Ted. This isn't going to be a handing out of your pink slip."

"I've been working on this newspaper for over twenty-five years and have never been in this office before," Cousins said, forgetting to use his cowboy lingo.

"My fault for that. I take it you and Richard Brand have become quite close."

" Yes, sir."

"The doctors at Howard University Hospital tell me he is going to be just fine. In fact, they are amazed at how well he is doing, considering his harrowing experience. He should be out of there in about a week and then home recuperating for a while. My guess is about a month before he's back to work."

"If I were to bet a peso or two, I'd say he'll be back in the saddle before a month." Cousins reverted to his normal language. "I ne'er worked with many men the likes of him before. Once he gets his hackle's up, he don't let go so easy."

"And that is what worries me."

"Sir?"

"I am putting you in charge. I want you to carry on with his work. If you need help, I can free up some staff for you."

Cousins was almost speechless. "In all the years of working on the *Gazette* I never was the lead person on any story. Sir, you don't have to worry about my writing or research. I have a college degree, and I don't write the way I talk."

"I know that. It is why I'm having you make all the decisions on this financial story until Richard gets back." Before Cousins could respond, the EIC said, "I know you don't want a byline, and that works for me. No one will know who is writing except us. You will turn in the work to me, and I will feed it through the system. We don't want another bombing to one of our best staff people. Do you have any questions?"

"Well, sir. I ne'er had no byline before, and it ne'er stopped me from writin'. I always say that the story is more important than any reporter's name. Yep, that's what I always say."

The EIC came out from behind his oak desk. "So why are you sitting here?" With a wave of his hand, he said, "Get out there and go to work. Oh, here is my first article about the bombing. I hope it agrees with you."

SUN GAZETTE

Open letter from the editor in chief:

Two days ago, one of our most respected reporters was the victim of a vicious car bombing. We are grateful he is still alive.

I am authorized to offer a fifty thousand dollar cash reward for any information leading to the arrest and conviction of the perpetrator or perpetrators.

Cousins read the excerpt. "I likes it jus' fine. I am proud to be part of this great newspaper."

FORTY-NINE

THE DC POLICE FORENSIC UNIT used every available means to follow up on leads of the bombing. To date, each turned out to be nothing more than bad information from individuals hoping for fifteen minutes of glory. The bomber did not try to follow up on his action and made no further threats to the newspaper.

Days passed, and the trail to the bomber grew colder until a lead came during a drug sting by the FBI. One of the lowlifes they apprehended traded a reduced sentence for information about the bombing. Hard time in a federal prison guaranteed a longer life than the threat of being tagged as a snitch in the local prison.

The interrogation uncovered a certain drug dealer using the stock market as a means of laundering profits. He was afraid Brand would unwittingly investigate one of his shell companies. The one characteristic all drug lords shared was their narrow mindset for profit; always make money and never risk losing it, even for the most inane reason. This drug dealer was no different. Putting fear into his enemies was his weapon of control. The car bombing fit his modus operandi perfectly.

Moving quickly, an undercover operation not only brought the dealer to justice but put a small dent in the drug trafficking all along the eastern coast.

THE WEEKLY SUPPLY PLANE MADE its regular drop, and the island trio went down to the beach to greet it. Along with the supplies was the mail pouch.

Phillipe opened the pouch, gave a resounding shout, and did a victory dance. It contained a letter addressed to him. "Look, Doctaris, this letter tells me I have finished my internship here on the island. It also says I received very high grades on my correspondence courses. Because of that, my college has awarded me a scholarship opportunity to select my practicum experience under a licensed veterinarian of my choice."

"If you have not made a choice," said Simi, giving him a hug, "I can help you at my university."

"No offense, Doctari. I would like to go back to Cape Town and work under Doctari Bob at Monkey Town. You know that while working on this island, I have been sending home enough money each month for my parents to buy a little house on the edge of the city where they can have indoor plumbing. I haven't been back for a long time. I miss my family very much and am anxious to see them again. This would give me a chance to see them and their new home."

"We both congratulate you on your hard work. We'll miss you very much when you go," said Siegal.

"It is customary for friends to give a graduation gift. Is there anything you want?" Simi asked.

Phillipe blushed. "I would like a plane ticket to Africa for my friend ... a girl."

"Have you been hiding something from us, you wild man?" joked Siegal. "Are you planning to capture her and take her back to your tribe for some ancient ritual?"

The remark was not so humorous to Phillipe. "I am already twenty. Well, almost twenty. In my country, I would be considered an old bachelor. Still, that is not the reason I am taking her back with me. I have been seeing her whenever we go to Nassau. We talk daily by email. We have become very fond of each other. She comes from a nice family. Both her parents finished high school. She is now attending the Seventh-day Adventist Church School in Nassau. I asked her parents' permission, and they said, 'Okay.'"

Siegal and Simi were truly surprised. This was the first time he ever told of his love interest. His education always seemed the only thing important to him.

"You don't have to sell us on her, said Simi. "We're happy for you. From my short contact with you, you have shown me a very mature attitude. If you are serious about her, then I wish you both all the luck in the world."

Phillipe relaxed. "Thank you, Doctari."

"Then it's settled," concluded Siegal. "Two first-class tickets to Cape Town are yours. Say, is she the nice young lady we met the last time we went on vacation together?"

"Yes, Doctari, she is the one. I hope to take her back and receive my parents' blessings, and then I will ask her to marry me. When I finish my internship, we plan to return and live here on the island. Her name is Gloria."

"Am I getting this a little turned around? Doesn't one usually ask the parents of the girl for permission?"

Phillipe smiled. "Every culture is different. We could just elope like our two monkeys did, hoping their two clans would accept them."

Both Siegal and Simi had a good laugh. Phillipe just smiled the smile of a young man totally in love.

"As long as I told you about my plans, do either of you have something in the mill?" Phillipe whirled his hands in a suggestive manner.

"It's almost the end of summer. I promised I would stay on till then. I still have responsibilities back at the Institute."

"You always know how to get right to the point," said Siegal. He looked directly at Simi. "I know we haven't talked about it ... but ... I hoped you would stay with me on a permanent basis."

The reality of reestablishing the mileage barrier between them didn't feel good to either. The past break was almost too large to repair. It was only the solitude of the island that made it possible to renew their bond.

Phillipe always had the knack of simplifying a knotty situation. "Doctaris, I have an idea. Doctari Block, you can go back to California by yourself for a while. And you, Doctari Siegal, can follow in just a few short months. By winter, I will be finished with my internship and plan to come back here and live permanently. It would be much less crowded for my wife, Gloria, and me if you were not also living here. That is, of course, if Mr. Danielson can figure a way to keep this island leased on a permanent basis as a sanctuary for our monkeys. I would have a wonderful place to live and bring up our children."

"Got it all figured, do you?" smiled Siegal. "You know, we still have a little mystery that hasn't been cleared up. We don't know who kidnapped Simi or why. I can't make any plans until they are solved."

"Don't worry, Doctari. You'll figure it out before I come back. I am sure of that."

FIFTY

Brand paced, limping about his apartment like a caged lion on three legs. He always viewed himself as a man of action. And now, he was sequestered by his doctors until he got better physically. The more he was told to relax, the higher his anxiety rose. He touched the automatic dialer on his cell phone. The person on the other end recognized his voice and accepted his request.

"I'll put you through, Mr. Brand."

The editor in chief answered. "Good morning, Richard. How are you getting along? I trust this little vacation is working well for you."

"You know damn well it isn't. I'm going stir crazy. I need to start coming in."

"The doctors say you're not ready. As much as I need you, I want all of you and not just the angry part."

"But I feel fine."

"Richard, my boy, you had a horrific experience. Take your time. That's an order."

Brand continued his argument. "There's still so much story to write. I can't lay the whole burden on Ted. He can't do it alone. Besides, he has never been a lead man before."

"Don't worry about him. He's doing great. We're giving him all the extra support he needs until you get back. Take it easy for another week. I won't take any other choice for an answer."

Brand had been following Cousin's articles and knew his boss was right. Still, every sentence used by the editor to calm him worked the opposite. The phone line went dead; Brand was left without getting in the last word. He poured another cup of coffee and turned on the television to the National News Channel.

For the past week, there has been unusual activity in pharmaceuticals. Several groups of smaller buyers have been seeking to buy quantities of Emphasis stock. It had been trading at near lows since its inception showing little interest during the past year. This recent interest has caused the stock to rise from $6.67 to over $9.00 per share.

Two years ago, Emphasis developed a computer chip to enhance male sexual ability. It was specifically designed for men with unusually small penises to enhance their capabilities without plastic surgery.

While women reported this augmentation was unnecessary for their needs, the psychological importance to the male vanity guaranteed the product's success. International interest in this product has made Emphasis the world's largest producer of all male enhancement products. Current sales exceed ten billion dollars this past year which is greater than the next three related companies combined.

The phone rang, interrupting Brand's concentration. "Hello?"

"Richard Brand?"

Expecting some sort of phone solicitation call, he replied, "Yes, please make this call brief. I am very busy right now."

"Sorry to bother you. This is Tom Danielson. Your voice didn't sound like you."

Brand's voice changed from sounding bored to being very friendly. "Tom, am I glad to hear from you."

"First of all, let me congratulate you on catching the bomber."

"You're welcome. But I didn't have anything to do with the arrest. Did you?"

"Maybe a little. What I really called about is to see if you are ready to dive back into work anytime soon?"

"I am. It's my editor and doctors who think I still need a few more days of healing. But my brain is well, and I am so ready to get to work."

"Do you think they would complain if we at least talked?"

"What they don't know won't hurt them. I'm going crazy sitting around this apartment. What do you have in mind?"

"I was going to explain before your accident. My team and I think we may be working in the same direction. Do you mind if I come over?"

"When?"

"How about right now?"

"I'll put out some snacks and boil some water for coffee. How soon will you be here?"

"I'm sitting outside your window using a cell phone. I'll be right up."

BRAND MOTIONED FOR DANIELSON TO take the soft chair next to the window. In minutes, the two men, who had never met before, acted as long-time buddies.

"How do you like your coffee, regular or decaf?"

"Either is fine." Danielson sat as Brand poured instant decaf. "I've followed your column for years. I like the honest way you editorialize as much as your investigative reporting style. Of late, your columns go deeper and are more introspective."

"You can blame that on my excellent assistant Ted Cousins. He's the best fucking researcher I've ever met."

"Hey. Maybe I can hire him away from you."

"Not even if my life depended on it." Brand put the conversation back on track. "You intimated before that we may be tracking the same stuff. My work is an open page. But I have no idea what you're doing."

"Several months ago, the fiancée of a very good friend was kidnapped. Her name is Dr. Simi Block. She's involved in a field called sociobiology."

"What the hell is that?"

"Don't ask. But it seemed important enough to have her kidnapped."

"I could use a bottom line here."

Danielson went into detail about all the events and about their unknown villain, Deep Pockets.

"All this is very interesting. Where do I and the newspaper fit?"

"It's not a 'fit' thing. It is a partnership. We both have a particular expertise that fits together. My headhunters are trying to determine who our villain is. My friend, Dr. Ross Siegal and his fiancée are trying to understand why she was kidnapped. And my job is to grease the gears, so everyone stays coordinated."

"I still don't see where I fit the puzzle."

"I'm coming to that now. We've compiled a list of possible names, all Americans, who are rich enough to pull this all off. So far, we have eliminated most professional categories except finance and the stock market. We believe our perp in involved in the markets."

"Now you really have me interested. I'm beginning to see the fit."

"When your accident happened, we felt sure we were on the right track except for one thing."

"And that being?"

"Our Deep Pockets is not a killer, or he would have killed Dr. Block. We have no indication killing was ever part of his plan."

"What makes you think your person didn't have the car bombing arranged?"

"We did some checking around and decided none of our possibles were the type responsible for ordering your car bombing. It had to be a gangland action. My perp is definitely a white-collar type. I checked with a couple of my informants and collected a name or two who might be involved. Then I just let the local police and FBI take it from there."

"You don't think your kidnapper is a gangster?"

"No, our kidnapper is much richer than most hoodlums and a whole lot wiser than the normal mobster."

Brand refilled his coffee mug. "You think I may know who your Deep Pockets is, don't you?"

Danielson nodded.

"For a minute, I was beginning to think you were accusing me."

"Hardly. I want you as a friend, not as an antagonist."

"I feel the same respect for you. Do you have a plan?"

"The meeting I invited you to was for developing such a plan."

"You have the complete cooperation of my paper and me."

"Perfect. We've talked enough for the time being. I'll be in touch real soon. If you come up with any clues, let me know. I'll have my headhunters send you a hard copy report of our investigation to date. Remember, everything we're talking about is off the record and can't be published. When we're through, you and your paper will get first crack at the story."

"You have my word."

The men shook hands, and Danielson left.

FIFTY-ONE

IT WAS EARLY AUTUMN. SPORADIC cloud bursts augmented a symphony of warm colors and aromatic smells of the fruit trees. Phillipe had left for Africa to begin his internship and have his family meet Gloria. Siegal and Simi took turns watching over the monkeys; while one watched, the other spent the day fishing or gathering fresh produce from their garden. The two monkey clans merged as one, with Cleopatra and Caesar ruling as the alpha pair.

It was during lunch one day that Siegal made an announcement. "While you were on the platform, the weekly supply plane came and left this letter. I decided to wait until you came back to open it."

"Who's it from?"

Siegal played the guessing game until Simi lost patience and grabbed the letter.

"It's from Sally and BF. I feel guilty for not writing them first." She opened the letter and started to read silently as a tease back at Siegal.

"Read it aloud, girl."

Dear Simi and Ross,

It has been a long time since we last communicated. We thought it might be time to get together again. And, since the two of you seem to be holed up on your godforsaken island, I guess we have to take the necessary steps.

Both BF and I have had a good year at the university. Now summer break is almost over, so we decided to come and visit you before jumping into our fall classes. Of course, that is if the two of you are not too busy and if you want us to come.

Actually, we decided not to wait for an invitation and are planning to come out the first week of September. Let us know by email if you plan to be somewhere else, like on the moon or Mars, and we can cancel. Otherwise, you have no choice.

Love, Sally

"Holy shit. That is next week. Look at this place. It's a mess. Ross, you have to do all the monkey business, so I can clean up this place. It isn't fit for a tramp, much less our very best friends."

ON THE NEXT WEEK'S SUPPLY plane, two best friends stepped off the plane. When the hugging finally stopped, they carried the luggage to the house.

Siegal said, "You got us at just the right time. Phillipe is in Africa, so we have an extra bed in the office for the two of you."

Surrounding a jug of iced tea on the porch, BF asked, "How are you getting along?"

Simi frowned. "Sadly, I have to be going back to Cal-Berkeley in a few days."

"Does that mean you're going to fuck up this relationship again?" asked Sally.

"Not this time," interjected Siegal. I think I'll leave this island to Phillipe after he finishes his internship. I will follow Simi to California. Her institute offered me a consultancy. I won't have to work too hard, and the two of us can be together."

"Are you finally getting married?" asked Sally.

"If she'll have me."

"Was that a proposal I just heard?" asked Simi rubbing Siegal's bottom tenderly.

Siegal nodded. Simi nodded her acceptance. The responses brought a new round of hugs and kisses. This was a momentous occasion for the fifty-year-old bachelor and a once proclaimed never to get married again divorcee.

BF said, "Now that the most important question is answered, tell us about what is happening on the island."

The four spent the afternoon and most of the evening discussing everything they learned about monkey behavior and relating it to human behavior all embellished by Simi's special sociobiological knowledge. The four sat barely three feet apart and were virtually yelling at each other, like teenagers at a slumber party.

The sky was already showing hints of morning red when they decided to take time and rest. It was noon when they rose again to start another day.

SIEGAL ASKED OVER BREAKFAST, "IS it fishing, swimming, or ...?"

Sally thought about the warm waters of the Caribbean. "Do beach rules require a bathing suit?"

BF said, "What difference would that make. Your bikini is so small; I can pack it in my shirt pocket."

Sally said, "I would like some swimming later. First, I want to see the monkeys. I love zoos, and yours is a free-range venue."

Simi said, "Then off to the observation platform. I'll pack some wine and cheese. We can be off right away."

Once at the platform, the conversation changed to Simi's abduction. This was the first BF and Sally had heard of the kidnapping, and they were stunned. They only knew Simi was not available at their first reunion on the island.

It has been two months, and your kidnapper is still on the loose? And, you haven't solved the mystery by now?" asked BF. "That's not like either of you."

Siegal rubbed his chin stubble, feeling the new set of whiskers he was cultivating. "We've considered everything we know about people, and we're still at an impasse."

"It's a fucking shame," said Sally. She had learned to curtail her gross language since joining a university staff, but among friends she could be her normal self. "Why don't we kick the shit out of the ideas like we did at City University? You know, use the Siegal method of brainstorming."

"She's right," added BF. "Tonight, when we get back, we'll do it, complete with papers on the wall and Simi managing the felt markers. It'll be fun."

"Good. I'll cook up some fish and my favorite banana salsa," said Simi.

"I'll help," said Sally. "We'll let the boys do the paper pinning while we do the fish panning."

"To the beach," yelled Sally.

They were off, dispensing their clothes on the sand as they rushed toward the water.

AFTER DINNER, THE BRAINSTORMING SESSION began. It was like old times. Only two things were missing. There was no pizza, and Siegal now held a glass of iced tea.

"Anyone up for offering a problem statement?" asked Siegal.

BF suggested, "What do we need to know to solve the mystery?"

The group sat in silence for about five minutes. Then the ideas rang out as quickly as Simi could record them on the sheets. Over fifty ideas were listed. Simi grouped the duplications, and the final total condensed to nine.

1. How many kidnappers are there?
2. Why did they need Simi when they had Sunada?
3. What special information does Simi possess?

4. Why such an elaborate abduction scheme on Simi?
5. What is the villain like?
6. What is the villain's motivation?
7. How many people will the villain's actions affect?
8. How can knowledge of motivation bring the villain down?

Siegal, toying with his new beard, acted pleased. "With this list, we can start making assumptions about the villain's personality. My friend Danielson is focusing on the specifics of what this person does. Between us, we can learn everything except his name and what he or she looks like."

"Let's do brainstorming part two," said BF. "I'm psyched."

"Me too," added Sally, "except I'm out of fucking beer."

"I can solve that," assured Simi as she went to the kitchen and brought out another six-pack.

"Okay, let's focus on item one. How many kidnappers are there?" read Siegal.

Sally asked, "Does it matter?"

Simi said, "If there is more than one, then we have a better chance of identifying the culprits. If it is one person, then the secret identity is easier to maintain. I propose it is only one mastermind."

BF said, "Then if our villain isn't a stereotypical criminal, we are thinking a white-collar criminal."

"No doubt about it," responded Simi. "And this is the first time this person has committed such a crime."

The group agreed.

Siegal started a new set of papers on the wall and wrote:

The kidnapper is probably a single, white-collar, first-time criminal.

He read the next item:

Why did they need Simi when they had Sunada?

"That's too fucking easy," said Sally. "Doc Sunada was hired to do the job, but he didn't have the right skill set. So, they used him to get Simi."

Simi jumped in, "And it almost worked. I really was sympathetic with Dr. Sunada. At the time I was rescued, I was ready to help him with anything."

"Okay, we can guess why they used Sunada, but why Simi?" asked Siegal. He felt he knew the answer but wanted the group to agree.

Sally said, "That's so goddamn easy to figure. She's an expert in this sociobiology thing."

Siegal explained, "And that ties in with the next item. Sociobiology involves the unique action between one entity and another. If you guys would have been here when Simi explained the unique actions between our monkey clans, then you would understand just how knowledgeable she is." He frowned. "We still don't know why our criminal needs this knowledge. Part of her expertise explains how people gain power. But there are other aspects."

"Like what," asked Sally.

Simi explained, "First of all, sociobiology explains why certain organisms behave because of their biological makeup. Now we add additional factors to this dimension, such as learning and other experiences in similar situations. The other side of the paradigm is the sociology part and involves how outside factors affect these certain organisms. Every reaction between biology and sociology causes further reactions. This goes back and forth ad infinitum to a point where everything one does can be explained scientifically."

"Holy shit. Then Simi is the unique person who knows how to figure it all out. This crook type wants Simi to give him the way to becoming invincible."

Siegal added to his wall chart:

> Simi is the one person to predict sociobiological behavior, probably making our villain invincible.

BF said, "Okay, the next question is why hasn't there been an attempt on anyone else in the same field?"

BF suggested, "It's because he thinks he already learned what he needs to know."

Siegal added, "Even if he doesn't know enough, his super sick mind tells him he can go it alone from here on."

BF jumped on Siegal's words. "Isn't that kind of Freudian for a strict behavioral psychologist to say?"

The group laughed for the first time in the meeting, signaling a need for a bathroom break.

Siegal, recognizing the signs, announced, "Session is over. Everyone, time for a midnight swim. We can work on the rest of the questions tomorrow. Remember, the two of you are on vacation."

The four working together seemed more play than work even though they fully understood the seriousness of the matter. That night, nothing more was said about the questions. Dr. Siegal's business office was closed for the evening.

SUN GAZETTE

The stock market remains unstable today. The strongest positive is pharmaceuticals, especially those producing personal enhancement devices.

FIFTY-TWO

THE DOCTORS AT HOWARD UNIVERSITY Hospital finally caved. It was not so much that Richard Brand was healed enough to be released back to work. They reasoned it was less intrusive to have a physical relapse than an embolism from the stress of keeping him holed up in his apartment.

Danielson took full advantage of Brand's release and arranged a joint sit down with his headhunters for one thirty the very next day. They convened at his favorite meeting place, The Smoking Musket Restaurant in Maryland. His stark office was too small for all of them. Besides, he had only one extra chair.

"My bringing you all together like this is unusual. It is my preference to keep all my assets isolated from each other for security reasons. But our problem is so interrelated I believe we can be more efficient working in concert." For the benefit of Brand and Cousins, he talked about Jamie and her team first. "They're a most extraordinary group when it comes to solving my quandaries. I never ask them how."

The group nodded silent approval at his attempt at humor as he introduced them by name.

Tim said, "You make us out like we're a group of undisciplined bandits."

"Whatever," smiled Danielson, turning to the newspapermen. "The man with the fresh scars is Richard Brand of the *Sun Gazette*. Do you want to introduce your colleague?"

"This old man is Ted Cousins. Don't let his looks fool you. He's a storehouse of information. They broke the mold after he was made. He, like you headhunters, helps me uncover facts certain people wish could be kept secret. I ask for the information, and somehow he gets it."

Danielson gave a hand signal, and the waiter brought out a pre-arranged menu. The group ate without discussing a word of business, a trait cultivated by Danielson. Once the dishes were cleared and fresh coffee served, the air settled and became serious.

"Richard," said Danielson, "why don't you tell us what you've been working on?"

"Okay. I've been investigating irregularities connected to high-level execs at several fortune five hundred companies. I discovered many activities by these CEOs verge not only on moral wrongs but some illegalities that should be investigated by the SEC. Their actions have created a great deal of unrest causing a high level of stock market fears. Any questions so far?"

"Doug asked, "Are you suggesting they're manipulating the market for their own personal gains?"

Brand nodded. "These bigwigs publish false profit reports. This initially sent their company's stock sky high."

Doug continued, "Is this what they call overvaluing a stock?"

"Exactly. Then before these false numbers can be found and corrected, the CEO sells off a large block of personal holdings at the inflated levels."

"And that's what you call insider moves?" asked Doug.

Brand continued, "Correct again, Doug. The sale of these blocks plus an examination of their books have caused major downturns in company valuations before anyone not in the inner circle can recoup their investments. The actions have left thousands of people out of work and retired folks without their hard-earned savings."

Cousins spoke up, "I don't get why we fit together. We at the *Gazette* are identifying crooked CEOs, and you all are worried about somebody active in the markets, Mr. Danielson."

Jamie said, "Maybe I can help clarify. Mr. Danielson brought us on board to find out who kidnapped Dr. Simi Block. Our research has narrowed the villain to be one of a few thousand or so possibles, very rich, and probably having some association in the market."

Danielson interjected, "I'm betting we may be looking at some of the very same people. By working together, we can eliminate duplicating our efforts."

"And you think that's enough ta join forces with each other?" asked a skeptical Cousins.

"Maybe," answered Jamie. "You at the paper are looking for bad guys in the financial world, and we're looking for one financially involved bad guy who kidnapped Dr. Block. Somebody who has changed his buying and selling habits enough for you to identify. For now, I think you have more for us than we have for you. I hope it is at least a decent tradeoff down the line."

Cousins cleared his throat. "Jamie, I knew there's something I like about you. You are pretty smart as well." Turning to Brand, he said, "I'm on their side, boss."

"And I'm with Danielson," said Brand. "What do we know right now?"

Kevin answered, "The elaborate scheme our kidnapper used tells us he is a stickler for details. He figures everything down to the nth degree. Next, he must be very rich because his kidnapping plan cost a small fortune. We also know he is a connoisseur of fine things such as wine. Deep Pockets, as we have nicknamed him, lives a very good life. But, as rich as he may be, we haven't been able to detect him through any sort of publicity, which is very unusual. Even his purchases have all been carried out through equally secretive means. Possibly even aliases."

Brand half smiled and half frowned. "Let me add this up. Excluding that you limited your search to about a thousand names, you're really nowhere near concluding your investigation."

Jamie said, "That's a pretty accurate assessment. Maybe working together, we can get closer and get our mitts on him before he can do more harm."

"Not maybe, missy. We'll get him, toots sweet," added Cousins.

Danielson said, "For starters, I would like you, newspapermen, to look over our list and identify any who fit your 'guilty of skimming' format. Also, see if any jump out at you as suspects in Dr. Block's kidnapping."

Jamie answered, "Our original list is one thousand plus, but we have pared it down to about fifty most likely names. If you can cull it further, we can research and interview them. Oh, and you can use us for information gathering on your own projects as a tradeoff. Is it a deal?"

"Deal," said Brand offering a fist bump. "I'm ready to start right now. Where is your list?"

Danielson slapped the table. "The newspaper twosome and the headhunting quartet are now a sextet. I like that." He looked at his watch. "I have to leave, but if you want, stay here for a while and work. The management won't care. They'll be happy to keep the coffee coming."

Danielson knew his headhunters worked better without him there. He suspected Brand and Cousins were much the same. "I'll be in touch."

FIFTY-THREE

IT WAS THE MORNING OF day two as the four friends ate fresh fruit, scrambled akee, and toasted breadfruit. The vibrant shades of the sunrise reflected over the sea and gave the food a magical touch. As soon as BF and Sally arrived the day before, it became evident that this was more a work retreat than a vacation. Simi and Siegal were in hot pursuit of Simi's kidnapper, and their friends were elated to add their minds to solving the puzzle.

Sally was the first to gobble down the last of her breakfast, "I'm ready." She was the youngest of the group, still in her late twenties, and enjoyed displaying her youthful vigor over the others. They quickly cleaned the porch area to the dismay of the local seagulls, anxious to gather leftover scraps. In minutes, they were perusing their brainstormed charts taped to the porch wall.

"Does anyone have anything to add from what we concluded yesterday?" asked Siegal.

"You remember the rules, boss," said BF, "We keep going forward. There is no retreating."

Sally said, "I feel Deep Pockets is fucking spoiled."

"Good point," concluded Siegal. "If he can't win honestly, he'll use any tactic. I believe money is his most effective weapon."

BF returned to his chair. "I have a far-out idea. I think he lost something and wants to get it back."

Simi nodded. "I never thought about that. He lost something, part a, and he's not used to losing, part b. It fits my sociobiological model. We're talking about a very possessive man."

Siegal wrote on the conclusions sheet:

> Villain is spoiled and used to winning. He is attempting to recover something and wants Simi's knowledge to get it back.

"Does anyone want to hazard a guess what he lost?"

"How about money?" said Sally.

"I disagree," said Simi. "He certainly had enough to carry out his elaborate plans thus far."

"Then he lost something else more important. Maybe he lost a family member or a close friend."

Simi concluded, "I don't think he lost somebody either. This person has little conscience to feel so bad about losing a person. It has to be something more personal."

Sally said," You brought up the question, BF. You're the philosophical one here. Give us your spin."

BF displayed his index finger to make his point. "I was just trying to think of what would motivate a man if it isn't money. The only thing I can think of is sex as a more powerful motivator. But why would anyone so motivated by sex kidnap Simi?"

"Thanks a lot," pouted Simi.

Sally eyed Siegal. "Is she really that good?"

"No comment." BF turned to Simi. "Did you, at any time, feel you were set up for some sort of sexual encounter?"

"Hey, you guys know I enjoy good sex. I think I would have known if they wanted my crotch."

"Seriously," said BF, "I don't think he has a lust for you, or he would have shown up as a stalker."

Siegal wrote:

> Our spoiled villain may be attempting to recover something he has lost. May have sexual implications.

Siegal said, "Our next point is to guesstimate how many people he intends to affect."

Sally said, "I think it has to be fucking big. If this bastard is just after a few, he could just pay to have them killed or paid off."

"Good point," agreed BF. "If his problem is that huge, then it is bound to affect a lot of people. I don't think he is planning a major war, only a little one. One that is focused and not a general one."

Simi suggested, "I agree to a point. But he may not be after a large number of specific targets. I think he is after a few who may be too insulated to get at them independent of any collateral damage."

Siegal wrote:

> This is a grudge affair. Many may be affected, but the action is targeted at only a few.

Siegal continued to lead the discussion. "You have any ideas on the time frame for Deep Pockets to make his move?"

BF answered, "His plan first surfaced even before Simi received her invitation to the symposium. He knew where this was going from the get-go. Simi's capture is only part of the plan. There has to be more, including some red herrings to throw anyone off the trail."

Sally looked at BF. "Do you really think this guy's plan is that complicated?"

"Absolutely. Whatever his motivation, it's been bottled up for a while."

Siegal asked, "You think his failure to complete what he wanted by abducting Simi only slowed him down?"

3333333333

BF nodded. "With or without Simi's help, he has to risk going on. He can't stop. I think it's all or nothing at this point."

Simi added. And, if we wait and see what it is, it could be too late. I said it before. The clock is ticking."

Siegal asked, "How much time do we have ... three months or less ... three to six months?"

In one voice, "Three or less."

"And now the most salient question," said Siegal, "How do our skills as behavioral scientists bring about the downfall of this perp."

The group went silent for a while. Then Sally said, "This looks like a problem for Super Simi."

Simi thought a moment. "So far, this unknown guy has me buffaloed. But, if using grudge as his motivation, the emotion is strong enough to make him nearsighted. It can be the flaw in his armor. I keep wanting to relate what I know about human nature and compare it to Hannibal. He was all-powerful. Then he changed something in his war plan. Something so minor, it was insignificant to him. General Hannibal fell to the untrained barbarians. We need to develop this Hannibal paradigm to defeat Deep Pockets."

"Our monkeys instinctively figured it out," proffered Siegal. "We intelligent beings should be able to do as well."

Simi continued. "We are no longer edge players but part of the barbarians. We have to determine who Deep Pockets' primary enemy is. After we determine that, we can start to make judgments about his weakness. It is all a matter of good timing and ..."

"And, a shitpot full of luck," added Sally.

Simi laughed. "I couldn't have said it better myself."

Siegal wrote:

Develop a Hannibal model.

Siegal said, "You guys came here for a couple of days of vacation, and all we did was work you half to death."

Sally responded, "Work? This was goddamn fun. We haven't worked together like this for years." She frowned, "I'm sorry that BF and I have to go back to our real lives. Promise to keep us in the loop."

Simi assured her, "Don't think we've finished with the two of you. I'm thinking that one day we can all be back together." The statement hit an emotional nerve. There wasn't a dry eye in the bunch.

Sally broke the melancholy. "Last one in the ocean is a broiled lobster."

She ran down toward the beach, taking off her clothes as she ran naked into the warm Caribbean water. She was followed in like form by the others.

They spent the rest of the day swimming and sunbathing. After the sun went down, they sat on the porch reminiscing about times gone by at City University.

MORNING CAME. SIMI AND ROSS were again alone on the island.

"Want to see how our monkeys are doing?" asked Siegal.

"Sure. You may even get lucky again," she winked.

FIFTY-FOUR

DANIELSON SAT IN HIS TEN-BY-TWELVE-FOOT office, far past the time most people were in bed. On one side of his folding worktable were pages of information collected from his headhunters plus the two new team members, Brand and Cousins. On the other side was all the information from Siegal and Simi. It included all emails to and from Sunada. Here were clues enough to track down his scoundrel, and he knew it.

"I'm in the home stretch. My bones tell me so."

He reread the latest fax:

> TO: TOM DANIELSON, S.O.B.
> Simi and I have been fortunate to have BF and Sally with us for a short vacation. We put our collective minds together and came up with some additional conclusions. I hope this report helps with the investigation.

Danielson found himself talking aloud as he flipped past the cover page and read the details again.

Our kidnapper is a loner, a very rich white-collar criminal with no prior convictions. Simi says Deep Pockets has a complicated mind and has planned an equally complicated crime. I get it. He doesn't want to get caught. No, maybe he knows he could be caught but wants to make sure his plan succeeds anyway.

Danielson reached for his pot on the Mr. Coffee maker and poured the last drop into his mug with the presidential seal on it, his one memento from when he was the chief of staff to President Thompson. The liquid that had been warming for most of the day had a stale taste. It caused him to grimace.

The part about this person's anger at the loss of something valuable instinctively stopped him. *What is so valuable that he would carry out his mission? I guess this loss happened recently—within the past year. Simi says we need to develop a Hannibal paradigm, whatever the hell that is. It's the way we can defeat him. And another thing she suggests is that time is critical and estimates we have only about three months to learn the answers.*

Danielson leaned back and pushed his speed dial. After five rings, the message came on.

Sorry, I am away from the phone. Leave a message; I'll call you back.

"Jamie, I received a fax from Dr. Siegal. I am forwarding you a copy. I think it's valuable."

FIFTY-FIVE

"HOW ARE YOU FEELING TODAY, sir?" asked a man in the dark pin-striped suit.

"I'm fine as can be expected, Paul," said the sickly man, wearing a royal purple robe over his imported silk pajamas.

"Are you pleased with the market today?"

"Its downturn is almost perfect."

"And your target stock?"

He nodded weakly. "Going as predicted. I plan on purchasing a large block of Emphasis under my name and several equally large purchases under my alias. Related company stocks are also experiencing increases. Other investors will follow the lead. Best yet, my cover remains perfect."

"The bandwagon effect, sir?"

A sinister smile showed on the frail man's lips.

"Shall I prepare lunch, sir?"

"Something light. Now I have to make some calls."

"Very good."

William Getsen III pressed a number on his speed dial. "Hello, my number is 1653B4. I wish you to purchase, in my name, ten thousand shares of EMPH at the current market price."

The voice on the other end repeated the account identification number and the order. One of Getsen's personal stockbrokers knew it was against policy to accept purchases by phone, but his knowledge of Getsen's health problems caused him to make an exception.

"That is correct. Thank you"

Getsen closed the call and touched another automatic number. He made three more buy orders to stockbrokers by the time Paul returned with lunch.

"I brought you some soup and a sandwich, sir. You must eat to keep up your strength. Do you wish me to hold all calls so you can rest?"

"You are my only friend. You take care of me like a mother hen. Yes, I can use the rest." In a voice that grew weaker each day, he reached toward his companion. "Should I no longer be able to carry on my business, I want you to know that in my safe is a list of offshore bank accounts. Open it. There are two legal documents on the lower shelf. You will need these along with my power of attorney. They will keep you very comfortable for the rest of your life. Now, help me to bed."

FIFTY-SIX

JAMIE CALLED THE TEAM TO gather at her apartment.

Tim, as usual, was the last to arrive. He dropped his gym bag in the corner. "What's up, boss? Your text sounded urgent. That means you have either some very good news or something very bad. Don't keep us in suspense. I reached the semis in the regional racquetball tournament and had to reset my court time."

Jamie handed each a copy of the report from Danielson. After giving them time to absorb it, she said, "As you see, it suggests the question: How sure are we that Deep Pockets is among our list of possibles?"

"He is if you ask me," said Doug.

The others agreed.

"I think so, too. The list is in the hands of Brand and Cousins to see if they have any clues to our perp."

"So, what do we do now? Sit on our butts and let them take over?"

"Don't get pouty," said Jamie. "Mr. Danielson is still our leader. I trust him to give directions. There is still work to do on our side. We can do some eliminating ourselves and see how it jives with the newspaper people. Our guy is too smart to be caught doing anything illegal. We should work that angle to eliminate our number of possibles. At some point, I'm positive he'll step over the line."

"Then," continued Tim, "all we have to do is wait and pounce."

"Waiting is not an option," answered Jamie. "Danielson's psychologists think we have less than three months to determine who this person is."

"I like it. We find out who he is. Then we go in with guns blazing. Bing. Bang. Boom," said Tim, pretending to fire his six-shooter and blow smoke from the barrel.

Jamie put her hand on Tim's shoulder. "Hold it, cowboy. If there's to be any shooting, then Danielson's raiders will do it. Remember how Doug got shot the last time. My guess is that he will be brought down intellectually and that means the brain trust guys, Siegal and Block will be the heavies."

Kevin added, "While you guys are playing cowboys and Indians, I've been looking down our list and comparing some of the things in Danielson's report. It was the question about Deep Pockets' motivation. Everyone on our list has greed at or near the top on motivation. But the psych guys don't think this crime is about greed. They think he lost something very valuable and is trying in some way to get it back, or at least get even. We have to find out what is so valuable to him."

SUN GAZETTE

A renowned psychologist was kidnapped this past spring. Through the use of high technology and some very fine detective work, Dr. Simi Block was rescued in a daring raid. However, the mastermind of this crime has not been identified. There has been a major undercover effort to find out who abducted her. We at the *Sun Gazette* are a part of this investigation.

Turning to the financial news, this week's market is taking some very interesting turns. The paradox is that there should be a general upside to it. Yet, the unexplained roller coaster continues. Pharmaceuticals show consistent gains independent of the other sectors. There is no concrete reason for it. Fisher Black, as far back as 1986, wrote about consumer noise in the *Journal of Finance* as the one major impetus that guides most day traders and small investors. It seems to be holding true even today.

One major noisemaker investor is focusing on pharmaceuticals. Others are being copycat investors hoping to make big gains. This is causing this sector to make larger gains than is fundamentally good practice. Early investors who helped initiate the noise stand to make short-term gains. Those that follow later are often at great risk of losing their investment. I comment on this because the market should be friendly for those who diversify.

FIFTY-SEVEN

A RED-EYED DANIELSON SAT IN his DC office. He barely slept since making a promise to his friend Ross Siegal and was not about to go back on his word. He said out loud. "I can start my own paper drive with all this hard copy shit. This is too much for one person to handle. I need someone like Cousins to make sense of it. It feels like I'm bouncing my head against a brick wall and no door to go through. What am I missing?"

Danielson thought of the last time he was involved with Siegal and the headhunters. It seemed so easy then. *All I did was have his headhunters discover Siegal's unusual leadership and special research abilities. Then, let Siegal run with it. All I had to do was grease a few wheels and open a couple of doors when things got too political.*

He jumped out of his chair. "I'm the wrong leader. Ross has to be the big gun." Danielson reached over a pile of papers and uncovered the phone hidden underneath. He pushed the familiar speed dial button.

"Hello? This is Phillipe. If this is a telephone sales call, we are not interested. We have plenty of whatever you're selling."

"Don't hang up. I'm not selling. I'm buying."

"Mr. Danielson, I recognize your voice. What can I sell you?"

"Can you sell me Ross for a few minutes?"

"He just went out back. You know. He will be back in a moment. He never takes long."

"Say, what are you doing answering the phone. I thought you were in Africa."

"I'm on holiday. I had a week off and decided to visit my monkeys."

"And how are they getting along without your expertise? Do we have any new ones lately?"

"I think one of our ladies is about to honor us." He paused in mid-thought. "I think I hear Doctari Siegal coming in now." He handed the phone to Siegal.

"Hello, Tom. To what do I owe this honor?"

"Nothing much, really. Have you talked with Simi now that she's back in California?"

Siegal knew Danielson never did anything without reason, even something as simple as a phone call. But he went along with the conversation. "She's back in the groove as if nothing happened. However, they keep a higher level of security around the lab now. Have you found anything more about Deep Pockets?"

"I wish I could tell you we found who kidnapped Simi, but I can't. Something's missing, and I can't put my finger on it. Our problem is we don't have the right leader on this. It's like sports. If the team is doing badly, they don't change the players; they change the coach."

"I feel a con coming on."

"Do you remember how we handled the last action?"

"Yeah. You conned me then, too. I could have been a happy research professor and maybe even married Simi with a couple of kids around my legs. Instead, I found myself running for my life."

"I doubt the kid thing. You probably would have died young from complications of your alcoholic liver. This one is not so dangerous. We were a great team then, and I think we must be the same great team now.

So, do I keep leading everyone down blind alleys, or do you take the reins and keep us on the straight and narrow?"

"And if I don't?"

"Plain and simple. If you don't, our villain pulls off whatever it is he or she is planning."

"You sure know how to sweet talk a guy. What's my first step?"

"I was thinking that you had never worked directly with my head-hunters. They're quite a group. Now I added a reporter and his assistant from the *Sun Gazette*."

"You did it again, Tom. I formally accept the dubious honor of volunteering—as if I had any choice. You know, we're about to be godparents again, and I don't want to leave the island."

"Then it's settled. We'll meet there. I can have everyone flown in. And, both you and Phillipe can be available as midwives. Do you want Sim there as well?"

"Are you kidding? It's her life we're talking about. Her special knowledge can be the very key we need."

"Then it's settled. You'll need a large catch of fish. There will be the four headhunters, two newspaper guys, you, Phillipe, Simi, and me. That makes ten—a pretty healthy group. See you in two days."

FIFTY-EIGHT

IT WAS HIGH NOON WHEN a twin-engine float plane landed and tax-ied on to the beach. Eight people plus the pilot disembarked. Phillipe greeted them at the landing site.

Danielson asked, "Any new arrivals yet?"

"No, Mr. Danielson. It will be very soon. One of the females is due any minute now."

"Good. I hope to witness it. Are the two lovers at the house?"

"Yes, sir, he is setting up a table on the porch for eating and work. He is making sure there is plenty of blank sheets on the porch walls for making notes. Doctari Block is making sure everything is nice and clean."

Tim, along with the others, stepped off the plane and looked around. "What's with all the chain link fencing? Is this the island of Dr. Moreau? We're not going to see half animals and half humans running around, are we?"

"Hardly," smiled Phillipe. "We use the fencing to separate us from the monkeys. I'll explain later when we give you a tour of the island.

FOLLOWING LUNCH, PHILLIPE CLEARED THE table, and their meeting began. Danielson, the recognized head, started. "All of you know each other third hand from your communications with me. This is the first time everyone is together. You all felt I have been the leader in finding Deep Pockets, and in fact, I have to a point. Now we have come to an impasse. We need a change on how we're doing business."

"Are any of us being downgraded or fired?" asked Tim.

"No one is getting fired. I am, however, downgrading myself."

"Then we're going on without a head, leaving only the other end of the horse," joked Doug.

"Wrong again. The best person to lead this group is our number one theorist."

All heads turned toward Siegal.

"I guess that means me. We organized this way once before, and it worked well in trapping an international terrorist."

Siegal had prepared for this meeting and knew he had to be definitive. It was not enough that Danielson named him to lead; it was how he managed the responsibility. He stood, went to the first sheet of newsprint, and outlined the new chain of command. "Tom Danielson stays as the central communications person. This lets him do what he does best and that is to mesh all the gears." He pointed to the second sheet already printed with some of his notes. "Most of this is old hat but it is a good way to start. These are some statements that we know or think we know about our bad guy. He wrote the following:

1. Very intelligent
2. Heavily involved in the stock market
3. Is an American and lives in the Northeast
4. A loner using loyal employees instead of paid cronies
5. Motivation is to get even with someone or something
6. Has legal knowledge which keeps him out of courts
7. He feels omnipotent and wants to stay invisible
8. May be already actualizing his scheme
9. We must stop him in his tracks

"Why do you think that last item?" asked Brand.

"I think I can answer that. He wanted me because of my special knowledge. He got some of that when I gave information to Dr. Sunada. But, since then, there is no indication that he has tried to get anyone else to give him information. That tells me our perp probably thinks he has enough to go it alone. And, knowing his style, he's not sitting idle. Our best strategy is to develop a Hannibal model to discover his weaknesses."

Siegal asked, "Am I missing anything?"

"It's inclusive to me," said Simi. "Everything but his name."

"On that, we're close," said Danielson. "Damn close. I feel it."

FIFTY-NINE

THE SMALLISH MAN, IN HIS ever-present pinstriped suit, opened the bedroom drapes. "It is a beautiful day, sir. Would you like to go out on the balcony?"

"No, thank you, Paul. I must complete my journal. The world must know who did this injustice to me and why."

"Very good, sir. I will be in my room."

William Getsen III activated his computer and forwarded to his last entry. He began to type:

> I never thought of myself as being so evil. Life-changing events have given me no other choice.
>
> It was one day before my tenth birthday. My mother had planned a wonderful party for me. We were going to have a pony ride and a magician. My entire class was invited.
>
> During lunch at school, I was given a note from Principal Gary asking me to visit his office. He met me at his door and had me sit down. He looked very grim. It was then I was told

of a boating accident. My parents were aboard. There were no survivors.

My brother, sister, and I were suddenly orphans. There were some aunts and uncles in various parts of the country, but they were never close to us. Coping with three children was too much for any one of them. The courts divided us among them. We only saw each other at one of those fancy summer camps for pawned-off children.

On his eighteenth birthday, my brother joined the Marines for one of those useless wars our president decided was important. He was killed in a friendly fire incident. My sister escaped her relative's placement by becoming pregnant and marrying the father. She divorced a year later and married again a year later. After a second divorce, she felt all was in vain and took her own life. Now at age twelve, I was truly alone.

Between detentions and expulsions, I finished high school and went to college pursuing a prelaw degree at a small private school in New Hampshire. From there, my improved grades earned me a scholarship to Harvard. I graduated magna cum laude and joined a small but prestigious firm in New Jersey. I became a successful litigator and a partner in the firm after just three years.

My requirement for winning became all encompassing. It precipitated a mental breakdown, and I underwent several years of intense psychotherapy. My senior partners urged me to retire and pursue a more peaceful life even though I was a relatively young man.

Therapy identified my compulsive desire to be the best at everything but did nothing to help control it. Winning was paramount. Success in both my law practice and private investments made me very rich.

I failed in only one phase of my life that I recall. I was never married. I was engaged several times, but they all ended badly. To feed my ego, I paid beautiful women to be around me constantly. Even then I continued to fail in my relationships. More rounds of therapy made me believe it was my physical inadequacies and not the women who were to blame.

It was this feeling of inadequacy that ultimately led me to my final downfall, a downfall that I cannot beat.

The typing stopped. Getsen pushed save on his computer and thumbed the call button attached to his wrist.

"You rang, sir?"

"Yes, Paul. I am very tired now. Help me to bed."

"Yes, sir. Do you want anything to ease your pain? Perhaps a morphine shot?"

"No, Paul. I can manage the pain. I must be aware during these final days."

SIXTY

SIEGAL THANKED DANIELSON FOR HIS promotion to lead the team and toasted everyone with his now favorite beverage, iced tea. "Exactly how was the list of possibles created?"

Jamie answered. "The list emerged from my team's research. We started with a request by Danielson to select one thousand very financially successful men living in the eastern United States. Is this the kind of response you want, Dr. Siegal?"

"Exactly. Now, how confident are we that our man is among them?"

"It works for me," offered Brand. "Every one of them is rich for sure. You don't get that way without winning the lottery or having a bit of larceny in your soul."

"I hate to disagree with my own boss. There's one thing missing in all these buckaroos."

"And what is this missing thing, Ted?" asked Siegal.

"All of them guys are workin' in too narrow a slot. I think this guy we're lookin' fer is more a freewheeler."

Doug nodded. "Maybe you're right. We did a lot of research. None hit the bull's eye. Only two or three have enough legal wherewithal to pull the whole caper off without a traceable team of attorneys and accountants. If any one of them used such a group, they would have been easy to track."

"Then where does that leave us?" asked Siegal.

Jamie said, "It means we haven't identified Deep Pockets at all, putting us back to step one."

"Or beyond," added Doug. "We're only guessing he is on the east coast."

Siegal nodded. "Is anyone here suggesting there is more than one person we're looking for?"

The group shook their heads.

Siegal continued. "One person makes sense. We're getting somewhere. He must be very rich for sure and probably working alone for his own cause. His motivation is not money. He is, or at least was, a mover and shaker in his own world. Simi, what does your expertise tell us?"

Simi thought for a moment. "About the only motivators stronger than money and power are hate and revenge. I think we are after someone with a deep sense of hurt who is very angry. Our culprit is trying to get even with someone or something."

"You know, Doc, I think you came up with somethin' we ain't talked about." Cousins held up two fingers and pointed to one with the other hand. "If he's a loner and knows so dang much about the law," he touched his second finger. "Then he must have been a lawyer in some respectable law firm. Probably even a partnership,"

Siegal's eyes brightened. "I think you hit it, Ted. My intuition tells me that he is no longer practicing. We need to find a person who's retired from his practice within the past couple of years."

Brand frowned. "I hate to act the pessimist, but I don't think that brings us any closer than we were yesterday."

Kevin said, "We may be missing another clue ... his age. I, for one, put him in his fifties or so."

Siegal asked, "Why so?"

Kevin continued, "I think he may have been forced into early retirement. Attorneys don't usually retire that young. From all I have read, the law profession can extend one's effective life far into the seventies."

Siegal wrote on a new sheet:

OLD AND NEW CLUES and ASSUMPTIONS

Retired (new)

Very rich (old)

Former partner in a successful law firm (new)

Works alone (old)

Angry and wants to get even (old)

Involved in the stock market (old)

Probable age in the fifties to sixties range (new)

Graduated from eastern law school (new)

Very intelligent (old)

Graduated in the top few of his class (new)

Cousins clapped his hands and said, "I ain't never been a big fan of psychology. All that mumbo jumbo stuff. You are somethin' else, Doc. Just when I think what you do is mostly bullshit, making profound statements only after the fact, you come out and make it seem so logical."

Danielson smiled. "Now you see why I wanted this man to lead us. He makes beef stew out of rock soup."

Cousins laughed, "Jus' what I was about to say myself."

Kevin opened his laptop and printed out their list of possibles. He searched them against their new clues. A few stayed till the very end. It was when they tested the names against the retired clue that the final few dropped out. "Either the clue is a false assumption, or we have to go down another research path to find our villain."

Simi scanned their list of clues. "I might have questioned one or two of the items, but being an attorney and being retired makes a lot of sense. Especially if we believe he's not getting outside legal help."

Siegal suggested, "I say we have to explore another avenue. Who has a thought?"

Jamie suggested, "I say we get a list of every major eastern law school and check out who graduated from them between twenty to thirty years ago. Then we put all their names on a wall and ..."

Doug blurted, "Throw darts?"

Jamie nodded. "You got that right. Seriously, it may be a viable strategy. My guess is we'll have about a hundred names from each class. Our computers can handle that."

Danielson was surprised how the list of a thousand names was so easily discarded after they had spent so many hours creating it. It didn't frustrate them at all. They just picked up the energy promoted by Siegal and moved with it.

Siegal, thinking about his Hannibal Clan, said, "Whoa. We need to slow down. First, we need more complete data before we can start making any conclusions. Two questions come to mind. We think Deep Pockets is a man. We don't have any name or face to prove it at this time. There have been many instances when women are the aggressors. Secondly, we can assume this person got a law degree from an eastern school because transmissions from Sunada's computer seem to indicate this. But servers can be from almost anywhere in the world."

Danielson nodded at Siegal's revelation. He felt it was fortunate their new leader was an experienced researcher. Ross Siegal knew the rules of good research, and this problem needed his skill level. The group sat in silence for lack of direction until Danielson broke the impasse. He said, "It's your lead, Ross. Where do we start?"

Siegal moved to the next blank sheet on the wall and started writing. "Here is my plan. If anyone has a better idea, then don't be shy about jumping in."

RESEARCH PLAN

Determine the top hundred law schools in the country

List all their graduates between twenty to thirty years ago

Keep the top 10 percent of each class

Eliminate all who have died

Review data for refining plan

Brand was skeptical. "Where do Ted and I fit into this picture? I like what you are planning, but I feel we're fish out of water. We're just reporters."

Siegal reassured them. "I know this is not the kind of investigation you normally do. This is the only way I know how to do it. Your knowledge of the different players will come in very handy and reduce the time needed for the digging out process."

Danielson smiled. Having Siegal lead the team was working. He knew both Brand and Cousins were indispensable parts of the team, and Siegal was showing his skill at keeping them both involved.

Jamie said, "Give us a day, and we can break down the possible names to a workable number. Other than one, what would be an acceptable amount?"

Brand responded, "I would like the number to be two if given a choice. Just joking, of course."

Danielson cautioned the team. "I can understand all your impatience for closure. I certainly respect your need to get through the deadwood and drive the nail into the hard lumber. I've worked with Ross for a long time. He doesn't take shortcuts if it means any chance of leaving out the most trivial clue. I suggest we let Jamie and her gang slug it out with the data and see where it goes from there."

Siegal looked at Kevin. "What do you think is a fair timeline to get the new listing?"

"One day is tough. By dividing up the work and using more than one computer, I think we can bang it out in two, maybe three days. Some of the graduate lists are buried in school archives and are harder to find."

Danielson, keeping the gears working in a smooth fashion, said, "Then make it no more than three. Simi judges our villain is about ready to strike a blow. We need whatever time we can get to counteract him or her.

"Good," said Siegal. "As soon as I get the information from the head-hunters, I'll pass it along to the rest of you."

DANIELSON, SENSING THE TEAM HAD done all they could at this time, said, "Phillipe, I think it's time for the bunch of us to get back to the mainland. Will you send for the plane?"

Phillipe gave his patented grin. "I already did, Mr. Danielson. I called the pilot when I went for the iced tea. Your plane will be on the beach waiting for you before sunset."

By sunset, only Phillipe, Simi, Siegal, and the monkeys remained.

SUN GAZETTE

This is Richard Brand, back at my desk for the first time since my accident. Thank you all for your cards and letters. There are enough to fill several storage bags. I will keep them forever.

Just before my accident, this department was investigating several CEOs from different companies. The plan is now to focus on whole sectors of the market that need investigation.

The first effort will be to investigate insurance companies. Their profit margins far exceed any good to the public they supposedly offer.

It must change by legislating rules closing loopholes allowing this to happen. The *Gazette* will provide the information. You, the public, must convince your state and national legislators to act.

SIXTY-ONE

WILY WILLIE WOKE, WELL-RESTED, AND surprisingly free of most pain. Without telling his employer, Paul had slipped morphine drops into his warm milk the night before at the suggestion of the doctor.

Paul had stayed most nights these past few weeks in Getsen's room. The doctor warned physical changes could occur without warning, and he did not want to leave his mentor alone. Over the many years, the two had developed more than an employer/employee relationship. Mutual trust and honest links were bonded with steel cables of friendship.

At the first movement of Getsen's hands, Paul was off his settee couch, pretending to be outside the bedroom. Getsen's stubborn independence fought the need for a babysitter.

"Good morning, sir. I trust you slept well. Can I get you some toast and coffee?"

"I am hungry. First, I need to finish my journal, then make some phone calls. Help me to my desk. Paul, we are almost through." He spoke as if they were co-conspirators. In fact, this was Getsen's revenge plan and his alone.

"Yes, sir." Paul left briefly, returning with breakfast and the morning supply of medications. "Remember, the doctor plans to stop by this afternoon. Don't overtax your energies. He likes you to be alert when he's here."

'Sir' was always how Paul addressed Getsen. Throughout his many years of service, he never addressed his employer in any terms of familiarity. Getsen hired him when he first began his law practice. Paul was a victim in one of his litigations.

"I'll be fine when he comes. Just help me to my desk."

Paul helped Getsen into the wheelchair by the bed and guided him to the computer.

Getsen reviewed his words from the day before. He was pleased with what he had written and pondered for a moment how to conclude.

In my entire professional career, there were few failures. Whenever anything did not go my way, I would create a plan to turn it into success. My calling could have been as a great mystery writer with involved plots, maybe as clever as Sir Arthur Conan Doyle.

At my peak, I commanded the highest fees of any litigation attorney. People paid them because I won. After a time, the challenge became less attractive. It seemed having my name on the case would move the opposition to seek beneficial settlements for my clients. I had to retire from practice at an age most attorneys are just reaching their peak. Some suggest it was my psychological problems that moved my retirement. This will be for others to determine. My firm paid me a great deal when I left and continued to do so just to have my name as partner emeritus on the office door.

I began collecting fine art and rare items of antiquity. This required me to travel the world and move into a new social circle. I found myself on the A-list whenever a suitable item was for sale. Price was never an object when I coveted something. I learned everything was for sale if the price was right.

At one time, I had many employees to manage my mansion and the acres surrounding it. I even hired a small armed cadre to protect me from outsiders. Yes, they were loyal, not to me but to my money. I released them all except my one and only permanent employee and friend, Paul.

My final enterprise was to move into the financial markets. I was very successful at predicting the ups and downs of the market. My singular investments were large enough that I quickly became a major player. At one time, I was offered a seat on the floor of the New York Stock Exchange. Still practicing my independence, I refused in order to stay under the radar. However, it did not seem to matter. If I selected a stock or bond, it became popular and always showed an upswing. When I sold something, the market would see this as a bear action, and the price on the floor would go down. Millions of people, including large brokerages, like lambs, followed my leads. I was Mellon, Getty, and Gates all rolled into one.

Getsen sat back in his wheelchair. He took a sip of the now cold coffee and finished his one slice of toast. Even this short amount of writing tired him. In moments he was asleep.

The next thing he was aware of was his physician visiting.

SIXTY-TWO

THE HEADHUNTERS GATHERED AROUND THEIR sophisticated array of electronic equipment in Jamie's apartment. They had no permanent office, and her place was a suitable site.

Kevin, the tech expert of the crew, was at the keyboard typing rapidly. "You know, by combining all the databases from the top law schools in the country as our data dump, we can collect every name from those graduating classes between twenty and thirty years ago. We are almost guaranteeing Deep Pockets will be on our list."

"Can we cut that list down a bit? We're talking thousands of names," said Tim. "I'm sure some of them have retired or died."

"No biggie," said Kevin. "If I use the database from the *Attorneys National Clearing House*, I can pick up anyone who is retired but maintain those with special status or emeritus standing."

"Fine for getting the names," said Doug, "I thought we were trying to get the list down to a manageable number."

"I can do that, too, adding a couple of filters. Social Security will have names of people in that age range who have died. We can highlight the top ten of each graduating class."

Jamie gave a small frown. "Okay, see where that takes us."

Keven's laser printer chugged out the list.

"Still too many possibilities," said Jamie. "What other limiting factors can we use?"

"I can sort the names anyway we want. We think Deep Pockets lives in the northeast and has been very successful. Income tax reports are public knowledge. I can tap into those. Another sort can be fine wine purchases. Give me a few minutes and see what comes out."

A few sorts later and the team had a couple of lists, each with under one thousand names.

"That's more like it," said Jamie. "Let's pair off and see what we find."

It was after midnight when an exhausted Jamie said, "I've had it. I'm afraid we'll make more mistakes from fatigue. Remember that old line from *Gone with the Wind*."

Doug agreed, "It may be another day for Scarlet O'Hara, but it's our red-letter day from Danielson."

"See you all at nine," said Jamie easing herself out of her chair where she showed the effects of sitting in one position too long.

AT NINE THE NEXT MORNING, Jamie had the coffee made, and Doug, the designated doughnut buyer, placed a fresh supply on the table along with some napkins.

It was after three when the last of the names had been reviewed.

Tim asked, "How many does that leave us?"

Kevin punched the total key on the special spreadsheet he created. "We're down to under two hundred."

"That's more like it," cheered Jamie.

Doug said, "I'm usually creative in these matters, but given our time constraints, I'm at a loss of where to go from here. Our usual process is to do face-to-face interviews. We just don't have the slack time."

"Well," said Jamie, "we just have to call upon the experts."

Doug smiled. "I'll get them on the phone."

There was a short pause. "They agreed to meet us at their newspaper first thing in the morning. I will relay our direction to Dr. Siegal."

SIXTY-THREE

"ARE YOU SURE YOU ARE strong enough today, sir?"

"It matters little how I feel." Paul could hear that Getsen's voice was noticeably weaker. "I have to finish. The doctor said my time is limited. I cannot slow the process."

"Yes, sir. Only ..."

"Only what, Paul?"

"Only you have always stayed strong and true to your course in winning the battles with others. It was the competition to win a case that drove you in the past. Your illness has changed you. You no longer worry about how innocent people can be hurt."

"Do you want out?" He gave a weak cough. "I can do it with or without your help."

"I haven't left you, sir. I was thinking more that you have left yourself. In the past, your only victims have been your direct adversaries. You have always shown a caring for others who could be impacted."

"See. That's where you are so wrong. My actions are mine alone. If people wish to follow blindly because of greed, then it's their own damn fault. Help me to my desk, so I can finish what I've started."

Getsen settled in front of his computer and resumed his typing:

My failure with women had to do with a hereditary lacking of my sexual organs. I remember hearing my father joking about his lack of size when talking with his friends, saying it never stopped him. He did not know I was listening outside his study. After each time, I would go to the privacy of my room and examine my own size, comparing it to some of the magazine pictures I had hidden under the dresser. As an adult, I became so obsessed that reaching a climax during sex or masturbation was no longer possible. The most competent prostitutes who formed a daily path to my door were unable to help my condition.

About three years ago, I began researching different methods of correcting my impotency. There were many choices—physical additions, air bladders with a squeeze bulb, and a prosthesis one could attach to hold my penis up. There were also drugs to increase blood flow.

Then I read about a new procedure. A microchip implant reacted to one's own emotional system coupled with female attraction hormones emitted during foreplay. The product would cause one's body parts to react in a normal way. It was guaranteed to work. The American Drug Administration did not approve this microchip for distribution. It was being made by an international company in South Korea. An Emphasis microchip implant was the answer, or so I thought.

I traveled to Seoul and talked with a surgeon willing to perform this procedure. We agreed on a time and price. I became the proud possessor of an Emphasis Penis Modulator microchip. I tested it several times while still in Korea with some professional help. The device worked perfectly every time. I returned each year for my physical review and new batteries. Everything seemed fine. The procedure cost me well over two million dollars and was worth every penny. My masculinity returned in every normal way. I even noticed how much longer I lasted during intercourse.

About a year ago, I began responding to male hormones as well as female hormones. It was to the point that a few drinks after a good foursome of golf with my male friends brought about erections. Company representatives of Emphasis and the surgeon who performed the operation refused to see me. Symptoms became more erratic. Now even my own hormones brought about uncomfortable erections lasting several hours. I found a surgeon in the United States who agreed to remove the microchip. But the damage was irreversible. My entire hormonal system had short-circuited. My vital organs were shutting down. I was doomed to fate, with only a few months to get back at Emphasis. My single goal was now to devastate the company. Destroy it completely. Make them feel my pain. Negotiation with them was no longer an option. I had to bring down Emphasis another way. My weapon of choice was the stock market. I used my buying and selling power in the market to turn their bonds into junk ratings.

My companion, Paul, suggested my drive is so strong that I care not what happens to anyone in any way. This is not true. My limited time left leaves few alternatives. I apologize for what will happen to many innocent people. But Emphasis cannot be allowed to exist and take advantage of another unsuspecting soul. Bankrupting Emphasis and putting them out of business will help more people in the future.

I leave this journal to explain my actions and let people make their own judgments. I do not want pity, only understanding.

Getsen clicked the save and print keys on his computer and then pushed the call button on his desk.

"You rang, sir?"

Getsen handed Paul the printout. "Put this in the safe. After my death, you must make it public. I need to place the last of my buy orders, but I am too tired. Typing the story has worn me out. Here is the list. You must make the calls for me. Use my account numbers 165383-165388. You already know the passwords."

"Very good, sir. I will handle it."

Getsen grabbed Paul's sleeve. "Promise you will follow through with my intention."

"I shall be there for you, sir."

SUN GAZETTE

The markets fluctuated wildly for no apparent reason. People were buying and selling at an alarming rate. The focus is of this fluctuation is mainly in the pharmaceuticals sector. The company showing the most movement is Emphasis.

SIXTY-FOUR

"HEY THERE, BUCKAROOS. WHAT'S HAPPENIN'? I know you didn't come here jus' fer our gourmet coffee."

"You got that right," said Jamie as she and her headhunters walked into Brand's office at the newspaper. "We promised Dr. Siegal and Mr. Danielson a name and went as far as we could by computer. Now it's your turn for some expert people's input.

"You need us fer the old-fashioned way of sleuthing," joked Cousins.

Brand put down his coffee. "What have you got?"

Doug said, "We're pretty good at finding people who fit certain characteristics. When it comes to finding one person in a haystack of needles, well ..."

Brand smiled, feeling the need to add experience into the equation. "Show us your list."

Doug reviewed their work using all the criteria given to them by Siegal and Simi. "We took a list of possibles every way we could think of doing. Each time we got a different set of names and a different number of possibles."

"Well, fellers. Let's get started. Toss out names and see if we know anything about 'em," said Cousins.

Kevin placed his printout of names with bios on Brand's desk.

"Hot damn. You fellers sure do lot of paperwork. Very impressive."

Jamie said, "We learned from experience never to throw out any data once it has been collected. It may seem cumbersome at times, but it beats trying to reconstruct it later."

Brand said, "Let me guess. You can build a profile and pick the people who fit. But you have no idea in hell who any of these people are. Right?"

Jamie agreed. "We feel very strongly that our perp is somehow associated with finance."

"And," concluded Brand, "you think we'll be able to recognize his name."

Jamie gave a hopeful nod.

"Well, if this person has been any kind of whale, you know, big investor, recently, we'll know him."

"We're hoping this whale, as you call him, is currently active in the market. That would make all our jobs much easier," Doug added.

The six poured over the names. Most were easy to eliminate. Some had considerable investment portfolios, but they were eliminated because they used money management firms to do their buying and selling.

"Are you sure these guys should be eliminated?" asked Brand.

Doug answered, "We think Deep Pockets works alone. If he is doing anything even remotely illegal, he doesn't want the obvious audit trail a money management firm would require."

Cousins nodded. "Okey dokey. We eliminate them folks. You guys are the profile pros."

By late afternoon, frustration showed on their faces. All the names were crossed off.

Cousins said, "It's like losing a super bowl game on the last play by passin' and gittin' intercepted on the one-yard line instead of runnin' it in."

Kevin shook his head. "I was sure our man is among the list. What have we been missing?"

Brand took two aspirin followed by a gulp of day-old coffee and slumped back in his chair. "I don't know about the rest of you, but I'm not totally well yet. I need my rest."

Jamie agreed. "I think we all need some rest. The four of us will go at it again tomorrow. Richard, if either you or Ted get any bright ideas, day or night, give me a call. Meanwhile, I will call Danielson. I know he won't be very happy."

BACK AT HER APARTMENT, JAMIE made her dreaded call. "Sorry, boss, we thought we had it nailed. All we needed was for Brand or Cousins to recognize the name. It was supposed to be a no-brainer."

"Don't give up yet. I know how good you are. He's on your list. I'd damn well bet on it."

"Then why didn't we find him?"

"You just weren't looking at the list from the right angle. I'll check with Ross and Simi to see if they have any ideas. There are too many good minds working on this to lose this one when we're so close."

THE SIX MET THE NEXT day at the newspaper, still in a quandary as to how to proceed.

Cousins was the first to offer an idea. "We're looking for a person who is very active at present. I think that's a mistake. From the list of possibles, several whales showed up as past investors. Now lookin' at the list of the present, most are still active. But one or two names are not. And still, our Deep Pockets is carrying out his dang scheme. One may stick out who is still buying blocks of a single stock. It is not enough to cause any investing notice. Yet, there are a number of new investors who are buying about the same number of shares. Ain't it possible that the old investor is using aliases to hide his identity? This could be enough to sway a specific sector."

Jamie said, "It is quite possible that our investor is still buying a lot of one a stock, and it doesn't show up as him being a whale of sorts. Do you think this kind of activity would urge tag-along buyers to follow?"

"You betcha, missy."

"I agree," said Brand. Give us a while to check out recent buys and sells. If anything shows up in a fishy way, Ted and I will find it.

SIEGAL'S CELL RANG WHILE HE and Simi were observing their monkeys. They were so confident the headhunters would find a name they took some leisure time to relax. Siegal punched the speaker button on his cell so Simi could hear. Danielson's voice was somber. He explained what Jamie had told him about what they found and what the newspaper team thought might be a fertile direction.

"What are you thinking, Ross?" asked Simi.

"It's not like him to call on such a downer. Tom always has a positive manner."

"I'm not so sure this time," said Simi. "The team is missing the boat somewhere, and I don't think it is because their thinking is that far off. You're right about one thing. Tom always has the answer. And that answer is you."

Simi thought for a moment. "The headhunters are numbers people, and the newspaper guys are fact seekers. Just suppose they have the numbers in place, and the facts are in a row as well. It's not in their nature to venture past that. They are missing what we can offer."

"And what is that, my dear," said Siegal, giving her a love pat on her bottom.

"Not now, hot pants. We must keep our minds clear. The answer is how Deep Pockets works. We're the missing link in solving this puzzle. We have to rethink everything we surmised about this guy."

"What have we missed? You're the one with the photographic memory."

"Thanks for the support. Let me see. We know about his age, profession, and that he is very angry at someone or something. What else?"

Siegal added, "Well, he has never been in trouble with the law and is a very private person."

"That's it," concluded Simi. "He is a very private person. That's the clue we have been overlooking. Being so private may be his strength and his weakness at the same time." She stood up and, without a word, started to walk toward the beach.

"Where in the hell are you going?"

She turned, "You are not the only person who likes to be alone to ponder. I'll see you in a while."

Siegal was aware of how Simi felt and knew enough to give her space. He remained on the platform until after dark when the monkeys were nested for the evening. He hoped the peacefulness of the platform would be his magic spot.

It was after midnight when Siegal heard Simi running toward the platform at full speed, or at least as full speed as Simi's pudgy legs could run.

"What? Are you all right?" he called as he saw her coming.

"I think I've got it," she exclaimed.

"You mean you figured out who Deep Pockets is?"

"Not quite." She paused for a minute to regain her wind. "Almost as good." Another pause for air. "It's the trait of wanting to be private. As a successful lawyer, he was very visible. And after retiring from law, he was also very visible in the stock markets. But now that he is on this get-even kick, being visible is not the way to go."

"Wait. I'm losing you. How can he stay so powerful in the market and be invisible at the same time? Danielson said that none of the head-hunter's list contains a current player."

"And, sweet bread of my life, that is where we have been missing the boat."

"Fill in the blanks. I'm still lost."

"We should be looking for a man who was very active in the recent past and is now inconsistently quiet or at least appearing to be quiet."

Without being aware of each other, the fact people and the theoretical people had come to the same conclusion.

Simi continued to explain. "It's so simple. He just has been using one or more aliases. Also, look for new big market players. The names may belong to the same person." Her excitement affected her intimate feelings. It was always at times like this that her sex drive became insatiable. "Call Danielson and tell him what we determined. Meanwhile, I'll be on the beach under a blanket waiting for you."

Danielson was not in his office at this time of night. Siegal left a short message. Thinking of Simi under the blanket by the beautiful Caribbean told him not to wait for his call to be forwarded. Opportunities like Simi's offer should never be wasted.

SIXTY-FIVE

SATURDAY MORNING AT THE NEWSPAPER, both Brand and Cousins were at their desks working. Sabbaths and other holidays meant little to such dedicated newspapermen. Deadlines were the only issue. And both men felt they were working on a deadline to determine who Deep Pockets was and help bring the mystery to a close. As two of the more highly regarded experts in the world of finance, Danielson had given them the responsibility to identify this person, and they had gladly accepted the challenge.

Late that afternoon, Danielson received their call. "Tom? It's Richard and Ted. I think we have your man."

"Good work. Give me a name."

"We're almost certain it's William Getsen III. Like Midas, everything he touched turned to gold. Both individuals and companies blindly followed his lead. In a very short time, he was rumored to have amassed several hundred million, maybe even billions. Then, at the top of his game, he virtually disappeared. That was about eight or nine months ago. We could not find his name on large or multiple buys after that time."

"Why him and not any of the other possibles we identified?"

"It was easy to eliminate most of them because they didn't suddenly drop out of the market."

"What do you call major players?"

"It's not what you may think," said Brand. "It isn't how much money they invest. It is more how their investments drive the price of an individual stock or segment of the market."

"How did you identify Getsen if he had not been a major player recently?"

"It's more a feeling you get when you've been in the business as long as I have. Here's how it plays out."

"You have my complete attention."

"A little over a year ago, Getsen invested several large chunks of money in one of the pharmaceuticals called Emphasis. They have been a hot item since coming out with a male sexual enhancement prosthesis. Just the act of him investing in Emphasis suddenly made the stock popular, and the price jumped significantly. Investors followed, and Emphasis and other related pharmaceuticals rose in value even more. You would have expected that if Getsen were working the market in a normal manner, he would sell off the stock for a nice profit. It would have kept him invisible."

"And?"

"The odd thing is he didn't. Instead, he backed off high volume buys but continued to periodically buy small blocks of Emphasis, we think as a smoke screen. He is neither selling nor in any way managing stock value changes. All this is very out of character for his business style. At this same moment in time, there were three high volume buyers who were previously unknown as whales which kept Emphasis stock rising even more."

"So, this is a red flag to your way of thinking."

"The clues can be easy to miss. He is not doing anything illegal or the like. His actions are low-key enough to pass under the radar if it was not for one of your clues about him. The one clue about him using one or more alias names was the key. Ted and I focused on purchases of Emphasis stock and found three new investors who began buying large blocks at the time when Getsen stopped. Then we put the calculator to the numbers. These investors made regular purchases that, if combined, would equal what Getsen was buying previously. Then to make it even more compelling, their purchases were all from some offshore wire transfers."

"Damn. You pegged him. Take the rest of the day off. You may also want to think about a week in Hawaii if we get this Getsen with his hands in the cookie jar. Tell me, what are any causal factors because of what he's doing?"

"Pure and simple," responded Cousins. "He doesn't own enough stock to manage the company. But he durn well owns enough to make the Emphasis Pharmaceuticals crash. Maybe even crash the whole pharma market as well. Wouldn't that be a pisser? His actions damn well would impact tens of millions of people around the world."

SIXTY-TWO

DANIELSON CALLED SIEGAL AND SIMI. "Congratulations, professors. With your last idea about Deep Pockets using aliases we pinpointed the bastard."

"Are you sure?" quizzed Siegal, afraid to believe his ears.

"On a scale of one to ten, we hit an eleven. Brand and Cousins did some fantastic research and found only one man on the planet that fits the total profile. His name is William Getsen III. I have my men tracing his whereabouts. He won't be hard to find. We already know he has a mansion in upper New Jersey and is probably living there under a false sense of security."

"Then the case is closed," said a gleeful Simi. "All you have to do is go in with guns blazing and bring him down."

"It's not that simple. He really hasn't directly broken any laws, for one thing. And we still are not sure why he had you kidnapped."

Siegal said, "Regarding Simi's involvement, I've spent the last few restless nights putting some order into this chaos. Let me go back and run this through both of you. Simi was kidnapped by Sunada on orders from Getsen. Why he didn't use Sunada to do his dirty work had me puzzled for a while? Sunada was a world-class motivator and seemingly had all the tools and willingness to do the dirty work for him. Again, so why Simi? Here is what I think. Sunada could motivate anyone to do his bidding. The key word is one. I think Getsen needed someone who would know how to motivate a group of like-minded people at one time. This is where Simi comes into play. She has the knowledge to do this. Ergo. Sunada was used to motivate Simi to do this. The question remains: Why? And after Simi was freed, why did he not go after another expert?"

"Good question," said Danielson. "I think some mitigating circumstance came into play causing him to change his timetable and attempt going it alone, probably using money as his weapon of choice."

Siegal asked, "What else do we know about this Getsen guy. Can Brand or Cousins give us more on how he normally operates?"

"I already guessed you would want to know," responded Danielson. "You being the behavior specialist and all. This is what they told me. I hope it helps. He is a loner most of the time. He probably needed Simi to ensure his success. What he normally does is buy quickly and sell just as fast when he feels the timing is right."

"And?" asked Siegal.

"And for some reason or other, he is holding onto his stock purchases. He's bound to make some drastic sell actions very soon."

Siegal thought for a moment. "By then, it will be too late. How are his latest stocks doing?"

Danielson replied, "According to Brand, these particular stocks have gone through the roof. Yet, he is still not selling them."

Then he's not doing this for the profit. Something else is in play," said Siegal. "Maybe the particular company is more his interest. What company did he buy into?"

"Emphasis. Before I called you, I did some research on them. They are involved in a product to enhance male potency. Does that make any sense to you guys?"

Simi answered. "Maybe he bought some of their product, and it didn't work the way he expected. This man, who goes all in on everything, wants vengeance. He wants to control the company in some way.

They messed with his male superiority. Sexual motivation is one of the strongest motivators in all of the animal kingdom."

Siegal added, "I'm not convinced we have the total answer. There has to be more than being dissatisfied with his sexuality to make him first hire Sunada and then kidnap Simi to get her to do his bidding. We're talking lots of money involved."

"I like the way you are thinking," said Danielson. "When you say it that way. My next guess is he wants to bankrupt them."

Simi jumped in. "Can't we just find a way to block him from selling? You know, like an injunction?"

"I also talked with Brand about that. Getsen really hasn't done anything in the market that is illegal. And we still haven't the smoking gun that ties him in with Simi's kidnapping."

Simi said, "Let me think. Up to now, he has been invulnerable, all-powerful, and acting without remorse. I feel he doesn't think anyone has an inkling as to what he is planning. His chink, this shortsightedness, is a weakness we can exploit."

"You mean like setting up a Hannibal paradigm?" Danielson asked. "Can we do it?"

Simi answered, "If we're using the Hannibal paradigm as a map, then it would be logical that Getsen wanted my skills as an insurance policy against getting caught."

"It's all becoming very clear," exclaimed Siegal. "Like Hannibal, Getsen hits hard at his enemies and destroys his targets. Getsen had not done the hard sell to destroy Emphasis, just as Hannibal added social reforms to uplift his enemies. The paradigm is a perfect parallel. It shows us a way to use this weakness to destroy his plan."

DANIELSON CALLED JAMIE TO BRING her up-to-date. "We are positive Getsen is our man. We still have to tie up a few loose ends before we can move in on him."

"Good. How can we help from here?"

Danielson said, "We have to be 100 percent sure of his connection to the kidnapping. Also, we have to have a feel for when he intends to act on his attack on Emphasis. That's where your team comes in. Don't tell me how; just do it."

JAMIE GATHERED HER TEAM IN her apartment. "We need eyes on Getsen for proof he's Dr. Block's kidnapper."

"What are we sitting around here for? Let's get started," said Kevin.

"Tim, check any public records we can find on him," directed Jamie. "His income taxes and other documents could be there."

Doug frowned. "I know. I get the dirty work. Looks like its garbage patrol for me. I'll also put a watch on his mansion and see who's coming and going."

Jamie laughed. "Don't gripe. We'll all help. Remember, our deadline is yesterday."

JAMIE MET WITH BRAND AND Cousins in one of the conference rooms at the newspaper.

"You're in luck," announced Brand. "We just filed our weekly column and have some open moments. Tell me. What do you think about fingering Getsen? I never figured Deep Pockets to be him at first. But then all the clues kept pointing his way, leaving no one else."

"You jus never know. Like a rotten peanut that's got a nice shell but is all shriveled up when you open it," said Cousins.

"What's really on your mind, Jamie?" asked Brand. "If you just had a question, it would have been easier to call."

"Cain't never pull the wool over his eyes," laughed Cousins.

Jamie paused. "Honestly, my mind is going in several directions at the same time. Whenever there is that thread dangling, I either have to pull it or snip it off."

"Sounds like you have more than one thread hanging," concluded Brand.

"I do indeed. Sometime back, it seems like an eternity now, my team identified over a thousand people, all of which could be Deep Pockets. We researched them and came up with a big fat zero."

"That sounds like pretty damn good research if you ask me," responded Cousins.

"The research was very good. My guys are experts. All our probables had at least one flaw. Some of them seemed to change their way of doing business, just about the time you fellows noted Getsen stopped showing up in the market."

"Hey, girlie. Are you suggesting there is some sort of action-reaction thing going on?"

"I don't have any hard proof. But you're right, Ted. I think there is. And if you ever call me girlie or missy again, I'll make you think you were never a man."

"Yes, ma'am. I learn very fast."

"Apology accepted. I really respect both of you, and I know it wasn't said in any kind of condescending manner. It's just a woman thing. But seriously, do either of you think there may be some kind of tie-in with Getsen and others you've been going after?"

Brand rubbed his still-healing wounds. "We can check the histories and look for any financial relationships that could tie them to this Getsen chap. We know a couple of them went to a conference hosted by Getsen. We won't find out about the others through the computer. We need to pare down the names manually."

Cousins said, "Give us a few names. If there is a match up, I say we have a fox in the henhouse."

Jamie opened her briefcase and fished for a paper. "Don't say I never come prepared. I have three that we investigated personally: Michael Sperling, an accountant from Philadelphia; Thomas O'Mally, a realtor from St. Louis; and Sam Blackman, a high-tech nerd."

"What a story. If they are actually involved as a smoke screen, this could be a Pulitzer," exclaimed Brand.

Jamie said, "You know you can't print it. At least for the time being. I am sure Danielson will release the story after we get Getsen with the goods. We don't want to compromise the criminal case against him on kidnapping. How long do you think it will take to get this information?"

"Not more than a day. One of the names is familiar. We have already done some groundwork on him," said Brand.

"So, what, gir ... I mean Jamie, else is on your mind?"

"I think that's it. You guys are great to work with. I'll be waiting for your call."

Jamie shook hands with Brand, gave Cousins a kiss on the cheek, and left. Her mind was still unraveling, but now with fewer loose threads.

SIXTY-SIX

EARLY TO BED AND EARLY to rise makes a man wealthy and wise, words William Getsen III always lived by even in his weakened condition. He should have included healthy. On his desk was his list of stock sells carefully diagrammed regarding when and where to move on them.

It was less than two years since his penile enhancement began to short circuit and destroy his vital organs. Emphasis refused any satisfaction. Getting even was his only alternative. Kidnapping Simi Block was the first action to ensure success. Controlling the pharmaceutical market was the second. The final timetable became set when specialists said his problem was irreversible and he had but two or three months to live. Now Getsen had less than eight weeks left to enact his revenge.

Acquiring large shares of Emphasis stock in his name and three aliases placed him in control of the company. He turned to Paul, who was preparing him for the day. "I have two choices. I can liquidate all my holdings at once, causing an immediate market drop and bringing about their quick and sudden demise. But no. That is too kind. I choose a slow end like I am experiencing. Using my aliases keeps me invisible from any legal intervention."

"Eat your oatmeal, sir. You need your strength."

Getsen continued as if not listening. "Forty days is all I need. Emphasis will fall into bankruptcy, a slow and certain death like my own. I'll first sell off the shares in my name. This will cause Emphasis's market value to drop almost imperceptibly at first. Then I will place the dagger squarely into its heart by selling all blocks held by my aliases. This will be seen by investors as a weakness in Emphasis. They will follow like sheep to the slaughter. Emphasis's credit will drop from an A-plus rating to a junk B-minus rating. No bank will offer loans to them. Emphasis will become paralyzed. And that will be my revenge for what they have done to me." He attempted to laugh but only coughed weakly.

This slow, methodical process was unlike his normal swiftness to act and was a complete change of behavior. It was the weakness Siegal and his team sought. It was the precursor to General Hannibal's defeat at the hands of his enemies.

"Mr. Getsen, sir, you will beat them. But you will also destroy the lives of many fine people."

"I can't give a damn for those people. They mean nothing to me. Their stupidity is not my fault."

"And the employees of Emphasis? They had little choice."

"None of them blew the whistle on the questionable results. They just followed, along thinking about their bonuses. They are no better than the rest. Don't go weak on me now. I have work to do."

"Yes, sir. Very good, sir."

He grabbed at his servant's sleeve. "Paul, should I at any time lose the energy to complete this venture, you must swear to finish. Do you swear?"

"I shall do my best, sir. I swear. I will come back in an hour and help you to bed."

Getsen turned back to his desk. He studied his plan again. He thought, "Paul is a faithful friend. I rescued him and gave him my home as his. Can I trust him to finish my fight? I am not sure. I have asked him to follow me even after death. I must develop a contingency plan."

As soon as Paul left the room, he began. An unfeeling smile spread across his face, the face of a man gone mad.

SIXTY-EIGHT

DOUG WAS IN CHARGE OF surveillance on Getsen's mansion. He tapped Tim as his relief backup enabling them 24/7 coverage. Doug parked his red pickup, carrying all his gear, out of sight behind a stand of trees just outside Getsen's mansion.

Doug's favorite equipment, purchased at an army surplus store, was his heat-seeking telescopes to monitor movement within the mansion. He waited until dark to set them up on the grounds near the mansion. Tim located the phone lines in the sewer system under the street and spliced a robot remote that relayed all messages back to Doug's computer. The final piece was their monitoring system to visually record all visitors through high-powered telescopes and motion-activated cameras with facial recognition apps. He then hacked Getsen's computer to gather any email messages.

Doug said, "All my high-tech gadgetry can take us only so far. We still must go trash diving, exchanging trash bags with dummy ones before they can be burned in the private incinerator." He called Jamie to say everything was ready.

"Now we wait," said Jamie.

THE DYNAMIC DUO FROM THE *Gazette* initiated their research on the business dealings Jamie had given them.

"Did you discover anything shady so far?" asked Cousins.

"Not really. They are all aggressive types when it comes to their business practices, but nothing we can peg as illegal."

"D'ya see any connects to Emphasis?"

"They all bought Emphasis stock as a healthy investment--nothing out of the ordinary. Only Getsen bought larger blocks. I don't think they were tied into Getsen's buy/sell scheme. My guess is they are unknowing contributors to Getsen's clever plan."

Cousins clicked on the large wall screen monitor to pharmaceuticals. The two sat, sipping their coffee as the screen tracked real-time sales. He focused on the lower corner to view Dow and NASDAQ numbers. "Everything points to a good day for the markets except for pharmaceuticals. They're radical as hell."

"Double-check to see if Getsen or his alias names are involved."

Cousin made some calls and scribbled down numbers as he listened. He turned to Brand and smiled. "Seems like Wily Willie is makin' his move. Med Alliances and Supreme Research both reported Emphasis is dippin' and divin' for no real reason."

"Nothing obvious," added Brand. "Check the names Med Alliance and Supreme Research gave you. See if any of them match up with the larger list the headhunters gave us."

Cousins studied the electronic data. "Curious. In the morning, Emphasis stock behaved like every other stock. It seems that each afternoon their value took a nosedive. Whenever Getsen's name appeared on the sell side, Emphasis stock dipped a little. Not so much to raise a red flag, but until he started doing this, all he ever did was buy."

"Very interesting," said Brand. "How big are his selling blocks?"

"It ain't how big. It's more that whatever Wily Willie did, people jus' followed like sheep. He still owns a lot of Emphasis."

"Danielson needs to be in on this. Getsen is making his move. We're running out of time. The crisis point is now. And the target is definitely Emphasis."

SIEGAL'S CELL RANG. IN FACT, it rang every fifteen minutes for the remainder of the day. Both Siegal and Simi were at the observation platform and had left their cells at the house. It was after the monkeys had nested when they returned and discovered all the phone messages from Danielson. Siegal dialed Danielson's private number. It was answered on the second ring.

"Where the hell were the two of you?"

"Sorry, Tom. We were shepherds tending our flock and forgot our cells."

Danielson didn't acknowledge the apology. "Getsen is making his move. We may already be too late to stop him."

Simi, listening in on the speaker, said, "Maybe not. Tell us what you know so far."

"All I know for sure is what Brand told me. Getsen is ordering some sells of Emphasis stock. My mind tells me Emphasis is his target for some reason. So far, it is only about a quarter of what he owns in his name."

Simi asked, "Does Brand think he sold some under any of his aliases also?"

"We don't think so."

Simi answered, "It may be good news. Still ..."

Danielson jumped on the word. "Still?"

"I'm surprised he didn't dump everything at once. That would have been his normal behavior of jumping in with both feet and making the kill short and sweet. I need to work on this. I'll call you back."

"We need answers fast. This isn't a semester term paper we're doing. There have to be answers fast. And, for God's sake, stay near the damn phone."

"JAMIE." IT WAS DOUG. HIS excitement was impossible to mask. "Sitting here waiting for something to happen, I played around on the internet. You'll never believe what I found in examining credit cards from Sperling, Blackman, and O'Mally.

"They all bought Emphasis stock? Brand already knows that."

"Better, they all took business trips at the same time to the same hotel in Washington state. There is also a ten thousand dollar entry on each one of their cards within days of their taking the trip."

"Interesting. But no cigar yet. What else?"

Doug continued, "It was a business conference which one hundred top executives across the United States attended according to the hotel registry. It lasted three days. Then thirty days later, two of the three attended what the hotel said was a follow-up meeting. O'Mally was invited but committed suicide earlier."

"Good going, Sherlock. Any tie-in to Getsen?

"The conference was sponsored by Wily Willie himself."

"Bingo. This is major. Check into Getsen's accounts for any ten thousand dollar deposits about that time."

"Shouldn't take more than a couple of minutes," Doug said. The computer did its business. "I couldn't find any deposits. He must be using an offshore bank. But I did find Getsen and an unknown companion had made the very same travel arrangements. That hardwires the four of them together."

"I'll ask Danielson to get a court order to access the hotel records during the same two periods. We may need to discover everyone who attended the two sessions for tie-ins with Getsen. I think he used the first meeting as a test of some kind. He needed the second to ensure his plan's success."

Jamie called Brand. "I'll be faxing you a list of names the hotel said attended the conference as soon as I get it. See what kind of unusual dealings any of them had in the stock market relating to pharmaceuticals. We are sure Getsen has some connection with Sperling, Blackman, and O'Mally. But what we don't know is if he had them do a special buy or if he was acting alone and they were part of his smoke screen."

SIXTY-NINE

THE SUPPLY PLANE LANDED TO deliver supplies. To Siegal, Simi, and Phillipe's surprise, Danielson stepped off the plane.

"Hi there, good buddies. I don't know about you, but I feel it is time for some face-to-face."

They did their regular hugs. Phillipe took Danielson's bags, placed them in the office bedroom, and brought out some fresh iced tea to the three now seated on the porch.

"Where do we start?" asked Simi, looking to Danielson for direction.

"That's not my job. He turned to Siegal as the crowned leader. "Well?"

Siegal scratched his balding spot. "I guess it is time to look at the facts and see which ones tie Getsen to the kidnapping."

Phillipe disappeared into the house and returned with some sheets of newsprint, felt pens, and masking tape. Taping several sheets on the porch wall, he said, "Maybe this will help, Doctari."

Siegal smiled. "Phillipe, you haven't been with me as long as the others, but I think you know more how I think than I do."

He uncapped a felt pen and poised himself in front of the first sheet. In a few minutes, they had a list of information, but nothing that gave any answers.

"Siegal concluded. "We know Getsen lost something and is blaming Emphasis. I think it is their product that has caused him to act the way he does. Tom, have the phone taps and lists of visitors collected from Jamie's team given us any new clues?"

"Not yet. I get hourly updates from the headhunters. We could know more at any time."

Siegal said, "We're past the time of guessing and making possible scenarios. Let's go on to a slightly different attack." Moving to a clean sheet, he asked the group to help list any connections Getsen had with Sperling, Blackman, and O'Mally.

"They were part of the guest list at Getsen's retreat in Washington state, according to the headhunters," Danielson said.

Siegal began writing, cataloging the thoughts and suggestions:

> *Getsen was in the hotel at the same time as the other three.*
>
> *After the first meeting, the three made very substantial and aggressive business decisions that were out of their normal character, reported Brand and Cousins.*
>
> *A follow-up meeting at which the three were invited had Getsen's thumbprint, reported the headhunters.*
>
> *During the interim between the first and second conference, Getsen, with his aliases, bought a considerable amount of Emphasis stock, reported Brand.*

Siegal concluded, "I believe those who were invited to the second meeting acted in a similar fashion to Sperling and the others."

"Did they all buy pharmaceuticals under Getsen's direction?" asked Phillipe.

"Probably not," said Simi. "Getsen's purpose with them was to make the market jump around and draw attention away from himself and what he's been planning."

"Is this enough for a call to action?" asked Siegal.

"Not yet," said Danielson. "We need to give Jamie's crew more time on their surveillance. In the meantime, I think the power of the press can slow him down a little and subvert his selling power. I'll see what Brand and Cousins can do to help."

SUN GAZETTE

Several weeks ago, I reported fluctuations in pharmaceuticals without any apparent basis. A certain individual, whom I cannot divulge at this time because of an ongoing investigation, has somehow manipulated large investors toward this particular segment of our economy.

Activity of this sort is called "noise." It is not a scientific term, but it simply means that people respond to rumors, innuendos, and false echoes. More than 60 percent of individual trading in the market is governed by this noise. The problem with this investment behavior is that by the time one hears of the news, it is old hat. The large investors have already made their profit, and the smaller investors are left holding a devalued stock.

If you have any trust in this columnist's integrity, you will take this advice. Don't sell any pharmaceuticals at this time. Keep your holdings. This will stabilize the market. You, the public investors, are the only ones who can stop such activity.

SEVENTY

KEVIN AND TIM SAT AT their stakeout positions, observing all activity at the Getsen mansion. Each hour they reported their logs to Jamie.

LOG SUMMARIES

Mail delivered to the front gate every day between 9-9:30 am. It is always the same: junk mail and the daily edition of the Times. It is picked up by a man in a pinstriped suit at approximately 10:00.

We overheard Getsen calling his caretaker Paul. This man is a trusted friend, caretaker, and generally whatever Getsen wants him to be.

During the morning of the second day, there were four phone calls to the same number, an offshore bank. Since then, there have been no other calls, either incoming or outgoing.

Each afternoon at approximately 1:00, an elderly man with a briefcase arrived. He was identified by his license plate as Dr. Franklin Kemp. Internet identified him as a semi-retired endocrinologist who only caters to a select few patients. Using electronic bugs, we've determined the purpose of the doctor's visits is more of a consultation than a treatment.

Jamie faxed the logs to Danielson with cc's to Siegal and Simi.

SIMI SHOUTED, "I THINK THE word for this information is eureka. These latest notes explain everything. I felt Getsen's anger was health related. Now I'm almost sure of it."

"What part of the play did I miss?" quizzed Siegal. "I'm still in the middle of act one where we determined Getsen is angry at Emphasis for some reason which we can only guess at. I feel I slept through act two, and it's now the finale."

Simi gave him a warm kiss on the cheek. "Maybe not the finale, but it is very close."

"I'm as much at a loss as you are, Ross," said Danielson, showing uncharacteristic excitement. "Go on, genius. Fill us in."

Simi took a sip of lemonade to tease her male counterparts a little. "First of all, the phone calls to an offshore bank are to sell more Emphasis stock; we need Brand to verify dates of withdrawals and purchases. Going on, Getsen wants to deliver Emphasis a slow and lingering demise. His plan is to use his aliases to finish off Emphasis. The daily and not periodic visits by the doctor tell us his life has been challenged. He now feels the need to speed up the process. His change in behavior is his Hannibal's weak link—his downfall."

"Doctari, I still don't understand why he focused on Emphasis."

"I think I can answer that one now," said Siegal. "The daily visits by the doctor, this noted endocrinologist, means Getsen is in worsening health. The absence of conversation between the doctor and Getsen indicates there is not much left to say. William Getsen III is dying, and there is nothing that can save him."

"And you think something Emphasis did caused this grave condition?" said Phillipe.

Siegal answered, "Whether it is true or not. It is what Getsen believes."

Simi interjected, "It is true. It has to be. He is almost at death's door now. Understanding how the man thinks, his plan is in fast forward, whether he personally executes it or not. If he cannot carry out his revenge, someone else has to be the one to do it. Being a loner, there is no other person he can involve."

Siegal was about to celebrate that. "We solved the puzzle and can now stop Getsen!"

This was when Simi said, "Try this one on for size. There is still one person who can finish out his plan. And that's his loyal friend and staff person, Paul, who has been there from the very first."

"You mean the butler did it, Doctari?" grinned Phillipe.

She answered, "Not exactly, but close, Phillipe. Remember my abduction? When the chauffeur came to pick me up for my supposed flight to France, I was alone in the back seat of the limousine. But when he helped me down from my apartment, there was a second man in the limo. The chauffeur forced me between them. The second man covered my mouth and nose with an ether-soaked cloth. Before I passed out, I got a glimpse of this man. He was dressed in a pinstriped suit. We also know that there was a man present in a pinstriped suit at the Washington state conference. The surveillance headhunters noted Paul, the butler, always wears a pinstriped suit. This is more than coincidental."

"Bless your photographic mind, Simi," said Danielson. "That's the thread that ties Getsen to your kidnapping and my legitimate reason to bring him down. Now we have to move fast before he can complete the plan."

"Do we really want to save Emphasis? Especially when they are delivering a faulty product?" Siegal frowned. "I guess we have to do the right thing."

Simi said, "I don't think we really have to do much of anything. Getsen, like Hannibal, set up his own paradigm for defeat. Emphasis will stay in business. He can't control the smaller investors. Brand and other financial experts will curtail that activity. And with the publicity newspapers offer, health organizations will be motivated to research Emphasis. We still need to stop Paul before he can dump Getsen's entire portfolio. There is enough of his holdings to place the entire pharmaceutical sector into a panic."

Danielson picked up his cell. "Lieutenant Goldberg, get your men together. Be prepared for a tactical assault stat. We are after two men, one who is very ill and another who should offer little or no physical resistance. It should be a piece of cake."

SEVENTY-ONE

BOTTOM FEEDERS ON ALL NEWS channels were having a field day since Brand and Cousins started breaking their story. All who were even remotely connected to the financial market, both domestic and abroad, requested public appearances. Their message to retain shares in Emphasis and other pharmaceuticals was repeated over and over. The bleeding of the entire sector completely stopped. The impending disaster was averted.

SEVENTY-TWO

LIEUTENANT GOLDBERG, THE LEADER OF Danielson's quick-strike force, and three of his NCOs, dressed in full battle gear, sat in Kevin's truck. "It's nice to see you two again. My men and I are here and ready."

Kevin said, "Let me bring you up to speed. About an hour ago, Getsen's private physician was here. He stayed a few moments and then left. He made a phone call in his car and drove off. Since that time, there has been no conversation or even movement in the mansion. The two individuals living there are in the bedroom. Getsen is in a prone position, probably on his bed. His butler, Paul, appears to be just sitting in a chair. I don't think they pose any armed threat."

"We plan to blow the front door open and rush the two in the bedroom. Your team has been on surveillance. Do you have another strategy?"

"I don't think you'll find much resistance. There may be some small armament, but we haven't detected any booby traps or the like in the mansion or on the property.

"Mr. Danielson would like us to take them alive so he can question them," said Goldberg. "I think we are overdressed. I wish we had some civilian gear."

Tim said, "I agree. I don't think they are well armed. Two of your smaller men can borrow Kevin and my extra clothing."

"Then it is agreed. Two of my men, dressed in civies, will attempt to enter from the front door. They'll pack small arms under their jackets or shirts in any case. My other man and I will set up in back, ready to assault the mansion if there are any signs of resistance."

The two men, no longer in greasepaint and wearing wires to connect them with Goldberg, approached the front gate and received permission to come to the front door.

Kevin's heat sensors showed the man in the chair getting up and moving to the massive double front door.

Paul opened the door. "You have come very quickly. Dr. Kemp called less than two hours ago." He ushered the men inside. "Please come this way."

The two raiders nodded, hid their bewilderment, and followed Paul to the upstairs master bedroom.

Goldberg monitored the two wired members' conversation. "Sir, we were let in as if being expected. Is this some sort of trap?"

Goldberg answered, "This feels vaguely familiar to when they found Dr. Sunada in his villa. Use extreme caution. Something is happening, and I don't know how to figure it out. Use any force necessary for your own safety."

Paul led the men to the master bedroom. There all questions were answered. On the bed lay William Getsen III. He looked calm, almost smiling. For the first time in over a year, he was completely free of all pain. His hands, clasped over his chest, held his typed journal.

"You are from the mortuary, I presume," said Paul. "Where is your gurney?"

"No, sir. We are ..."

Just then, a second ring was heard at the gate. "We are from the mortuary and have come to collect Mr. Getsen."

"Two more from the mortuary? This is very strange," said Paul. "Who are you two?"

Then the phone rang in the bedroom. "Am I speaking with a gentleman named Paul?"

"That is correct."

"I am Tom Danielson. We have been working on the case of the abduction of Dr. Simi Block. We believe you and Mr. Getsen have been involved in a complicated scheme, which includes both her kidnapping and stock market manipulation. You are under arrest and will have to go with the two gentlemen there. Do you need to call anyone, perhaps an attorney?"

"Mr. Danielson, my employer died this morning. I am waiting for the mortuary to receive his body now. I will go with these gentlemen as soon as Mr. Getsen is taken away."

SEVENTY-THREE

SEVERAL DAYS LATER, BACK ON Little Dead Man's Cay, a group of thirteen people gathered on the beach for an old-fashioned clambake. Many were meeting for the first time. It was Danielson's style to keep everything on a need-to-know basis. But this group had now become family. Included in the group were Goldberg, the four headhunters, Brand, Cousins, Siegal, Phillipe, and his future bride, who had just returned from Nassau where she was planning her wedding. And, of course, Simi, whose adventure began it all.

"I usually don't get in at the tail end of a mission. My men go in, clean up any rat's nest and leave. I never realized so many people were involved," said Goldberg.

Danielson said, "I imagine this may not be the last time we meet. You will be there should the need arise."

"We all came out in one piece this time," remarked Jamie, toasting her glass filled with the island's official drinks, lemonade and iced tea. "We headhunters relish these few days on the beach before getting back to work again. My team has a few contract proposals in the holding file. But, if you ever need us again, boss, we'll be there before the phone rings twice."

"And there will be a time. I promise," answered Danielson.

"Tell us. Is this Paul character going to jail for kidnapping, or at least securities fraud?" asked Phillipe.

Danielson answered, "Probably not. The journal in Getsen's hands explained why he did what he did. His illness pushed him to insanity. Paul confessed everything. His testimony helped make the case even stronger against Getsen. Paul was just an overly willing pawn wanting to please his benefactor. I'm confident he will live a law-abiding existence with the money and possessions Getsen left him."

Danielson turned to Siegal and Simi. "What's going to happen with the two of you? Are you guys going to screw it up again?"

"Hardly," said Simi. "I made that mistake once, but not again. I have to go back to Cal-Berkeley for now. I will change that if Ross wants me to be here."

"That's not going to happen either," jumped in Siegal. "The university made me an offer to be a professor and work on more research. As soon as I wind things up here on the island, I'm going back to civilization. I can't remain here and ask Simi to give up all she has worked for. Does anyone know how I can get rid of a few very well-behaved spider monkeys where they will be properly treated?"

Phillipe displayed his toothy grin. "No problem, Doctari. If Mr. Danielson can find a way to keep this island intact, my wife and I could manage it all. You know, the way Missy Ro does it in Africa. We could build a few tourist huts and run a gift shop. That could help pay for the rental to keep this island."

"A great idea," said Danielson. "I think the tourist idea works. We are close enough to a great vacationing country just north of us called the United States. I wager you would have more reservations than you could ever want. At the same time, this place could develop into a free-roaming research center for the study of primates as Ross initiated. I think you could manage it all, of course, with an on-site vet and business manager.

The only requirement would be that any of us can visit you as guests once in a while."

Phillipe was speechless. He jumped up and did a victory dance. The others rose and followed him around the beach, jumping into the water at the conclusion.

They reemerged from the water after some juvenile antics and toweled themselves.

"I guess that about wraps it up," said Danielson.

Brand frowned. "Maybe I'm just a bonehead reporter. But I don't see how we helped you so much by letting out that series of stories and interviews about holding onto Emphasis stock."

"That's easy to explain," said Simi. "Let's go back to the Getsen character. Remember the story of the great and cruel conqueror Hannibal. He gained the reputation that no enemy could stand up to his mighty army. Then, at the height of his strength, Hannibal was defeated. Getsen failed the same way. Can anyone guess why?"

"He changed his game plan?" suggested Goldberg.

Siegal explained, "Exactly. Hannibal's normal plan would be to go in hard on anyone who posed a threat, kill the warriors and enslave the women. Getsen used the same technique and controlled the markets. If Getsen had carried out his actions by selling everything at once, he would have succeeded in destroying Emphasis and possibly much of the drug market. But, like Hannibal, he had a blind spot and chose to take Emphasis down slowly and painfully. This gave us the time to stop him by having small investors hold on to their stocks and wait out the crisis.

And he was probably only hours away from succeeding," added Danielson.

"The Hannibal paradigm," Phillipe said with a toothy grin.

ABOUT THE AUTHOR

HERB PADZENSKY, PH.D., HAS A Psychology degree from Denver University, and has written several textbooks used for college credit. His best known, *Goalguide*, is part of a six-set, self-paced manual directed toward developmentally disabled instruction.

In his early years, Padzensky left high school because of his reading, writing, and speaking disabilities, spending most of his life embracing the challenge by becoming a stand-up entertainer and educator. His love for all forms of puzzle solving helped him develop quirky, out-of-the-box thinking, making him uniquely suited to write intriguing psychological thrillers.

Padzensky's writing includes several one-act plays and short stories. *RATS: A Ross Siegal Psychological Thriller* pits university professor Dr. Ross Siegal against heinous villains worldwide. He currently lives in Denver with his wife Ro.